CLEAR
SKIES,
NO
WIND,
100%
VISIBILITY

CLEAR SKIES, NO WIND, 100% VISIBILITY

THÉODORA ARMSTRONG

This edition published in 2013 by
House of Anansi Press Inc.
110 Spadina Avenue, Suite 801
Toronto, ON, M5V 2K4
Tel. 416-363-4343
Fax 416-363-1017
www.houseofanansi.com

Distributed in Canada by
HarperCollins Canada Ltd.
1995 Markham Road
Scarborough, ON, M1B 5M8
Toll free tel. 1-800-387-0117

House of Anansi Press is committed to protecting our natural environment.
As part of our efforts, the interior of this book is printed on paper that contains
100% post-consumer recycled fibres, is acid-free, and is processed chlorine-free.

17 16 15 14 13   1 2 3 4 5

Library and Archives Canada Cataloguing in Publication

Armstrong, Théodora
Clear skies, no wind, 100% visibility / Théodora Armstrong.

Short stories.
Issued also in an electronic format.
ISBN 978-1-77089-102-9
I. Title.
PS8601.R5954C54 2013   C813'.6   C2012-905957-9

Cover design: Marijke Friesen
Text design and typesetting: Alysia Shewchuk

 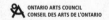

Canada Council   Conseil des Arts
for the Arts   du Canada

ONTARIO ARTS COUNCIL
CONSEIL DES ARTS DE L'ONTARIO

*We acknowledge for their financial support of our publishing program
the Canada Council for the Arts, the Ontario Arts Council, and the Government of
Canada through the Canada Book Fund.*

Printed and bound in Canada

For my parents

and for J, with love.

CONTENTS

RABBIT

I WRAP MYSELF IN our scratchy curtains and watch Mom from our front window. The glass is freezing. I can feel the cold without touching anything. My brother, Matt, is sleeping on the couch behind me. He's snoring and his shoes are still on. His jacket is on the floor beside him. He looks ready for a quick escape, but he's been here for a while now, almost a year. He has a toothbrush Mom bought for him. He's hung a movie poster in his bedroom, *Scarface*. I guess that's a good sign.

It's too early for visitors, but Mom is in her fuzzy blue robe and thick woolen socks, talking to our neighbour on the porch. I don't know his name, but sometimes I see him early in the morning walking to his car in a suit and tie.

It snowed last night—the first snow—enough to get to my ankles. Mom's breath is thin like a beautiful bubblegum balloon, reaching out and almost touching the neighbour before vanishing.

Mom comes back into the house, all the cold running in with her. She can't see me behind the curtains. She stands watching Matt for a while. I wish I could snore like him, like a bear asleep in a cave. I poke my head around the curtains, moving them carefully so I don't wake up Matt. "Get a move on," Mom whispers. "I'm giving you a ride to school this morning."

I SIT IN THE car while Mom warms it up. I'm in a white envelope being mailed to China or Peru. She knocks ice and snow off the windshield with her mitts. Usually I walk to school— it's not far, four blocks on the other side of the mall, but the mall is a long block and counts for at least two. I want to ask why I'm being driven to school, but weird things early in the morning always mean bad news. Mom keeps forgetting things, running back and forth from the car to the house. She spills her coffee getting into the front seat and swears. For a minute I think she's forgotten I'm here.

There are a lot of people on our street this morning. Most of the time our streets are empty. In the morning or at dinnertime cars are in and out of driveways, but there are never people on the sidewalks. Sometimes I feel I'm the only one who walks on our street. But this morning people are out, walking in groups of four or five, holding steaming cups of coffee, calling greetings to each other. They look like carollers, but I've only seen carollers in my Christmas books. At the end of the road, police cars are parked around the brown house with the windmill on top. Mom slows down as we drive by, and for a second I think we might stop to join everyone, but instead we turn the corner and head toward the school. "There was a girl that went missing last night," Mom says. "She never came home from the mall. Did you hear anything?" I shake my head no.

Along the river, the tree branches are heavy with snow. There are police cars here too. I turn up the heat, hot air blowing in my face. Mom turns the dial back down.

NOT MANY KIDS AT school know about the girl, so at recess I tell everyone. I say what she looks like even though I've never seen her. She has long blond hair in braids. Her eyes are green. She was wearing a jean skirt and winter boots. Everyone crowds around me in a tight circle. They go off to make other circles. Soon everyone is in circles.

After recess, Ms. Peterson makes a special announcement to the class. She uses the word *abduction*. She tells us what to do if we meet a stranger. We don't take candy. We don't tell anyone our names. We scream. People turn to stare at me, their eyes huge like moons, and it's official now: I told everyone first.

SAM'S MOM IS GOING to take me home before she takes Sam to his swim lesson. Sam's in my class, but we never play together because he plays kickball every day, even in the snow.

When they drop me off they walk me right to my front door. Matt cleaned off the stairs this morning and all my footprints are gone. I feel grown-up taking out my key chain with the blue dolphin and unlocking the door. Sam doesn't have a key chain or a key, and he was looking at mine while we waited in the schoolyard. He was pretending to make the dolphin dive in the snow, but I was afraid he'd lose my keys and I wouldn't be able to go home, so I took them back.

We talked about the girl. She's not really a girl. I'm a girl; she's a teenager. But everyone calls her a girl—that poor girl, that innocent girl. Mom told me a bit and Sam told me the rest, but no one really knows anything about her. Someone took her while she waited for the bus in front of the mall. She went to Ferndale High. I don't think I knew her, but one day I might have walked beside her without realizing. She screamed a lot. Lots of people heard her, but everyone kept drinking their tea and watching their television shows. Sam says he heard her, but I think he's lying. Mom says she thought it was teens down by the river goofing off.

Sam and I stand by the front door staring at each other while Sam's mom looks around my house. She wants to know where my brother is and I tell her he gets home from the glass factory at four. When I picture the glass factory I see nothing but stacks of window panes. Once Matt picked up a sheet of glass with unfinished edges and slit his palms open. Mom says he's lucky to have his fingers. You're supposed to wear heavy gloves at all times. He was at home for a month with fat white bandages around his hands. He liked to pretend they were boxing gloves. He still has the scars.

When Sam's mom leaves she tells me—same as Mom did—not to open the door for anyone. I hear them wait until I turn the lock before they make their way down the steps. I run to the front window to watch their car pull away from the curb. Sam watches me from his window. I make the blue dolphin bob up and down as if the windowsill is an ocean.

I TURN THE HEAT up as high as the dial will go. There's a heat vent beside the sliding doors in the kitchen that look out on our backyard. I sit there with a box of Froot Loops and let the hot air puff out my T-shirt. The house is quiet like a forest. I feel like animals are hiding everywhere, under the sofa, in the cupboards, behind the doors. Matt isn't home yet and because of the snow it'll take him longer than normal.

If Matt gets home before me, he's usually on the deck with his .22 rifle. I like to sit on the vent and watch him. Matt just turned twenty. We had meatloaf on his birthday and Matt ate seconds. Last year, we didn't get to celebrate his birthday because he was living in Port Alberni with Uncle Pat and working at the lumber mill. Before that he was with Grandma Alice in Vancouver and before that I can't remember. The last time he left, he didn't say goodbye. Mom forgot to tell me he was gone because he comes and goes as often as cats want out. One day I asked her where he was and she looked dazed. She said: *Oh, honey.* She said people need space to breathe and I thought that was pretty obvious. Everyone needs space to breathe or else they'd be dead.

But Matt always comes back—one day he opens the front door and he's here. There are twelve years between us. Mom says that makes him responsible for me.

Matt likes to shoot soup cans from the deck. He stacks the empty cans on tree stumps at the back of the yard. They're old and rusted together, the labels peeled and curled—beef barley, cream of mushroom, chicken noodle. I make the soup when Mom's late from work. Behind the stumps are trees and behind the trees is the river. After you cross the river you get to the mall.

It takes Matt a long time to shoot. He aims carefully, adjusting his arm a lot. The bullet flies when I least expect it, but it never makes me jump or even blink. He almost never hits a can.

Sometimes while I watch Matt, I blow my breath against the glass of the sliding door. I blow a lot at once, covering a large area, then I draw quickly before the glass clears again. Sometimes I plot out maps, how far Matt has to shoot to hit the cans. Or I'll draw the face of someone I hate at school, then I don't mind when the glass clears. Sometimes I draw Matt's girlfriends with big breasts and knock on the window to get his attention, but he never turns around.

Everyone has walked into these sliding doors. Mom likes them really clean. Once I got knocked out. I was running and looking at something on the TV. We are as dumb as birds, I guess, but our necks are too thick to snap.

The front door opens and I hear girl laughter and Matt stamping the snow off his boots. I peek around the edge of the island between the kitchen and the living room. Matt's standing beside a girl who's unlacing her boots. When she bends down he sticks his gloved hands under her skirt and she swats them away while she loosens her laces. "Quit it," she says, but she's laughing. The girl graduated from my elementary school last year. She used to have no boobs. She was bad at sports. Once her class was playing baseball outside and the ball hit her in the nose. She had blood down the front of her shirt and a black eye for over a week. I was going to the washroom and saw her walking quickly down the hall with Mr. O'Brian holding a hanky to her nose. She was crying and I thought that was stupid.

She looks the same now, but with breasts. Not bloody or crying or anything, I just mean the same face and the same haircut. She's wearing a puffy jacket and under her skirt her legs are bare and red with goose bumps all over — chicken legs.

She and Matt don't see me sitting on the kitchen floor as they go into his room. The girl is giggling like something's funny, but I can't hear them talking. I crawl to where I can see past the door, lying down on my stomach. I'm wearing a white shirt and the kitchen is all white just like hunting in the snow. Matt's sitting on his bed with his head tilted to one side, watching the girl. She's between his legs with his hands in her hair. He starts grunting, moving his hips and pushing down on her head. She makes a choking noise and then climbs up on the bed beside him. He sits there, his penis straight up and shiny. I slide back behind the counter, my breath stuck in my throat and my palms sweaty along the linoleum, but then I look again. The girl lights a cigarette, drops it and laughs before picking it up. She rubs a spot on the comforter. Matt stands and zips up his pants as he leaves the bedroom, and I leap back to my spot on the heater, my heart thumping the way it does when I run around the yard three times.

He plops down on the couch and turns on the TV. I crunch my Froot Loops a little louder. Matt turns to look at me, "How long have you been sitting there?" I shrug. "I've got a girl here. Hang out in your room." I shrug again.

The girl comes out of his bedroom and smiles at me in a practised, older-person way, "This your sis?" She doesn't recognize me, but I didn't think she would. Matt flips the channel to hockey without saying anything. The girl snuggles into him, but Matt likes a big space between him and whoever else is sitting on the couch, so he moves over and she stays put. She watches him more than the TV. You could drop something on Matt's toe and he wouldn't notice. The girl leans over the back of the couch, looking at me with owl eyes. "Police think it's someone in town took that girl," she says. Her cigarette is still dangling between her fingers, the smoke reaching way up, touching our ceiling. "Someone who was following her to and from school."

I shrug and look out the window. In the yard snow falls off the trees.

"They won't find her," Matt says, flipping channels.

"She's dead, for sure," the girl says.

I want to stick my tongue out at her, but I'm too old for that now.

Heavy feet come up our front steps and someone bangs on the door. The girl shrieks and then laughs again, grabbing onto Matt's arm. "That was freaky," she says. "Who is that?" The banging gets louder and she turns to look in the direction of the door, her face suddenly going white. "It's my dad." I wonder if she has X-ray vision.

"Dawn, go to your room," Matt says, taking the girl's hand and leading her to his bedroom.

The house is quiet again. Now there are people hiding. I eat my Froot Loops and wonder if the Dad has a gun. If he does, will he shoot Matt or will Matt get his gun and challenge him to a duel?

A man walks up the back porch steps. He doesn't have a gun. He's mostly bald and has delicate glasses. The steps are slippery and he walks slowly, holding the railing. Instead of winter boots he's wearing brown loafers that are very wet. They look like the soft nose of a dog. He peers through the sliding doors, a white blotch from his breath growing and shrinking on the glass. He knocks loudly before noticing me sitting on the vent and squats down so we can look at each other face to face. His eyes are dark as rain puddles and there are deep wrinkles criss-crossing his forehead.

I leave my box of cereal and run to my bedroom, slamming the door. The only sound is my breath whistling through my nose. I reach down inside my pants and tuck my hands between my legs. I fall asleep on top of the covers.

WHEN I WAKE UP the sky's dark and Mom's back from her shift at the hospital. I walk into her room and she's sitting on the edge of her bed, pulling off her pantyhose. She wears the same kind every day: bare nude control top, the Leggs brand. In the morning, when she has on a new pair, I like to rub against her. I can tell how her day went by her pantyhose. In the summer, clouds of dust puff up as she pulls them off. Once there were flecks of blood down the backs and she wouldn't tell me what happened at the hospital. Today the snow is melting in Kelowna, car tires turning everything into wet mush along the sides of the road. I watch as she slides the thick elastic top down her hips and grabs at the stained toes, pulling inch by inch. Muddy water marks dot the nylon, but no runs. They can be saved, thrown in the sink to soak and hung on the shower rod. I hope I never have to wear pantyhose and go into town.

"What did you have for dinner?" Mom asks.

"I fell asleep."

"You feeling okay, hon?" She puts a warm hand on my forehead. Her skin is dry and scratchy. I shrug my shoulders and back flop onto the bed. She likes to pull out a thermometer for the show of it, giving it a shake and popping it in my mouth. I stretch out and work the glass tip around with my tongue.

"Don't fool with it. Keep it in one place."

She pulls off all her jewelry — one ring, pearl earrings and a gold chain with a thin cross. I used to think a man had given them to her as presents, but when I asked one day she said it was Grandma's old jewelry and when I was old enough I could have it. She stretches out beside me on the bed and pulls the thermometer out of my mouth, holding it up to take a look. "Normal," she says.

"I knew you'd say that."

"The thermometer doesn't lie. You're a normal kid. What kind of soup do you want?"

"Tomato," I say, following her into the kitchen. She pulls out a pot and a can opener from one of the drawers. "I got a big heating bill today," she says, punching the opener into the top of the can. "Know anything about that?"

"No."

"You haven't been touching the thermostat?" She cranks the opener and loses the lid in the liquid. There's a knock at the front door and Mom goes to answer it. I hop up on the counter to fish the lid out with a fork, but it keeps slipping back in. When I look down the hall Mom's talking to a man in a dark coat. He says they found the girl down by the river, close to the dam. Mom says *God, God* and then her voice floats away. "I keep thinking, if I'd gone out to see—" Mom says after a pause and the man clears his throat. He asks her questions about the members in our family and takes notes in a book. Mom twists her hair and answers yes or no. She tries to close the door gently, but the man keeps his boot in the doorframe. "Just a minute," he says and he smiles. I slide quietly along the wall toward them. He asks Mom if any of our family members spend time in the area around the river. "No, we don't," she says. I stand beside her and they stop talking and smile at me. The man takes his foot out of the frame and Mom closes the door carefully. "Who was that?" I say, following her back to the kitchen.

"A police officer," Mom says, pulling the lid out of the can.

"About the girl?"

"About the girl."

We stand in the kitchen listening to the clock while Mom stirs soup, swaying from side to side like she's listening to the radio. "Matt had a friend over today," I say.

"Did he?" She stops swaying and looks up at the ceiling.

"And the girl's dad came here."

"Really?" She turns to give me a look that says, *I know there's more to this story*. A crinkle, like a little worm, forms in the middle of her forehead.

"But I didn't let him in."

"Why not?" she says. She's not looking at me, but I can tell she's listening carefully because she tilts her head in my direction.

"You told me not to."

"I said strangers."

"He's a stranger."

"Well." She scrapes the inside of the empty can. "Well, well." It's something she says when she runs out of words. She twists her hair again, this time in a knot on top of her head. "Have people been saying anything to you?"

"Who?"

She looks at me and shrugs. The hair unravels and falls around her shoulders. "Kids at school."

"About what?"

She turns back to the stovetop and talks to the pot. "Sometimes your brother makes the wrong choices, but he's a good person."

"I know."

"Don't let anyone tell you otherwise." She stirs the soup. Her hips move from side to side. Bubbles pop and send splatters over the stovetop.

"Can I sleep in your room tonight?" I say.

"If you have a bath."

I LOCK THE BATHROOM door behind me, checking it twice before turning on the tap and letting the tub fill. I dip my toes in first then stand ankle-deep while my feet adjust to the heat. Slowly I lower myself into the water. When I was younger Mom wouldn't let me lock the door, in case I slipped or drowned. She promised not to come in, but she always did, saying, *I'm covering my eyes, I'm covering my eyes,* searching like a blind lady for whatever she wanted.

When I turn off the tap I hear sports on TV. Channels switch, flicker, flip. "People talk," Mom says, over the noise of the announcer. "People make assumptions."

"You're paranoid," Matt says, laughing the way he does when he thinks someone's stupid. Scores ring out on the TV. The tips of my fingers are white. They're wrinkled like they could be picked apart.

"Pay attention to me," Mom says. The TV noise goes dead.

"Give me the fucking remote."

"Be quiet."

"F-off."

"Dawn will hear you."

"Fuck Dawn."

I disappear under the water. There could be more bubbles in here, but it's too late once you've poured the bath. The dead girl floats into my head, her skin white and picked apart like the tips of my fingers. I wonder: if the girl was in the river, why didn't it carry her away? The river never freezes. When I come back up from the water Mom is knocking lightly on the door. "You okay in there?" I keep myself as quiet as possible. I keep the water quiet around me. I hold my breath and watch the door. "Dawn?" The doorknob jiggles and Mom shouts. "Dawn, answer me!" Her body thuds against the door, trying to force it open. "What?" I call, splashing in the water.

"Why didn't you answer me?"

"My head was underwater."

"Don't do that again." Mom is so close I hear her lips brush the door, her body against the wood. Her breathing makes me feel lonely. I blow bubbles in the water until she goes back to the kitchen. My hands glide over the skin on my stomach. I don't like that part of my body because there are no bones to protect it. The skin is pink from the heat, and soft—rabbit skin. Rabbits are too squishy and terrified. They're always running. My nails dig into my tummy, leaving rows of white moons.

WE LEAVE EARLY AGAIN this morning. Overnight everything has turned to ice. Mom and I hold hands down the sidewalk and I take long, skating steps, but Mom squeezes my hand and tells me to stop. She's wearing nice clothing and dressy shoes that are too slippery for snow. She says she wants to give the lady in the brown house our condolences. "They found that poor girl dead"—that's what Mom said this morning. When I asked where, she thought for a second then said, "Down by the river." She wanted Matt to come with us, but he didn't come home last night.

We used to go for walks along the river before Mom got her job in Kelowna. Once we saw a dead bird. It was black like it had been stuck in the oven for too long, but I can't imagine a dead girl. There are always teenagers down there, wild like packs of wolves. They always seem hungry, but all they do is smoke. I never look at them when we walk by. When we had our dog, Tucker, we would take him for walks along the river, where he'd sniff out beer bottles and sometimes find clothes or a shoe. Matt would come with us, taking the leash and walking ahead. Tucker would look back to make sure Mom and I were still there, but that was a long time ago. Matt watched the groups of teenagers like he was hungry, too. One day he knew some of them and stayed down there while Mom and I took Tucker back home. That night Mom waited for him, pulling back the curtains, but she got used to it. After that we didn't walk down there much.

I don't tell Mom about the dream I had last night about the poor dead girl. She was running and I was chasing her. I was angry, but I kept forgetting I wasn't supposed to be. I was trying to tell her something, throwing my arms up and yelling. She kept running and falling. She had rows of bloody moons down her stomach. She didn't have blond hair like I thought.

We get to the brown house and there are colourful cards and flowers all over the front steps. It's like a candy machine exploded. We have to step carefully around them. Some of them are buried in the snow, wet and soggy, the ink running so you can't read people's words. Mom finds a spot for our flowers in a dry corner near the door. She puts them down gently and we start back down the stairs without ringing the bell or saying hello. It seems too quiet to make any noise at all and I don't even like the sound of my own steps crunching down the walk. When we get to the street I hear a window opening above us. A woman sticks her head out, pushing the window with her flat hand. "What are you doing?" I stare up at her, my mouth open to the sky. "What are you doing here? Where were you when she was screaming?" the woman yells at us. "Get out of here."

Mom stiffens and takes my hand. I can't look at her. We turn around and walk away.

IT SNOWS AGAIN. SAM stays after school so I walk home by myself. It keeps snowing again and again, like the town is trying to be new every day. Or maybe it's trying to be the same. I can't imagine anything quieter than snow falling off trees, and white piled on white makes no difference.

I take the shortcut through the mall parking lot even though Mom doesn't want me going that way. There are too many cars, too many doors that could open with people waiting to snatch me away, but it's cold and I want to get home quickly. When I get to the mall only a few cars are parked near the doors and a snowplow clears spaces, piling white hills around the lot. The automatic doors swish, opening and closing as people hurry around inside. Matt's car is in the lot parked sideways, but it doesn't matter because there are no lines for the spaces. I brush the snow off his bumper and sit down, waiting for a ride. Once he picked me up from school and we went to A&W. We didn't go through the drive-thru, we sat inside to eat our burgers. When our fries were done he bought us more to share so we could stay longer.

Matt comes out of the mall with the same girl, the girl from the house, and they walk along the covered sidewalk. I can only see them from the chest up because of the snow piles. Matt climbs the bank and holds out his hand to the girl. She's wearing the same short skirt. A car door opens near them and the girl's father gets out. They all stand staring at each other without saying anything. I have one of those bad feelings you can't ignore, so I start walking toward them, calling Matt's name. The dad holds out his hand to the girl, but she jumps away and slips on the ice. Her skirt lifts up and I can see her purple underwear. Matt tries to help her, but she pushes him away and hops off the snowbank. She doesn't cry or look back at him, but walks to the mall entrance, disappearing into the warm, colourful air. The dad is shouting, pointing his finger at Matt, and I start to run.

"Go home," Matt says as I stop in front of him, before I

even have a chance to speak. He doesn't look at me. The mall parking lot suddenly feels bigger, like it's spreading.

"I want you to stay away from her," the dad is saying. His voice is so shaky I think he might give up. Matt looks away from the father with a smirk on his face. He smirks at the snow, he smirks at the mall entrance, he smirks at the snow-plow circling. I step closer to Matt, standing between him and the father. "I don't need this," Matt says, smiling at the snow on the ground. His warm breath floats down on top of my head. When he turns to walk away the dad reaches out and puts his hand on Matt's shoulder. "She's my daugh-ter." The words are gentle, but Matt turns and shoves the dad. "Worthless punk," the dad growls, slipping on the snow. "You're nothing. You're a loser." The words fly out of his mouth. Matt looks down at me, and for a moment, I think he's going to pick me up and carry me to the car, but instead he punches the dad in the face. It's not something I expect. One second Matt is standing, arms loose at his sides, the next he is throwing the punch right over my head. The father falls against one of the snowbanks and everything freezes. Matt is breathing hard, his shoulders rising and falling. He looks right through me and then walks quickly to his car, shaking out his hand. The engine revs and his car slides from side to side on the ice, skidding out onto the road, but there's nothing for Matt to hit even if he wanted to.

The father takes a handful of snow and holds it up to his nose. His glasses fog and there are drops of blood at his feet. "Your brother is a pervert," the dad says, through the snow. He looks right at me when he says the words, but I don't blink. I spit on the ground, aiming the glob near the dad's shoes. I was saving the saliva in my mouth without thinking, swishing it around with my tongue. A shock cuts through my body, breaks me in half, leaving me standing off to the side, watching. I can feel the curl in my lips, hot words in my mouth, ugly and new. "You fuck off."

"You're not so different from him, are you?" the father says, shaking his head like I'm a shame. He looks at the bloody clump of snow in his hand and I squint at the parking lot. The man in the snowplow waves at me and I wave back. The dad doesn't say anything else. He puts new snow on his face and gets into his car. "Go home," he says, before he drives away.

I stand in the parking lot by myself. The plow is on the other side of the mall. I don't want to go home, but there is nowhere else to go. I take off running because it's cold. There's nothing in the air but the sound of my breathing and the word *pervert, pervert, pervert*. No one is at the bus stop. The neighborhood houses look abandoned. The curtains are pulled shut like eyes sleeping tight. When I get home my lungs are burning and snot runs out my nose. I can taste it on my upper lip. Matt's car isn't in the driveway. There are muddy tracks from the tires, tracks from Matt's boots in and out of the house. His room is messy, clothes everywhere. In the bathroom, his toothbrush is gone. His gun is gone. His *Scarface* poster is still there.

I get my box of cereal and turn up the heat.

ONCE, MAYBE LAST WINTER, I watched Matt from the trees and he never found out. He had only been back a while. I came home from school early to see him, the thighs of my snowsuit rubbing. The noise was annoying. I lay down in the snow behind our house, in the middle of all the tall pine trees, waiting for him to come home. There was no snow falling that day. Everything seemed frozen together. I even felt frozen together. Like if I went inside and sat on the heat vent, I might fall apart. I fell back, lying there for a while, trying to see if I could melt snow off the trees by staring at it long enough. It didn't work. I lay there until Matt came out. The sliding door swished open and closed. He shot three times and hit nothing. I could hear the bullets zip through the trees above me and get lost.

I go lie in the backyard like I did that day. I pretend I'm hunting rabbits. It's harder than you think. Rabbits turn white in the winter and everything else is white. The sun shines white rays and if you look hard at anything you go blind.

Matt's been gone a week. Mom called around, but no one's heard from him. When he comes back I might ask him to take me rabbit hunting. Then we could have rabbit stew for dinner instead of canned soup. I would stand over the stove stirring for hours, and by the time Mom got home from work the house would be full of the smell of meat. We'd all be at the table. The smell would be so good, Matt would have to sit down. We'd be so busy chewing, no one would talk.

I imagine Matt and me crouched down in the snow, our elbows propped up, our guns ready. I'd see it even though everything would be white on white. I would squint my eyes and shoot. Matt would laugh in a good way like he couldn't believe it was me. I would pick the rabbit up by the ears. The ears would be the softest things. The rabbit would be heavy. I would have to hang on tight.

FISHTAIL

TED CAN SEE THE vague outlines of the girls' heads bobbing around the foggy car as he stands beside the ticket booth, shouldering the cellphone to his ear, trying to focus on the numbers his client is shooting at him while he waits for the vending machine to finish spitting out its last drops of coffee. Getting away early on a Friday afternoon isn't normally done in Ted's office, but it was his managing partner at the firm who suggested the trip. "I have a nice plot of land on Quadra I just put on the market. Five acres," Jim said. "You should go take a look." Jim offered his cabin, suggested Ted take Heather and the girls. "Those kids'll be grown in no time," he said. "Take a holiday while you still have your hair." Ted didn't see any reason to tell him the girls were already grown, Leslie in her last year of junior high and Anna in her first year at Camosun College. Sometimes he finds it hard to believe himself. In the mornings, as he checks his shave in the mirror, he likes to appreciate the clean-cut features he sees reflected back at him, though lately he's been taking a closer look and finding some unsettling evidence of decline: a softness in the skin under his eyes, a fine webbing of spider veins around his nose, a slackness along the line of his jaw. He's in the habit of giving his face a couple of brisk slaps in the morning, like saying: *Hey, smarten up!*

The girls didn't want to come on the trip. Convincing them took some arm-twisting, but he knew how to lay it on thick: How often were the three of them together without Heather? When did they ever get to enjoy quality father-daughter time? How will they feel when dear dad is old and grey? "You are grey," Leslie said, "and I feel fine." "It's called salt and pepper," Ted replied.

So far the trip lacked the camaraderie and good humour he was hoping for. He hadn't anticipated the dim panic he felt during the drive up along the Island Highway. His usual tricks with the girls weren't working. Anna sat sullenly, refusing to crack a smile as he went through his standard comedy routine, and Leslie bounced and chattered in the back seat like she'd had a bag of sugar for breakfast. He can't calm Leslie the way Heather can—a hand between the shoulder blades, soft words, kindness. At home the girls hole up in their rooms behind closed doors. On occasion a head pokes out with a demand or complaint; he obliges. Conversation takes place during commercial breaks or chauffeured trips to the mall. But Ted is confident that once they reach the island and the girls are surrounded by forest and salt air, everything will sort itself out.

He waits for the last of the coffee to splash into the cup before heading back to the car—he will need every drop. The dull clutch of a headache is tightening the base of his skull. He gets back just before his lane starts loading onto the ferry. The client on the phone is looking for an informed answer and Ted gives him his standard investment banker's dictum on maximizing profits —*higher risk, higher return,* words applicable in most scenarios. The rain is coming down hard now, fat drops they were lucky to avoid on the highway. As he opens the car door, he's hit with the damp, flowery smell of the girls' mingling perfume.

"Oh my God, Dad! Where were you?" Leslie says, gripping the back of Ted's seat and giving it an aggressive shake. "The ferry's leaving." He holds a finger up to his lips, pointing to the phone. She leans forward, positioning her nose an inch from his face, her cheeks puffy and red with excitement. She holds an imaginary cellphone up to her ear and pretends to have an animated conversation. In the rearview mirror, Anna rolls her eyes.

"We're getting onto the ferry now. I'll be back in Victoria on Monday," Ted says into the phone. "All right —I'll call you back in twenty minutes." He puts the phone on the dashboard. "Seatbelts," he calls into the back seat.

"Why?" Leslie rolls down the window and ducks her head out. "We're next."

"I thought I was going to have to drive on without you, but you didn't leave the keys," Anna says without looking at him, her finger tracing swirls in the condensation on the window. "You should always leave the keys." She reaches over and yanks on one of Leslie's belt loops. "Sit down. Quit being such a little shit." She's been taking harsher tones with her sister, but it might be what Leslie needs. Ted remembers road trips when they were girls, with their armies of stuffed animals and whispered secrets. A distance has grown between them lately, one that only seems to make Leslie crave her sister's attention more. "Hey, remember that trip to Tofino? That was fun," Ted calls into the back seat. The memory is vague at best in his own mind—he's grasping.

"Oh right, when I was like three," Anna says.

"I wasn't even born yet!" Leslie laughs and punches the seat. "Yeah, Dad. I remember that trip. I was in the womb. It was warm and red. It was a great trip!"

"Oh, come on," Ted says, and he laughs too.

Leslie hangs out the window again and shakes her bum in Anna's face. Anna gives her a hard smack on the butt cheek. "Bitch," Leslie screeches and the muscles in Ted's neck tighten. "Leslie, get in," he shouts. She ducks back into the car, her face speckled with raindrops that she wipes away with the sleeve of her sweater. Ted fumbles for the keys in his jacket as the brake lights of the car in front of them light up and engines rev. "Okay, we're off," Ted says, turning on the car and taking a sip of his coffee. His headache has gone from dull to throbbing. He's hit with the sudden wish for a couple drops of whiskey to sharpen the taste of the drink, anything a little stronger. He thinks about the four bottles of wine tucked into the cardboard box of provisions in the trunk. The car in front of them inches forward and the driver behind them honks.

"Dad, oh my God! Go already." Leslie gives the front seat a hard kick and lets out an annoyed sigh. "Jesus, Mary and Joseph," she says and then bursts into giggles, turning to Anna for a reaction. The car honks again.

"Asshole," Anna says, under her breath. She wipes away the condensation on the back window and gives the driver the finger. Leslie bites her lip, cheeks puffing out again as she tries to hold back her laughter. Ted gives Anna a look in the rearview that says *mind your sister*, but he can't help a smile.

As they cross the loading ramp onto the ferry, Leslie holds her breath, her face turning pink, and for several seconds there's silence in the car. She slaps Anna's knee to encourage her to do the same, waving her arms above her head insistently. Anna's gaze remains fixed on the lineup of cars ahead filing onto the ferry's deck, but Ted hears the sharp intake of her breath. Beneath the loading ramp the dark water surges.

Whenever they cross onto a ferry, everyone in the car is supposed to hold their breath—this is their strange family ritual. The girls created the game and when they were young Ted played along, but he doesn't bother anymore. They invented it so long ago they've forgotten its origin, but Ted remembers. As they pull onto the deck Leslie exhales dramatically. A young ferry worker motions for Ted to roll down his window. "We're going to get you in a little tighter," the boy says. Ted backs up the car and pulls hard over to the right. "How much room do I have?" he calls out the window. "You're good, keep it coming," the boy says, and taps the hood of the car when he's close enough. The girls are quiet again and Ted catches them staring at the boy. He's around nineteen and smiles at Anna as he walks by. Ted turns in his seat to give the boy a harder look. "What are you girls staring at?"

"Nothin'," Anna shrugs and Leslie turns a shade of red.

The ferry shudders to life and pulls away from the dock.

"I'm stuck," Leslie says, looking out the window. "There's no room to open the door."

"It's a ten-minute ride," Ted says. "Close your eyes and we'll be there."

"But I want to get out!" Leslie rattles the door handle.

"There's no passenger cabin," Ted says. "Everyone stays in their cars."

"I want to walk around," Leslie whines. "My legs are cramping."

Anna scrambles through the space between the two front seats and slumps down in the passenger side, bringing an arm up over her face. The skin of her forearm is translucent, a flawless white threaded with blue veins. "Seriously," she mutters. "She doesn't shut up."

"We're going to have a nice weekend," Ted says, tapping Anna's knee lightly.

The rain has stopped and the island is circled in a thick mist hanging low along its shores, the green hump of its back breaching the haze like a whale surfacing. Leslie is finally quiet and Ted, the full weight of the workweek suddenly hitting him, leans back in his seat and closes his eyes.

Many years ago a minivan plunged off the loading ramp of a ferry leaving Tsawwassen. There was a reason Ted couldn't remember: rough waters, a careless worker, a mechanical malfunction. The van sank in the deep water where the ferry berthed, and got trapped between the massive hull of the boat and the barnacled underwater pillars of the dock, making the rescue difficult. There was a family inside: three children, a mother, and a father. The father was the only one who survived. He managed to pull out one child, a daughter, who died later in hospital. It took them several hours to haul the minivan to the surface. What could anyone do? A car fills quickly. Water makes movements slow. A scramble over the seats takes forever, like a thick-limbed nightmare. Ted can't imagine the feeling of failure that must haunt that father. Heather used to use the story as a warning, a way of keeping Leslie and Anna quiet in the back seat. That's when the girls started holding their breath.

OVER DINNER LAST WEEK, Ted told Heather about the property. He recounted Jim's description of the five acres of untouched land, the hundred-year-old trees, the salmon fishing, the cliff that drops into a clear, calm bay. He didn't tell her about the weathered Adirondack chair he imagined set near the edge of the cliff, where he could have his morning coffee and look out at the ocean—he kept that one for himself.

"What do you think?" Ted said.

"Sounds like an oasis." Heather picked up her fork and poked it around the plate without picking up anything.

"I could use a new project." Ted leaned back in his chair, hands behind his head, and looked around the room. "There's not much left to do around here."

"Sure," Heather said, raising her eyebrows in agreement. "You like to be busy."

Ted and Heather own a house in Fairfield, a three-bedroom revamped 1920s heritage home on Wildwood Avenue, a short drive to Gonzales Beach and Beacon Hill and an easy commute to Heather's dental practice and his office in downtown Victoria. When they moved in, Heather had the house repainted and chose an imperial green with a red trim for the windowsills and front door. It's not a colour Ted would have chosen, but it's grown on him and suits the neighborhood, and he has to admit the house looks exceptional during the holidays. His favourite part of the day is the short trip from his car to his front door; along the walkway, with a quick stop at the mailbox, the clack of its little metal door, and up the steps until the moment his feet rest on the welcome mat.

"I think I'll take the girls with me," Ted said. They had stopped eating, but their plates still sat in front of them, the food long gone cold and both Ted and Heather too tired to clear the table. Anna and Leslie had excused themselves. From upstairs, pop music blared, commingling with the sound of the television downstairs.

"Would you like to come?" he said.

"Pardon?" For the first time during the meal, Heather looked directly at him. Sometimes he had the urge to reach out to her, give her a shake, shout: *Wake up.*

"Sorry, I was thinking of something else," she said, scraping the food to one side of the plate.

"Can you get time off work?" Ted popped a cold carrot into his mouth, not because he wanted to eat it, but for something to do. He had the urge to spit it out, but realized that would be ridiculous and instead held it in his mouth for a moment before crunching through it and swallowing. The carrots were undercooked.

"Maybe," Heather said. "Although I could get some stuff done here while you're gone." He didn't picture Heather getting stuff done. He pictured her making tea and wandering around the house, forgetting her half-empty mug somewhere to get cold and heating the kettle all over again. He imagined cold cups of half-finished tea all over the house. He had a suspicion she was cheating on him or thinking of cheating on him. He had acted the same way two years ago, when he was thinking of cheating on her.

"Not next week but the week after," Ted said.

Heather carried the plates into the kitchen. "For how long?"

"Couple days." Ted sat back in his chair and considered getting up to help, but he felt too comfortable and instead watched Heather move around the kitchen.

"I think I'll stay. I could use the time," she said, scraping off the dishes. "Don't let Leslie eat a lot of junk. She's gaining weight again. I'm going to have to put her back on that diet."

Ted didn't argue with the diets; he let Heather do as she wished. She was convinced Leslie's "episodes" were the result of poor nutrition. Ever since the social worker had paid them a visit, Heather had been taking out stacks of books from the library: *Superfoods for Special Kids, Brain Foods for Teens, Healthy Diets for Super Kids.* Ted thought these so-called "episodes" — the screaming and the violence — were nothing more than the antics of a spoiled brat. Leslie was immature, afraid to grow up; she still played with Barbie dolls at fourteen. It was ridiculous, Leslie calling child services for a slap across the face, making them sit through a family assessment, the counsellor's critical gaze, the long pauses as he cautiously chose his words. Ted would never forget the look of distress and satisfaction on Leslie's face when he opened the door to the man with the guarded smile and the file folder. Her expression read as both a question and an affirmation: *I can do this to you.*

Heather hadn't been the same since, hadn't been the same with him since. It was an embarrassment, two professionals being interrogated like that. It was as though she blamed it on him, somehow — his late nights and extended workweeks — but he wasn't the one who had raised his hand and he wasn't the one who had called child services.

Ted got out of his chair and went over to Heather, who stood at the sink rinsing the dishes. "Maybe the trip will cheer Anna up," Heather said. "She's been miserable to me."

He leaned into her, bent to her ear. "Anna's fine. She's always fine," he whispered. "She's the good one, remember?" Anna was the child who sang you songs while she helped load the dishwasher, who left her dirty boots at the door, who cleaned her plate without bribery. Leslie was the child who ate glue.

"I don't know if I'd go that far," Heather said, shaking her head. "I think she might be flunking out of Camosun."

"Anna got straight A's in high school. She's adjusting." He wrapped his arms around her and laced his fingers near her stomach. "The trip will be good for both of them. I'll talk to them, straighten things out. We'll eat vegetables all week-end." He kissed the back of her neck. "I'm trying to make you happy." Heather gently unlaced his fingers and lifted his arms off her, continuing to rinse the dishes. Her lips pressed together in a tight smile. "What's the joke?" Ted asked.

She shook her head. "Nothing. Take the girls. You'll have fun."

THEY'VE ONLY BEEN DRIVING along the winding island road for ten minutes when Anna starts to groan in the back seat. "Pull over. I'm going to be sick."

"Carsickness is all in your head," Leslie says.

"Shut up. Dad, stop."

As soon as Ted pulls over Anna throws open the door, stumbling along the side of the road, clinging to the long grasses beside the ditch. Leslie hops out of the car and scans the bushes, looking for the best blackberries and popping them in her mouth. Ted flips open his phone—the screen shows emergency service only. His client will have to wait.

Mist hangs back in the forest like a curtain, creating a sound barrier, leaving everything dewy and still and filling Ted with an unjustifiable sense of hope—for what, he has no idea. Maybe the property, the potential summer house. This part of the island is sheltered from the winds off the strait, the branches of the towering evergreens fossilized in their still-ness, not a quiver in their needles. Something in the air—the smell of fir—is stirring good memories, and when the inevit-ability of his own death suddenly grips him, Ted reassures himself, knowing that when that day comes, he'll be able to look back on this trip with a sense of accomplishment: he'll buy the property, hand down a parcel of land to his girls. It's as though he has woken clear-headed from a bad sleep. He hasn't felt this way since Anna and Leslie were young, when Ted and Heather would take them island-hopping in the summer, spending a week ferrying around the Gulf Islands. The girls loved the ferries; they would stand out on deck at the bow, mouths wide open in the salty wind. Anna could name all the islands they passed—Pender, Saturna, Mayne. One summer, for no special reason—either he or Heather was busy with work—they stopped going, and they haven't been back since.

Leslie opens her stained hand and offers Ted a selection of plump blackberries. He thanks her and pops one in his mouth, savouring its tartness. She eats the rest of the handful, dark purple juice oozing out from between her lips. Ted laughs and puts his arm around her, pulling her toward him and giving her shoulder a squeeze. "We haven't done this in a while, have we?" he says.

"It reminds me of something." Leslie wipes the juice off her lips with the back of her hand and cranes her neck to take in the tops of the trees. "Did we come here when we were kids, like, on this exact road?"

"Not here," Ted says. "This is all new."

Anna walks back toward them, pale and unsteady.

"Did you puke?" Leslie asks, getting back in the car.

Anna follows her, getting in the front seat. "Keep going, but don't take the turns so fast."

"A deer!" Leslie says, pointing to a doe nipping at the underbrush along the edge of the forest.

"I'm sure we'll see lots of them," Ted says. "They don't have many predators here."

"Am I supposed to keep my eyes open or closed?" Anna asks, her eyes squeezed shut.

"It's so cute. Come on, Anna, look," Leslie says, shaking her arm.

"Fuck off," Anna shouts, shoving her sister to one side of the car. The sharpness in her tone shocks them all into silence for a few seconds. Ted turns on the engine and the deer runs into the forest, vanishing behind the wall of fog.

"Why are you so pissy?" Leslie says, her voice quiet and hurt.

"Leslie, don't say pissy," Ted says, turning back to the road.

"Anna can say 'fuck off', but I can't say 'pissy.'"

"The cabin's on the edge of that hill." Ted points up ahead.

"Where's the ocean?" Leslie asks.

"The cabin's not on the ocean. It's on a lake."

"Oh." Leslie sounds disappointed. Anna lurches forward in her seat with her hand over her mouth. "Stop the car."

THEY EAT AN EARLY dinner of cold cuts, bread, and sliced tomatoes with salt and pepper. The girls become quiet and sullen in their new environment. Leslie's giddiness disappears. They're both disappointed the cabin has no television. Ted made a production of the bicycles propped up against the garage awning, taking one for a quick circle of the front yard as the girls stood, arms crossed, unimpressed.

Ted and Anna drink wine out of mugs because they can't find glasses, and Ted gives Leslie two small tasters. This perks her up right away and after the first sip the chatter starts once again. She hoots like an owl, saying, "Listen. It's weird. It's so quiet. *Hoo, Hoo.*" Over dinner their conversation is self-conscious, but loosens up as Ted pours a second glass of wine for Anna and himself. When he mentions Leslie's "boyfriend on the ferry," she blushes and Anna teases her ruthlessly. On the bookshelf Leslie finds a deck of cards and hands it to Ted. "What do you want to play?" he asks as he shuffles them, enjoying the sound of the deck breaking.

"Go Fish," Leslie says. She reaches for the wine bottle and Ted stops her, placing his hand over hers. "I don't think so," he says.

"Come on. You barely gave me any."

Ted looks to Anna who shrugs and looks around as if to say, *Is there any harm, here in the middle of nowhere?* "A drop,"

Ted says, pouring a finger of wine into her mug. "Don't tell your mother."

Leslie grins, pleased. Her teeth are red.

THEY PLAY CARDS ON the porch for the better part of an hour, shouts of *Go Fish* echoing across the lake, before Ted leaves the cabin, driving back to the ferry dock in search of cell reception and a pie for dessert. He buys blueberry at the market and tries his client first, getting voicemail, and then calls Heather. Her tired voice makes him instantly sleepy. "How are the girls?"

"Good. In fact, they're great. Leslie's at least trying to behave."

Heather laughs softly on the other end of the line and for a little too long; Ted starts to think the joke may have been about something else. "It's quiet here without them," she finally says.

"It's quiet here too." When he says these words, Ted's eyes go instinctively out to the ocean, where the last ferry of the day is loading. He suddenly feels paranoid, as though at this very moment, Heather may have a naked man in bed beside her. "You'll have to come with us next time."

"Can I talk to them?" she says, ignoring his offer.

"They're at the cabin. There's no phone, no cell service, no TV. It's rustic. I came into town to buy pie."

"What about Leslie's diet?"

"We're just having some fun."

Silence fills the phone line. The ferry leaves the dock and sends a puff of smoke into the air.

"I should go," Ted says, suddenly feeling restless and annoyed. "I should too."

Neither one of them says goodbye.

TED CAN SEE THE cabin from a fair distance along the road. The lights in all the rooms are blazing, the cabin's reflection flickering on the surface of the black lake. He has an urge to abandon the car and walk the rest of the way, take in the night sky and the smell of the firs. His buzz is wearing off and his true urge is for a walk with a half-drunk bottle of wine. He drives the rest of the way to the cabin, and as he steps out of the car, he can hear the girls laughing the way they used to when they were small, their fast-paced babble like humming-bird wings, out of place in the dark evening. He stands in the driveway for a few minutes trying to catch bits of their conversation, but most of what they're saying is nonsensical.

When he walks in, the bottle of red wine they drank from at dinner is empty on the kitchen table and the girls have uncorked another. They sit sprawled out on the floor, playing cards and laughing hysterically. The energy in the cabin has changed since he left, the playfulness replaced by something frenetic, wild.

"You brought pie," Leslie squeals, snatching it out of his hands. "What kind?"

"Pay attention. Count your cards," Anna says, grabbing Leslie's ankle. Leslie yelps and her cards flutter to the floor. "I don't care about cards," she says. "Let's eat pie."

Anna flops back on the floor and, spreading her arms wide, yawns at the ceiling. "All you do is eat."

"Did you let your sister drink all this wine?" Ted says, picking up the almost empty second bottle.

"It wasn't that much," Anna says, coming into the kitchen. "Is that the first bottle?"

"No, the second," Ted says.

"Oops," Anna giggles. "It was like a little itty bit. It's fine," she says, waving dismissively.

Leslie walks unsteadily into the kitchen and pulls a large knife out of the drawer, too large to properly cut pie, and starts trying to slice a huge wedge for herself. "It's fine," Leslie parrots, though Ted is pretty sure she's not following their conversation, judging by the single-mindedness with which she devours her dessert. She offers a forkful to Anna, who shakes her head. The bite of pie falls to the floor and Leslie scoops it up and pops it into her mouth.

"Ew," Anna says, leaning in to her sister's ear to make pig grunting noises. Leslie places her plate on the kitchen counter and pounces on Anna, putting her in a headlock. They end up spinning on the kitchen tiles, their arms wrapped around each others' necks. Ted pulls Leslie off Anna and holds her back as Anna gets to her feet. Leslie gets an arm free and flings it toward Anna, catching her on the cheek, and Ted grabs Leslie's arm and wrestles it against her chest. He turns her around and gives her a gentle shove into the living room.

"You touched my boob," Leslie screams at him, her face contorting so he can't tell whether she's going to laugh or cry. "Child molester. Rape. You rapist."

"Oh, why don't you go call child services then," Ted says, flinging his arms up in frustration. He can feel it all of a sudden — the flash of heat that made Heather lash out.

"Fuck you," Leslie shouts, red-faced.

"Up to your room—now," Ted says. He tries to grab her again and slips in his socks on the kitchen floor. He slams his open palm down on the counter. "Dammit, Leslie."

"I don't have a room here," Leslie screams.

"Then pick a bed and stay there."

Leslie goes stomping up the stairs and slams a door. A few seconds later the door opens. *"Hoo, Hoo, Hoo."* The door slams shut again. Anna rubs her cheek, where a red spot is forming.

"See," Ted says, "that's what happens when you let your little sister get drunk."

"Whatever," Anna says, pushing past him and heading toward the stairs.

"I don't think your mother would like this display of yours." Ted stands in the middle of the living room, folding his arms across his chest.

"Well, good thing she's not here," she says on her way upstairs.

"Anna." Ted follows her. "We're talking."

"She's looking for your fucking attention, Dad," Anna says, turning so they face each other. "Just like Mom. It's pretty fucking simple, really." She smiles unkindly before turning to run up the rest of the stairwell.

"Anna," he says, grabbing her to get her attention. The thinness under her sweater shocks him enough that he drops her arm. "You used to be a sweet girl," he says.

"And now what am I, Dad? What am I?" He stares at her blankly, her pale face. "You don't even know," she says, before leaving him on the stairs alone.

SOMETHING WAKES HIM IN the middle of the night. He was having a dream he was in the city and the city went dark. In his dream he stumbled through rooms feeling for light switches. When he wakes up, he believes for a moment that he's still in the blackout. The stillness and darkness are complete and for a moment he has trouble breathing. Then he remembers he is in a cabin on an island in the middle of the woods. Lying still in the bed, he's aware of his wilting erection, an erection that has no reason to be there anyway and makes him miss a Heather that no longer exists, a younger Heather before the children were grown.

He hears a door close softly—one of the girls in the kitchen, probably Leslie, going for her second helping of pie. He listens and thinks he hears footsteps outside on the gravel. There are no cars on the dirt road at this time. There's no reason for anyone to drive out here. He can hear some rustling out front, maybe a deer searching for food along the front hedges. He gets out of bed and opens the bedroom door quietly, standing there for a moment, letting his eyes adjust to the dark. The door to the girls' room is open. He can make out Leslie in one of the beds, her long dark hair a black halo against the white sheets, her limbs hanging off all the edges. He walks into the room and tries to make out Anna's shape in the bed beside Leslie. He creeps closer, trying to see a leg or arm poking out from under the comforter. He isn't convinced the bed is empty until he touches his hands to the cold sheets. Leslie tosses in her bed, mumbling, "Dad? What are you doing?"

"It's okay. Go back to sleep." He makes his way downstairs without turning on any lights, using his hands along the walls to guide himself.

On the front porch, he scans the bushes for deer or raccoons, but there's nothing. He tries to remember if there are bears on Quadra and recalls a story about them swimming the short distance between here and Vancouver Island. He grabs a rake by the door and walks out, standing quietly in the middle of the front yard until he hears something—a quick breath, a cough, a sigh. He pulls open the door of the garage with a slow creak. Inside he's surprised by a darkness that's even darker. There's a soft glow like embers in a tiny dollhouse fireplace and the smell of burning plastic.

"Anna?" He hears a crinkle of aluminum and coughing. In the corner of the garage, he can begin to make out the silhouette of Anna's body. She's sitting on a crate, her dark hair hanging around her face. "What are you doing?" Anna stands quickly and brushes off the back of her pants. "Nothing. Nothing," she says, walking past him. She makes her way across the grass, unsteady. He can see her clearly now, his eyes adjusted, the yard almost luminous after the total darkness of the garage.

"Anna," he says, his voice pleading in a way he doesn't expect. She stops in her tracks, but doesn't turn around. Her body sways gently from side to side. "What are you doing?" he says again. She turns toward him, her eyes wet and sparkling under the moon, her fingers picking at the skin of her lips, and they stare at each other. She's having trouble focusing on him, her head bobbing up and down, looking behind him, at his feet, at the sky. He can't find the words he needs. "What were you doing in the garage?"

"Hm." She presses her lips together and tries to look at him. Her eyes close and she says nothing for several seconds.

For a moment he thinks she's fallen asleep, until her eyelids flutter and she squints at him with a soft smile. "Nothing."

"Anna." He takes a step toward her.

"Dad! Jesus!" Her eyes bulge and she bites down hard on her lower lip. "Jesus!" She turns her back to him and runs her fingers through her hair, tugging in frustration. "Why are you here?" She starts to walk toward the front door.

"Where are you going?" he says. She doesn't answer him. "Are you going back to bed?" He follows her dark shape into the cabin and up the stairs to the bedroom, where Leslie is now sleeping. She climbs into bed and covers her head with the sheets. "Anna," he whispers.

Leslie rolls over and groans. "Dad, you keep waking me up."

"Go to sleep," he says. He goes back to his room and sits on the edge of the bed, listening. For several minutes he hears nothing, and then Leslie's soft snoring. He waits in the dark for a long time before heading down to the kitchen to collect the plates drying on the rack and put them back in their rightful places in the cupboards. From the rack he pulls a mug with the words *World's Best Grandpa* and fills it to the rim with wine. He sinks into one of the oversized sofa chairs by the window and looks out at the porch, the dock, the silvery shimmer of the lake. The absolute quiet is strange, as though he's suddenly lost his hearing. His eyes register the world in front of him and expect something—some proof of existence.

He lets the wine travel slowly over his tongue and coat his tight throat. It was easier to make the girls believe he could protect them when they were young. Back then his existence was enough to reassure them. One day when the girls were very young, they were driving toward Uptown Mall to go

Christmas shopping. Heather was dozing in the front seat, a Christmas list in her lap, and Leslie and Anna were sleeping in the back, small enough to still be in car seats. It was raining hard, the highway covered with puddles, and in the distance traffic had come to a standstill. There was construction on the highway and ahead of them a sea of red tail lights glowed in the dreary afternoon. They were the last car in the long line, and as they slowed down, Ted pumped the brakes, checking the rearview mirror as any good driver would. That's when he saw the sixteen-wheeler coming down the hill toward them. It was still several hundred feet away, but he knew it wouldn't be able to stop—it was coming too fast. As his eyes searched the sides of the highway, trying to find a place where he could pull out of the way, the truck fishtailed, coming toward them sideways. It all happened in slow motion, in a vacuum of sound. At that moment Anna woke—she couldn't have been older than five—her bright eyes watching him in the rearview mirror. She picked up on his fear and turned to see the truck, but she didn't cry out. She didn't even look scared— she looked at him. She sat up very straight and watched him. Past her head he could see the truck sliding toward them, and though he was still afraid, he felt calmer. He took his foot off the brake, ready to drive into the ditch, but before he even turned the wheel, the truck veered and careened along the shoulder of the highway, coming to rest a safe distance away from them.

When he turned around to check on Anna, she'd already closed her eyes and gone back to sleep. Her reaction gave him confidence in her, but also in himself. Back then he believed that together they could handle almost anything.

TED WAKES UP WITH a headache, a pain starting in the tightness along his shoulder blades and working its way up to his temples. He pulls on his sweatpants and laces up his old sneakers with the hope that an early-morning bike ride along the logging road will clear his head. The girls are still in bed, content in slack-mouthed sleep, their faces younger somehow. He half-expected Anna to be gone, though he's not sure why. There would be nowhere for her to go. Her restful presence in the bed makes him question last night's events, whether or not he dreamt the entire thing.

Ted stops at the bay window in the living room to look out over the backyard and down its steep slope to the lake. The clouds remain dense, the day never breaking through the morning light's first struggle. On the edge of the property, a deer noses in the salmonberry bushes, its gait twitchy as though it's ready for a getaway at the slightest breeze through the treetops. He steps closer to the glass and the deer vanishes into the bushes, its soft brown flanks camouflaged by the branches. Ted realizes he would be a terrible hunter, and this makes him neither happy nor sad.

Outside the air is still damp from a heavy morning rain. Ted opens the garage door and steps inside. It's mostly empty, with dusty shelves at the back and milk crates stacked in one corner. He goes over to the spot where Anna was sitting the night before and gets down on his knees, scanning the dirt floor for any sign, a bit of tinfoil, a butt, ashes, anything to give him a clue as to what she's been doing, but there's nothing. There's no sign of Anna in this garage. He picks up some of the dirt and sniffs it—ordinary dirt, not drug-laced junkie dirt. He brushes off his hands and goes to pick up the bike in the grass.

Ted follows the logging road in the direction of Jim's real estate property. He can't remember the last time he went for a bike ride, but judging by the tension building in his shoulders and chest it's been a while. His calf muscles tighten. He should've stretched before, but he's too stubborn to stop now—he digs his feet into the pedals and pushes on, whizzing past undergrowth thick with dewy ferns. Birds call out from somewhere deep in the trees.

He should have checked the garage last night or searched through Anna's pockets for that tinfoil, figured out what she was smoking. Heather would have done it differently; she would have grabbed Anna by the shoulders and demanded an answer. She would have pulled her into her arms, held her tightly, smelled her hair, slapped her. She would have tried to get a sense of what was going on.

The road in front of Ted winds down a long hill. He picks up the pace, focusing on his loud, uneven breath. Suspicions flash through his brain, but they come too quickly and then disappear: Anna's long absences, her vanishing hunger, her vanishing body, her chewed lips. Everything is wrong somehow; he sees it now like a doll built from mismatched parts, the limbs too thin, the head too large. Her eyes are wrong. The wheels pick up momentum, flying as he surrenders control, his hands braced on the rattling handlebars. He can hear a rumbling behind him and he pumps the brakes, moving over to the side of the road. As he stops and catches his breath, a logging truck roars by, coming so close he can smell the freshly cut lumber. He clutches his hand to his chest and takes in deep ragged gulps of air. He has a sudden urge to reach out and grab onto one of the chains keeping the logs together, to go off flying with the truck through the forest, though common sense tells him what would actually happen: his arm ripped out of its socket, the rest of him left on the bike alone on the road. The truck's momentum catches him off balance and his foot slips into the ditch, tipping him over into the tall weeds.

He pushes the bike out first and then clamours up, wiping the dirt off his legs and arms. The truck has already clattered down the rest of the hill and takes a sharp curve at the bottom of the road. It looks unstable enough to go hurtling right through the forest, but somehow stays on course, keeping its load in position. Ted bangs his fist on his chest, trying to ignore the pain shooting through his shoulder: a sure sign of a heart attack. He lets his vision blur with the throb of blood rushing through his head. He could die here on this logging road. Someone would find him. Wrap him in a blanket. Put him in the back of a pickup and tie him down with rope for the long ride back to the mainland.

Behind him he can hear laughter and the whistling spokes of a bicycle wheel. "Are you going to keel over?" Leslie shouts, braking beside him with a spray of dirt. He can feel the muscles around his heart slacken and, with his daughter as a distraction, the pain in his shoulder disappears.

"I didn't know you were following me," Ted says, embarrassed, hoping Leslie didn't see him fall into the ditch.

"Why didn't you wake me up? I thought we were all going together?" She gets off the bike and pulls her ankle behind her, stretching first one leg and then the other. "I tried to get Anna up, but she was bitchy."

"Don't say 'bitchy.'" Ted wipes the sweat off his forehead. "You both looked tired. You girls had a late night."

"I'm not tired." She smiles shyly at him, completely different from the tipsy, belligerent girl last night.

"Well, let's go, then," Ted says, starting down the road. Without discussion they both decide to walk their bikes. After several minutes of silence Leslie asks, "Do you know where we're going?"

"I think this is it, up ahead." Ted veers and climbs up a steep dirt driveway that disappears into the forest.

The site is barren, cleared of all vegetation, with huge mounds of earth along the edge of the lot. Tall firs stand around the perimeter of the property like mourners at a burial. There are still stumps to be dug up, and rusted machines — forklifts and backhoes — are parked along the driveway, looking as though they've been there for years. Ted sits on a stump to catch his breath. He's still sweating. He watches Leslie walk slowly along the edges of the property. "We could put a pool here." Leslie stands at the back of the lot in the middle of an empty square of mud.

"So, what do you think?" He follows her gaze to the tops of the trees and watches her eyes focus on something distant, maybe the possible view of Cortes Island and the water. He is having trouble visualizing anything different, anything beyond the trucks, stumps, machinery, and porta-potties. He can't picture his Adirondack chair, or rather he can't picture himself in the chair. He had it drawn out in his mind, but now he sees nothing but the bare trees, the stripped branches, the mud and sky.

"We could cut down those trees there, I guess," Leslie says, pointing to the left of the bulldozer. She looks out at the land, indifferent, uncommitted. She can see it, but he guesses she isn't sure she likes it. "I don't know. It's kind of a long way to come," she says.

"You think?" He knows she's becoming a smart young woman, albeit slowly—but sooner than he probably realizes, she'll be smarter than him. She lies back on a large stump and looks up at the sky. "It's kind of far for a weekend place."

"Hm," he thinks, sitting down beside her. "You're probably right."

"Maybe look on Salt Spring." She smiles at him. "Sorry, Dad."

"What are you sorry for?"

She sits up and tugs self-consciously at the back of her sweatshirt, trying to cover the gap of bulging flesh above the waist of her jeans. She's dwarfed by the sawed-off tree, sitting like a little girl, with her knees tucked into her chest. He gives her a gentle pat on the back. She shrugs her shoulders. "Nothing, I guess. I wanted to like it too."

He rests his arm across her shoulder for a moment and then pulls her close in a hug.

"Dad," Leslie says, laughing uncomfortably, "you're squishing me." He pulls away and they sit quietly.

A wind passes through the trees, picking up Leslie's hair as though she were sitting at the bow of a boat. It moves the branches of the huge firs and gives the two of them a better view of the ocean.

THEY DECIDE TO GO home early. Anna stays in the bathroom until Ted is outside honking the horn, and when she comes out they barely exchange a glance. The girls sleep during the ride back to the harbour. The thick smell of a night of drinking hangs in the car and Ted rolls down the window for some fresh air. The ferry shakes as it pulls away from the dock. A tugboat presses along beside them, a sort of sentinel, heaving headfirst into the oncoming waves. It rides each swell to its crest, suspended for a moment mid-air before plunging down the other side in a wake of white foam. The island is still covered in mist, still circled by a grey ocean. The fog has lifted slightly and the rocky shores are visible, littered with washed-up logs; their gnarled branches and stumps look like limbs and torsos in the muted light.

Ted looks up into the rearview mirror and catches Anna watching him. Fear flickers across her gaze, changes her entire face for a quick second, and scares Ted enough to catch his breath in his throat. He looks away, and when he looks back Anna's eyes are closed. Her face is new in a way he can't identify; there is something unrecognizable there. He can hear the nasally inhale of her breath, the feather-light rasp he'd never detected before, the sound like an engine rattle to him now, a broken-down thing. She looks so serene he can almost convince himself he imagined her eyes opening and all along she's been sleeping peacefully.

As they unload from the ferry, Ted holds his breath.

BACK ON THE ISLAND HIGHWAY the rain starts again. Ted turns on the windshield wipers and the CBC. He opens the window a little wider and takes deep breaths of the wet, evergreen-filled air. The mountains are still covered in patches of snow, but the poplars are dripping with red catkins. He decides not to tell Heather about the weekend, about Anna. He'll tell her the property was a dud. He'll tell her the girls enjoyed the fresh air, they should get away more often, next time Heather should come. The rain turns hard and Ted rolls up the window, clicks the windshield wipers to their top speed. He'll say those things, but he won't believe them. This will be the last time.

A transport truck approaches in the rearview mirror and passes them on the left. As it overtakes them, the car rattles gently. He's aware of the weight of the steel chassis, the spin of the tires, the phantom feeling of impact. The truck's wake kicks up a slap of water against Ted's windshield as it shuttles past. Even though he anticipates it, he still jumps. He's blinded for a few seconds. The wipers go *swoosh*, *swoosh* across the glass. And just like that, everything slips away.

WHALE STORIES

THE SCRATCHING OF THE pine needles on the roof woke William from a dream that left his armpits damp. The wind crawled through the trees, weighing down the boughs, forming fierce patterns on the wall above his bed. An empty pillowcase tacked up with two pushpins covered the bedroom window. His mom hadn't found time to buy curtains yet. They didn't have a kitchen table or a TV or a couch or a doormat. The bed and breakfast was bigger than their house in the city, and for now most of their furniture went into the guest rooms.

There was something else — another noise, some sort of animal snuffling and pawing at the side of the house. Shaking himself out of his covers, William flipped on the bedside lamp and checked the alarm clock. It was already nine-thirty. He pushed the pillowcase aside and opened the window an inch. The wind cried through the crack, spitting salty air into his face. There was a clatter of garbage cans below and he caught sight of a scruffy tail disappearing under the porch: one of the wild dogs again.

At the end of the yard, the huge arms of the pines rolled like they were trapped in an underwater storm. The clouds collected in dark barrels along the mountainside. He could see a small section of the beach through the thick cover of pine trees, the waves reaching up, breaking, and then dropping onto the grey sand. William yanked the window shut, rattling his rock collection, which sat in a tidy line on his windowsill. The rocks came from Australia, Africa, South America. His father was a geologist and travelled all over the world collecting samples from the different continents. The travertine rock—William's favorite—fell to the floor, ricocheting under the bed, but he had no time to find it this morning. He dressed quickly, pulling on his dark blue sweatpants and a grey sweater. He had planned to be up hours earlier, before his mom and his sister, but he hadn't slept well last night. He kept hearing footsteps and voices in the upstairs bedrooms. He still wasn't used to the B&B, the strangers in the house moving around at all hours. The floors were rough and creaky, and it took him a while to figure out how to sneak around soundlessly. When the guests left for their daily outings he would open the doors to their rooms—something his mother had warned him not to do. He only ever took two and a half steps into the room and from that point craned his neck to get a look inside their suitcases.

In the mornings, William's mom left their breakfast on the kitchen counter or in the oven to keep warm while she bounced back and forth from the kitchen to the dining room, serving the guests. Her cheeks were always pink and she smiled widely, with only a small crinkle of concentration on her forehead. She did look happier to William, but only when she was working, cleaning up or listing the best spots to go kayaking. The guests came from all over—Ohio or Toronto or Oslo. His mother told him once that instead of opening their home to one traveller—his dad—she could now open it to all of them. William sometimes felt like one of his own rocks but much bigger, rooted in the middle of the ocean, with people from interesting places drifting past on their way to somewhere better. His mother kept saying this was her dream, something she never could have done if she was still living in the city with William's father.

In the kitchen his younger sister, Miriam, sat on a chair, her plate of waffles balanced on her knees, the plate looking dangerously unstable each time she cut herself a bite. William could tell Miriam had already spent most of the morning outside. Her jeans were grass-stained and she was wearing her yellow rain hat. This was probably her second breakfast.

"Where are you going?" she said.

William grabbed a waffle from the counter and ate it standing up. "To the beach."

"It's going to rain."

William shrugged.

"Why do you have to go to the beach every day? I found a hollow tree. Just past the road up there," she said, motioning behind her with her fork.

"Good for you," William said, stuffing the rest of the waffle in his mouth.

"I can show you where it is."

William ignored her, gave her a half-hearted wave goodbye, and headed outside, grabbing his pocket knife before shutting the kitchen door. He kept it hidden in his rain boots by the coat hanger. His father had given him the Swiss Army knife last year on his ninth birthday. It had come all the way from New Zealand in a large yellow manila envelope with his name written in big capital letters across the front. His mom and dad had fought about it over the phone, about whether it was an appropriate gift for a boy his age.

The wind tugged at William's wet hair and crept up the sleeves of his sweater, sending a shiver down his back. He took the porch steps two at a time and bounded for the forest. Now the tree trunks swayed back and forth, their bare, spiky tips slicing through the dense fog billowing off the ocean. Usually it took him a while to cover the distance between his house and the water's edge because he often stopped to watch a beetle's progress or to unravel the tight coil of a worm with his finger, but this morning he hurried along the path, anxious to get to the beach. William scowled as he hurtled past one of the B&Bers standing in the backyard—a birdwatcher with expensive-looking binoculars. He couldn't understand why his mother loved to share their space with these strangers. Back in the city, they'd had a large, fenced-off yard where there were never any birdwatchers getting in his way or little kids wanting to play little kid games or kayakers flapping around in the water like angry birds. Whenever there were children staying at the B&B, his mother coaxed him and his sister into playing with them. Miriam seemed to like the other children, drawing them into make-believe games in which she often chased them, pretending to be an elephant or a rhinoceros. Miriam, in fact, seemed lonely and sad when the children were gone, but William preferred to be alone. Most of the time the children were much younger than him or had no interest in rocks or traps.

First thing to do this morning was to sharpen a stick. William wasn't sure why, but he had a feeling. The wind had knocked down lots of branches, so it wasn't hard to find a good one. He positioned himself on a rock with the branch laid across his legs and whittled the wood to a sharp point. A ragged dog, its grey coat matted with dirt and burrs, ambled over. William stiffened as the dog sniffed at his stick and his feet. He was wearing sandals and the dog gave his bare toes a lick before trotting toward the beach.

The dogs were a problem in the area. His mom said it was probably cottagers bringing their pets on holiday with them. Maybe the pets ran away or the owners were cruel and didn't want them anymore, but the dogs were left behind. They bred and there was a pack of them now, all mutts, dogs turned wild. He never touched them. Many of them had sores or bits of their ears missing. Their eyes were shifty and they panted even when they weren't running. Usually they left people alone and you'd only see them when they went rummaging through the garbage cans. At night it was hard to tell them apart from the coyotes. William was sure he sometimes heard them following him through the woods or watching him while he was on the beach. Some of the other residents would shoot the more troublesome ones, but no one really felt good about that. There was always a lot of talk in town about what to do about *those damned dogs*. Everyone called them *those damned dogs*. Even his mother, and she never swore.

The second thing William had to do this morning was to check the hole. He walked up the beach toward the rocky outcrop to the west, whacking with his new spear at the tall ferns that grew on the outskirts of the sand. The waves had left deep tidal pools along the rocks and he splashed through them, scattering tiny fish and sending crabs scuttling to their hiding spots. He loved the sound of their legs scratching across the boulders. On any other morning he would have stopped to peer into the puddles, maybe sent Miriam for an empty ice cream bucket so they could collect specimens. Miriam was meticulous about it, counting each crab, noting the ones that were missing legs or had odd markings, and giving each one a name. But this morning he was in a hurry. He wanted to get to the hole as quickly as possible.

He had visited this part of the beach every morning since they moved to the Sunshine Coast. It had taken him a long time to dig the hole. And it had taken him a while to pick a good spot. He chose an area protected by a rocky outcrop that stretched right into the ocean and hid the beach from view. He dug a couple of small trial holes and decided on a spot near the treeline where the sand was still damp but where the hole wouldn't fill with too much water. The first week he started digging right after lunch and only stopped when it was dark and he could hear his mother's voice yelling *bedtime*. He had worked straight through the noon heat, taking breaks every fifteen minutes and running into the ocean to splash water on himself. In ten minutes he'd be dry again and by the end of the day his body would have grown a second, salty skin. The first week had been hard work.

The second week it rained and he was down in the hole every day with a bucket trying to keep it from caving in. He found an old abandoned shed back in the forest. It was covered in moss with half the roof sunk in and the windows thick with spiderwebs. He pulled some old boards from the siding, dragged them through the forest, and propped them up along the sides of the hole, trying to hold up the walls. Since then, luckily, there'd been a dry spell.

In the third week, with the weather hot and sunny again, the hole was deep enough that it provided a little bit of shade while he worked. The challenge in the third week had been getting in and out of the hole. One day he had dug so fast and deep that he couldn't get back out. For a while he had been convinced he had captured himself. He screamed for ten minutes straight and no one came. Then he sat and cried for another five. He imagined Miriam peering down at him with all her questions and then going to tattle — or worse, the B&B kids wandering over and staring with their googly eyes. They would think he was some sort of treasure or a wild sea creature, wet and thrashing, trying to get back to the water. Finally he discovered he could claw his way out, but that meant partially refilling the hole.

The next day he rigged a long rope he found in the abandoned shed to a nearby tree and used that to get in and out. The rope was dry and brittle, but it held. When the hole was deep enough — almost two feet taller than William — he covered it with large branches. He warned his sister not to go to that part of the beach. He told her there was a dead whale with its eyes pecked out, and that it stank so bad you would throw up on the spot if you went anywhere near it. She kept away from the whole area, but every few days she would ask him if the whale was still there. He would tell her about the carcass in different stages of decomposition: the tail munched away, the fin all droopy and slimy, crabs happily eating away the huge whale tongue. Miriam would listen to his stories and wrinkle her nose. Sometimes she'd gag or pretend to plug her ears. One day, he guessed, the whale would disappear and he wouldn't have to lie anymore.

He never worried about his mom wandering in that direction. She liked to walk east, probably because it wasn't so rocky. The beach stretched out smooth and glossy at low tide, as if the land and water were one. William's mother warned them to be careful walking out on the sand. The ocean could be tricky, could sneak around you until you were left standing on an island, alone. Miriam had become uneasy about this and kept one eye trained on the ocean at all times when she was looking for shells.

Their mother's walks were a habit now and came after dinner without any announcement. Miriam and William were never invited along and knew not to ask. For the first few evening walks, Miriam would clutch the porch railing and cry, believing their mother was never coming back. But now they barely blinked as she quietly escaped the house. Every once in a while, though, William still followed her, but always at a distance, watching her from the forest. He would crouch behind the tall ferns, his breath shallow and painful in his chest. She stopped at a different spot every time, and when she found her spot, she would sit on the beach and sink her hands deeper and deeper into the sand, staring out at the water. Sometimes she sat for a couple minutes and sometimes she sat for an hour. The longer she sat at the beach, the greater the chance she would cry. When she was finished, she stood and wiped off her bottom, but with her hands covered in sand she usually just made it worse. There was always sand in the house. She made William and Miriam take off their sandals and hose off their feet before they came in, but she never noticed when she tracked the sand in herself.

For the past two weeks, William had been waiting and hoping. He hoped that at least something small would fall into his hole, and if he was lucky something bigger. He wondered about the hole at night when he was in bed. Sometimes the wind tricked him and he thought he heard a yelp or crying. On those nights he hardly slept, waiting for morning to come so he could go check out his catch, but there was never anything in the hole. A few nights earlier, he had an idea that came from watching one of the B&Bers fishing that day, something important he hadn't thought about before: the hole needed bait. While no one was watching, he slipped the rest of his bits of beef from his dinner plate into the pocket of his shorts, and while his mom took her after-dinner walk he ran to throw them on the branches covering the hole. He'd done this every night for the past three nights: chicken, fish, and last night, pork.

William had dug a hole once before, when he was much younger. Actually, it was his father who had done most of the digging, with a small plastic shovel that came with the beach set his mother had bought for him. They had gone to Spanish Banks for the day. His mother was pregnant with his sister and lounged on the beach blanket his father had set up for her under a tree. William spent the entire day running back and forth between his parents at top speed, helping his father with the digging and pressing his ear up to his mother's belly. His dad kept saying, "We must be on our way to China."

That night his dad had to explain that China was actually very far away and that it would take years of digging to get there, that it was much quicker to fly or take a boat. But William was disappointed. He felt misled. Looking now at the speckled rocks half-buried in the sand, he tried to remember where his father was at this moment. Digging somewhere in New Brunswick, he guessed. He was fairly sure that was the last place. When they moved, they left all of his father's clothes and books. His mom said it was easier for their father's work if he left his things in the city.

"HI," A SMALL BOY said.

William had been planning his attack should he find something in the hole, and he almost walked right into the kid. The boy was definitely one of the B&B guests and a couple of years younger than William—young enough that his parents still dressed him. William could tell by the way the boy's shirt was tucked in and cinched with a miniature belt. His hair was carefully combed to the right side of his forehead. He was in gumboots, standing ankle-deep in a tidal pool, pushing around a large bit of Styrofoam with his foot.

"Where are you going?" the boy asked.

William was surprised by the question at first, but realized he must have been walking with purpose. "None of your business."

"Can I come?" the boy asked, looking hopeful.

"No." They stared at each other blankly.

"I made a boat. It was for the crabs to float on. But I can't find any," the boy said, motioning to the large piece of Styrofoam.

"Doesn't look like much fun."

"Nah, it's not really. You want to help me sink it?"

William didn't bother answering. He raised his stick and whacked the boat, sending bits of Styrofoam flying everywhere.

"Wait for me," the boy yelled, running to the beach. "I need a stick, too."

William paused mid-strike and waited for the boy to return with his stick. The two boys swung and swung until all they were hitting was water, and tiny Styrofoam islands floated all around them.

"It never sinks," the boy said.

"Nope." William brushed bits of Styrofoam out of his hair. "I gotta go."

"Where are you going?"

"I told you already. It's none of your business." William started back on his course toward the rocks. The boy followed behind him for a ways, and when the boy didn't turn back William swung around to face him. "I said don't follow me." The boy took a couple more steps and William realized maybe the boy was older than he thought, just small for his age. William raised his stick. "Don't follow me or I'll stab your neck."

FROM THE TOP OF the rocky outcrop William had a good vantage point. He could see the boy walking back to the bed and breakfast—probably to tell on him. And he could see the hole. Something was different from the day before. The branches had shifted—only slightly, but he could tell they had definitely been moved. The meat was gone. Maybe the wind had moved the branches or a bird had tried to pick up the meat. Or maybe something had fallen in. He scrambled down the rock and ran toward the hole, sliding into a crouching position. As he leaned over, he accidentally kicked some sand over the edge. A faint shuffle and a sigh escaped from the depths of the trap. He sat back a moment and thought about the sound, listening for something else. His entire body shook with expectation and fear. His hole had trapped something; he didn't know what to think. In his hurry he had dropped his stick behind him. He ran back to grab it and crouched down again, taking deep breaths. Slowly, with his eyes squinted in anticipation, he began to pull the branches away gently, one by one, setting them down in the sand behind him.

The creature at the bottom of the hole was shadowy, but he could still make it out: a dog. A small one, maybe a year old. It was grubby, a mutt like all the others, its brown-and-gold coat spotted with bits of rough skin from too much scratching. But it was still alive and that wasn't what was supposed to happen. The dog was lying in a few inches of murky water. The ocean had seeped into the hole over the past week, bit by bit. The sand William had kicked in was scattered across the dog's belly and on its face. Its front legs seemed to be bent back too far and it was blinking, trying to get the sand out of its eyes. When he had imagined the creature in the hole it was always dead. Most of the time it was a skeleton with bleached-white bones and he took the skull home and put it on the steps of the porch. Other times it was a bit messier and he had to do real man's work. The pocketknife came out on these occasions, but the thing was always partly decomposed.

It was never a broken thing. And it was never a crying dog. The dog had started to whimper and give little yelps. William walked the circumference of the hole and came to the conclusion that the dog was dying. He turned from it and ran.

Back over the rocks he slipped and fell and didn't feel a thing, didn't even check his knees for gashes. He could still hear the dog's whimpers. He ran across the length of the beach and up the path to the B&B. He ran through the empty living room and into the dining room. There was a family sitting at the dining room table: a mother, a father, two girls, and the boy from the beach. They stared at him in stunned silence. The boy grimaced. William's mother was laying out one of her many maps of the area.

"What have you done?" she gasped. Her face crumbled and William was sure his mother already knew everything.

"I'm sorry, I'm sorry," William choked, out of breath from running.

"Oh, your knee. What a mess, come here. Let me have a look."

William had forgotten his knee. He looked down. Bits of gravel were embedded in the pink flesh and the blood had spilled over the torn skin and trickled down his leg. It made him ill to look at his own blood and the tissue under his skin.

His mother pulled him into the kitchen, away from the guests. She picked him up and sat him on a stool, ran a clean cloth under the tap and pressed it to his knee. She carefully cleaned around the edges and patted the raw centre, gently picking out pebbles with a small pair of tweezers.

"Always into things." She frowned, trying to look stern. She rinsed out the cloth and ran it up and down his leg, wiping off the blood. The cloth was cool. It felt wonderful to him. He wanted to take it for the dog.

"What happened?" she asked.

William shook his head. "I slipped on some rocks," he whispered.

"Well, you have to be more careful." His mother inspected his knee once more. "I never get to do this anymore. You're getting too big." She took a large box of Band-Aids from one of the cupboards and sealed up the cut. "Be more careful next time," she said, patting his cheek. "Why don't you play inside now."

WILLIAM WENT BACK TO his room to take a nap, but he couldn't sleep. He remembered his rock and slithered under the bed on his stomach. He carefully placed the travertine back between the whale-shaped sandstone and the almond-sized quartzite. He ran his hand along the windowsill, gently brushing the rocks with the tips of his fingers, watching them spin slowly. He had placed the quartzite in his mouth once and chipped one of his molars. He picked up the travertine and licked the smooth surface ringed in rusty reds and ambers.

Whenever his father returned from one of his trips, he would pull a new rock from his shirt pocket. Sometimes he would give William a rock right in the middle of the airport with William still wrapped around his neck in a hug. Other times, William had to wait until they reached the parking lot, aware the entire time of the hard lump pressed to his chest as his father carried him to the car. And sometimes his father forgot all about the rock. The next morning there would be a stone sharing William's pillow. He could see his father's long fingers with their carefully clipped nails—he kept them very short to keep the dirt from collecting under them—turning the rocks gently as though they were fragile as eggs. He would smooth his fingers over their surfaces, giving them a particular sheen. Over time they dulled and William would rub them furiously with his own fingertips without any results. Licking them was the only way he could get them to shine. Miriam never got rocks as presents from their father. She got notebooks or fancy pencils, and once she got a large shell full of the sounds of the ocean. Later their father explained that the shell did not contain the sounds of the ocean, but rather the sounds of the inner workings of their own ears—their blood and bones.

William opened the window and stuck his nose outside. The wind had let up and the clouds hung low and full. A stillness had fallen over the beach, the occasional lap of a wave the only sound, no longer rhythmic but stuttering and sad. William knew he had to go back, but he didn't feel like hurrying anymore.

WHEN HE REACHED THE hole the dog had stopped crying. It was lying quietly, taking in shallow breaths. Another, older dog lay near the hole, tongue hanging out sleepily, spotted belly exposed. William kicked sand on the old dog and it raised its head a moment before letting it drop back with a thump. He yelled at it and hit it with his stick.

"Get out of here, mutt. Stupid shithead mutt, move."

The dog rolled over onto his back, panting heavily up at

William, its paws swimming in the air. He kicked more sand on the dog. He kicked sand everywhere: at the old dog, at the dying dog. The dog in the hole started to whimper again and then yelp, short, piercing cries that bounced across the water. William sat down and pushed at the sand with his feet and hands. It only took him twenty minutes to fill the hole. Much less time than it had taken to dig.

AS WILLIAM CLIMBED BACK up the rocks, a light sprinkling of mist coated his face and arms. By the time he got to the top it had started to rain—fat, silly drops that hit him in the eyes and trickled down his forehead in streams. When he touched his face, he could feel the red heat of his cheeks. He had the same wetness in his underarms as he'd had this morning. He stopped at the edge of the rocks to take a few deep breaths. Miriam in her yellow rain hat was trudging up the bank toward the house. He turned and watched the rain patter over the mound where the hole used to be, the drops smoothing the surface until that part of the beach looked exactly like every other part of the beach. He stayed on the edge of the rocks until his jeans were soaked and the flush had drained from his cheeks.

WHEN HE GOT BACK to the house, Miriam was sitting on the floor in the living room, braiding a blonde girl's hair. The girl sat poised, one knee bent, as though she was ready to bolt instantly, but Miriam still had a firm hold on one of her braids. The other stuck out crookedly from the back of her head. It looked painfully tight. The bang from the kitchen door woke his mother, who was napping on the couch beside the two girls.

"Is the whale still there, William?" Miriam said, without looking at him. She was still focused on the blond girl's hair.

"The whale?" he said, confused for a moment.

"Yeah, the dead one. I saw you by the rocks."

"No," he said. "No, it disappeared."

"What whale?" his mom said, sitting up now on the couch. The left side of her face was lined with sleep creases.

"There was a huge whale down that way on the beach with no eyes. The birds ate its eyes." Miriam said. She finished the braid and the little girl instantly stood and ran into the dining room without saying goodbye.

"A dead whale? Why didn't you tell me about this?" His mother looked worried.

"William said it was a secret. He said if you smelled the whale, you'd barf."

"William, where on the beach was it?"

"I don't remember."

"Past those rocks," Miriam said. William bent down and pretended to be busy taking off his shoes. He picked at the knots in his laces.

"Well, I hope you didn't touch it. William, take those sandy shoes outside." His mother sank back down onto the couch and curled up like she was getting ready to go back to sleep. "How could it just disappear?" she said, through a deep yawn.

William pulled off his shoes and looked at his hands. He had sand under his fingernails. "It doesn't matter," he said. "It's gone now."

THE ART OF EATING

CHARLIE BEAULIEU DOES NOT notice the day's unusual weather. As he drives to the restaurant, he does not notice the wind wrestling the trees into dramatic bows all along English Bay. He does not see the crazed kids sprinting along the edge of the shore, shouting in glee at the sheer size of the crashing waves. He misses the sight in the park across from the ocean of the remaining fall leaves shooting out of their once-tidy piles and forming miniature gold-brown tornadoes across the lawn. Bombing down Denman Street in his second-hand Honda Civic, he fails to see the light angling through the dark clouds gathering against the mountains. He doesn't feel the frigid note in the air or notice the birds fleeing for shelter. Charlie rolls the window down an inch to air out the smell of stale cigarettes clinging to the car's upholstery. He stares dully, straight ahead, trying to ignore the unease beginning to brew in the far recesses of his brain, and ashes his cigarette out the slit in the window. The damp November air rushes through the crack and tickles his ear with its *swip swip* whisper, but

Charlie Beaulieu does not notice any of the day's remarkable happenings — the wind, the birds, the riotous ocean — because Charlie is thinking hard about how much he is worth.

"FOR YOU," AISHA SAID earlier that afternoon, holding up a cheerful yellow letter. She was standing at the foot of their bed in bra and sweatpants, pumpkin-baby belly exposed, holding the usual assortment of bills and grocery flyers. A frown creased the smooth perfection of her forehead. Charlie had the urge to rub it away with his thumb to preserve the suppleness of her skin. "It's from your dad," she said. "Look at the return address." She held it out to him and he squinted at her for a moment — his father had died eight years ago.

"That's not funny, Aisha," Charlie said, taking his glasses from the bedside table and putting them on.

"Why would I joke about something like that?" she said. She placed the letter gently in his lap as though it might contain dangerous materials. Charlie picked up the envelope and ripped it open. A peacock proudly fanned its train across the front of the card. Inside it read, in his father's messy scrawl, *Bon Anniversaire. Tu as bien fait,* and was signed *Papa,* which was unusual because it was his mother who had always taken charge of the cards — birthdays, Christmases, graduations — writing the sugary words of encouragement and signing them, *Maman et Papa.* Above his father's message was a hastily scribbled date: August 11th, 1995 — over a decade ago.

"Well?" Aisha said, impatiently rubbing her belly.

"It's Mom." Charlie got out of bed and pulled on a clean pair of black work pants. "She's losing her marbles. The card's ten years old." Charlie had cleaned out his mother's storage space several weeks ago and brought some boxes to the care centre for her to go through. Her mind was going soft, so he'd thought sifting through the old family letters might be good for her, jog her memory out of its stupor, but it had only been making her do strange things.

"What does it say?" Aisha sidled up to him, leaning over his shoulder to get a closer look.

"It says nothing," Charlie said, stuffing the card in his pocket. A pain was creeping up his sternum. "It says happy birthday."

THE CIVIC SPEEDS THROUGH a yellow (red) light, barely missing several pedestrians entering the crosswalk, before pulling onto Georgia Street and crawling to a stop in the line of slow-moving bridge traffic. Later today at Marinacove, he plans to ask Susan, the manager, for a raise. Charlie practices his monologue, breaking occasionally to give himself a significant look in the rearview mirror. He does notice a few things this afternoon outside the orbit of his own large head. He notices that his hands smell like dirty dishrags. He notices that someone in another car sees him talking to himself in the rearview, which makes him stop his monologue and scowl into all his mirrors to make sure no one else is looking at him. He notices that he looks hung over and pale from lack of light, which makes him look like his father. This doesn't reassure him, because in a couple months he will *be* a father.

When Charlie left the apartment this afternoon, he barely even noticed Aisha sitting at the piano pounding out Brahms.

"Don't bother saying goodbye to us or anything." *Us* meaning Aisha, her piano, and the little barnacle she is hosting. She had turned herself around on the bench so she could send a withering look his way, her dark hair swaying just above her derrière, while she played a twinkly little tune with her pinky. She isn't happy with him. He's been leaving for work earlier and coming home later. He had to re-enter the apartment and kiss her forehead or else the look would've soured into something more threatening while he was away at work. Pregnant women are like that.

"Bye bye, barnacle," Charlie said to Aisha's belly.

"Don't call the baby that."

The piano materialized last week, the last installment from her former abode, towed and heaved by two lithe, ropy men, friends of hers, so-called musicians. He had never seen musicians built like that. The barnacle materialized eight months ago, and despite undeniable evidence, he is having a hard time believing it's actually there. Not here yet, but *there*, in that contained antimatter pod. Some days he stands in the middle of his living room, staring at the piano, wondering how all this had happened. An overflowing shoe rack in his front hall, underwear hanging from his towel racks in the bathroom, a pile of half-read baby books stacked on his bedside table — she is spreading over all of his stuff, over him, like spores on a week-old loaf of bread. He drew the line at Scaredy. The cat and Aisha shared almost the exact same hair colour. It gave him the heebie-jeebies. He'd find himself talking to the cat as it sat up on the counter, or shooing Aisha's head out of the bed. He didn't need that kind of confusion in his life. He told her he was allergic to the cat — in a way he was.

Charlie can see a corner of the yellow envelope sticking out from behind the sun visor. He brought it with him because Aisha is a snoop. He should dismiss the card as nothing more than an example of his mother's steady decline, void of meaning in spite of the fortuitous timing, but he was unsettled by his father's kind message turned sour. *Tu as bien fait.* Whatever Charlie had done so well back then had quickly come undone. He knew why the card was never sent. It wasn't because of absent-mindedness; his father never forgot anything. Ninety-five was the summer Charlie lost his job at Le Remoulade, the city's shining star of fine dining. It was the job his father never thought Charlie would have. It was his *bien fait.* He was thirty-six at the time — at that age his father already owned his own restaurant. Charlie spent four years at Le Remoulade, moving quickly up the ranks to First Cook. Under different management he'd surely have gone quite far in the establishment, and he doesn't mind taking credit for the fricassée de veau au basilic they still feature on their menu. Charlie's contract was "severed" during a period where he was having issues containing his abuse of certain substances, enjoyed with other staff members who will remain unnamed. His dismissal created quite a proliferation of hearsay among the insidious restaurant insiders, hence the reason he now found himself in a kitchen on the outskirts of the city. Despite everything, he still remembers those days with fondness — late nights wandering the strip, bursts of impromptu song, gropings of just-over-age servers at the Roxy. He's nostalgic for those early mornings, zigzagging home through the Granville Street trash (animate and inanimate) as the sun began to burst over the buildings. On occasion, he'll bestow his new staff at Marinacove with a story from those bygone days: the time he accidently snorted crystal instead of blow and was up for three days straight working doubles; or the time he was so trashed during dinner service, he burnt the bottom of his pan and sent the entire pot of artichokes in garlic saffron sauce right across the kitchen, narrowly missing six staff members. He had wanted to burn them all—or so he tells the story.

After his release from service at Le Remoulade, there was a brief stint of house painting, which inadvertently led to real painting and an unexpected epiphany: Charlie was an artist. He gave up cooking, charged a small fortune on his credit card for supplies, and spent his days covered in assorted colours of cracked and flaking paint, body painting large swaths of unstretched canvas spread across the floor, strutting around the house naked, drinking his whiskey-spiked morning (afternoon) coffee, and squishing his cigarette butts (and butt cheeks) onto the canvas. It was only after his father's death that he got hungry and went back to food. Besides, the paint dried out his skin and a friend informed him that the cigarettes squashed into canvas had been done over fifty years earlier. He worked at a Brazilian barbeque where they carried meat around the dining room on long spears, a Japanese-Italian fusion restaurant where an octopus alfredo was the most popular dish, and a bubble tea café—during his darkest days—where he spent his shifts scratching the itch inflicted by his paper hat and attempting to solve the mystery of the *boba* bubbles. And then he finally landed his position as head chef at Marinacove.

An extra lane opens on the bridge and the traffic breaks up. The Civic goes shooting through the causeway, evergreens on either side blurring into a long green tunnel. Charlie moves into the middle lane down the Lions Gate Bridge, taking in the West Vancouver mountains and the mansions creeping up the slopes. At the base of all that luxury, a short drive down the hill from the Trans-Canada Highway, across the train tracks and past the main thoroughfare on a quiet street overlooking the ocean and the bridge, is Charlie Beaulieu's restaurant. During the summer months swarms of sunburned bathers from the beach spill over onto its patio, but once the deck umbrellas are stacked in the corner and the chairs are tilted against the tables to prevent pooled rainwater from rotting the wood, the stream of diners quickly dries up and the only customers left are the regular patrons: the elderly, ruled by habit or limited mobility, and the wealthy, too nervous to cross the bridge and leave their little hamlet of multi-million-dollar homes.

Today he will sit down with Susan to negotiate a salary increase, because Charlie feels he deserves more. He knows food and he loves food and he's a big man because of it—not morbidly obese or anything, but a bit of a fatso. When Charlie came to the restaurant three years ago, the menu was all over the place—eggrolls alongside pierogi, an Indonesian stir-fry next to a pasta bolognese. The previous chef had been fired after he went across the street for a midnight dip in the ocean with some of the underage staff members and then left his wet underpants to dry in the back hall. Charlie's fairly sure he's looking pretty good by comparison. A few days ago he organized an early-morning tasting for the staff. He stood in the middle of the dining room and recited the menu changes as though he were reciting a love poem, everyone squinting at him from under baseball caps and hoodies. The room smelled strongly of a night club—booze and body odour and smoke—until he brought out his food and then the room filled with the aromas of bouillabaisse, salmon terrine, quiche lorraine, and filet mignon. He recited the ingredients and preparation of each dish to the frantic clatter of cutlery. It was like watching a pack of hungover hyenas—save Rose, who ate nothing, and Susan, who sat in the middle of all the chaos eating like she was completing a business transaction, neat mouthfuls chewed precisely. After each robotic machination she would make a note next to the item on the menu. What could she have been writing? Bouillabaisse: sublime. Risotto: transcendent. Duck confit: orgasmic. How could one describe such pleasure with words?

He's been composing different speeches all week, fine-tuning his approach, but the birthday card has unhinged something inside his brain, caused a short-circuit that has eaten a smouldering hole through his grey matter, and now everything is tumbling out of its compartments, collecting in a big messy pile inside his head. The idea of sorting through the disarray is making Charlie feel unbelievably tired, and he is tired most days; tired of ungratefulness and gluten allergies and Atkins regimes. Charlie's fatigue is profound and feels like old deep-fryer oil pumping through his arteries. When he pulled out of his underground parking spot this afternoon and drove by the liquor store at Davie and Thurlow, he felt the pull of a super-magnet, the same super-magnet that pulls the escaped IV-wheeling alcoholics from the hospital down the street to the liquor store's front door in search of cheap whiskey. Some days he feels no different than those parched men hobbling along the sidewalk, clutching the back of their hospital gowns to keep their bare asses from hanging out.

The Civic zips down the alley, thumping over the speed bumps, and pulls into the small parking lot behind Charlie's restaurant. Back here there is no hiding the truth. Seagulls dive-bomb the garbage bins and scatter the remnants of last night's dinner service all over the lot. The paint is peeling and a faded sign from days gone by advertises Cheap Gyoza Tuesdays. A broken grease trap leaks a rank odour akin to death. There's always a cluster of angry and bedraggled wait-staff smoking on his back steps. It isn't a sight that promotes the appetite. Any tiny morsel of hope Charlie may have mustered while driving to his restaurant is always shattered when he pulls into his parking spot. They irritate him, the squawking seagulls and the squawking waitstaff. *Ack, ack* — scavengers, all of them.

Of course, technically Marinacove is not Charlie's restaurant. It's owned by a group of has-been sports stars with shares in three different establishments in the Lower Mainland. Mostly they remain anonymous, but once a year the Logan Group calls a meeting to discuss something pointless like bringing pierogi back onto the menu. He dreads those meetings — those square-shouldered thick-necks coming in to tell him how to run the restaurant. If he were in charge of the place it would never have become this cesspool of miscreants and deadbeats wallowing in their own puddles of worthlessness.

Charlie lugs his tired body up the back steps of the restaurant, the loitering of unkempt staff parting for him as choruses of *hey, Chef* bubble around him. He grumbles as he elbows his way through—his usual shtick—and they all grin good-naturedly (save Rose) like he's some sort of cartoon character put on this Earth for their entertainment. He's already picked out a staff member to yell at tonight: the teenage dishwasher sitting at the bottom of the steps, looking pale and water-logged, as though he's just been pulled from the ocean.

Charlie pulls his toque down over his ears. A gust of wind blows in off the water, the cold biting at his earlobes. He's more exposed to the elements with his bald head, more vulnerable to illness.

"Chef, guess what I found in my pocket this morning?" Martin, the bartender, says, rooting around in his brown leather jacket. You can never tell Martin is drunk until, at 3 a.m., you find yourself standing next to him at the twenty-four-hour Chinese buffet while he builds a teetering pile of ribs on his plate. "Bones." He pulls out a couple to prove his point. "Dry ribs. Were we at Fortune House last night?"

"I was here last night," Charlie grumbles. There's something about the way Martin looks today—something in the plum-coloured circles under his eyes—that's making the pain in Charlie's chest worse. Charlie and Martin have spent many an evening together when neither could find any good reason to go home. The night always ends with Charlie standing at the entrance to some downtown alley, yelling at a drunk-deafened Martin wandering off to something more sinister.

Their baker, Tara, hasn't lifted her head off her knees yet. He gives her a nudge with his boot, but she doesn't move. Rose stands next to Martin, smoking and chewing gum at the same time. "Like menthol," she explained to him once. Charlie nudges her for a cigarette even though he has a nearly full pack in his back pocket. "No," she says, scowling at him. She reminds him of a cigarette—skinny, dirty, stinky, but still appealing in a way he could never explain. She's added to the sleeves on her arms, swirls of stars mingling with twisting koi tails. He glares at her tight-lipped, dagger-eyed face and vaguely recalls a remark he made to her last night, something off the cuff, something about intelligence and a sack of bricks. "Don't say no to me," he says. She yanks out a cigarette and throws it at him. She's the only one who refuses to call him Chef; she calls him Charlie, that is *if* she's speaking to him at all. She's above it: above taking requests, above scraping people's leftovers into the garbage, and Charlie has a strong hunch she also feels she's above him. He puts the cigarette to his lips without looking anyone in the eye. James, one of his kitchen runts, whips out his lighter. *Asskisser,* Charlie thinks as he leans the tip of the cigarette into the offered flame, catching the fire before a gust of wind blows it out. "Looking a little tired, Chef," James says.

"It was a late night," Charlie says. Rich, one of their First Cooks and an exchange student from Japan, beams at him. His hair stands straight up from his head and even in the wind remains immobile. Last night, he emptied the hot deep fryer oil into a plastic bucket, which meant Charlie was at the restaurant until the wee hours of the morning, drinking wine and jingling his keys while he watched Rich bop around the kitchen cleaning up the mess. The grease had melted the bottom of the bucket and poured out over the floor, also melting the bottoms of Rich's shoes. It was difficult to get angry at him, because he spoke very little English and was also an unnaturally happy person. A bubble of chaos followed him wherever he went, and yet he was the only cook in Charlie's kitchen who never cracked under pressure.

The cigarette doesn't calm or ease the strain on Charlie's lungs. He smacks his tongue against the pasty roof of his mouth. The birthday card has made him aware of a foul taste he suspects may be his life rotting away from the inside out. He's parched, but he's decided not to drink today. He wants to preserve an edge for negotiations. He hacks and spits into the ashtray can. "Fortune House," Charlie laughs hoarsely, trying to distract himself from his thirst. "I was so stoned there one night. Was I with you?" he asks Martin.

"Could've been." Martin smiles at the memory he may or may not have.

"The two-foot tower of chicken feet in the middle of the table," Charlie says. "Did you help me build that?"

"Yeah, yeah." Martin grins, nodding his head.

"This story again," Rose says, rolling her eyes.

"What's up your butt today?" Charlie turns to glare at her.

"You got kicked out. For some reason you were barefoot. You walked into a club, cut your foot, ended up in emerg, tetanus shot. Hardy, har, har." She gets up, brushing dust off the back of her black pants and flicks her cigarette butt over the railing. "I'm fucking bored," she says, stomping up the steps and slamming the back door behind her.

"Oh, stuff it, Rose," Charlie calls after her, spitting into the garbage again. He briefly indulges a fantasy of flicking his cigarette butt into the bird's nest she's concocted with chopsticks at the nape of her neck. He imagines it stiff with hairspray. The fire would be quick, merciless.

Susan's wife pulls into the parking lot and Susan climbs

out of the passenger side, barely able to get the door shut before the car goes peeling out again.

"Finish the story," Martin says.

"Naw," Charlie says, with a shrug. "It's been told."

Susan strides toward them wearing a short skirt, a loose-fitting blazer, and sunglasses, even though the sky is dark with clouds. The consensus among the staff is that Susan is certifiably insane, yet people are still attracted to her in the way eyes are unwillingly drawn to an eviscerated creature on the side of the road. She's only been at the restaurant for a few months, but Charlie already knows intimate details involving her sex life, gynecological exams, and bowel difficulties. She spent the last five years managing one of the top fine dining restaurants in Toronto, and her first week at Marinacove she walked around with a look of horror on her face—horror at the rude pops as wine bottles were uncorked, horror at the elementary way in which the napkins were folded, horror at the wet rings left from napkinless glasses. Her mission is to keep the bread-cutting board continuously crumbless. She keeps a razor in the back for the days when Martin forgets to shave, which are most days. She likes Rose for some reason, even though Rose is a terrible server, lazy and prone to rude-ness and unwilling to carry more than two plates at a time due to weak wrists. Rose has to take air out back at least once a night, but never clues into the fact that her lightheaded-ness may be attributed to the serious lack in her daily caloric intake. She and Susan seem to share an affinity, though, for ridicule and laughter with a serrated edge. Susan's laugh belies her fine-dining background; there's something rough there, guttural, something that hints at small towns, strip malls, and truck stops. It makes for an odd juxtaposition with her shiny suits and blond-highlighted hair. Charlie pretends not to hear Susan calling him in her sing-song, sugar-drippy voice. This is not a good sign. Usually he and Susan mutually ignore each other. He smokes hurriedly and shuffles inside so he doesn't have to say hello back.

As he clomps through the hall toward the kitchen, he accidently steps on Aisha's ultrasound photo, which has fallen from the corkboard. She pinned it there for him when he admitted to not knowing how to tell the staff about the incoming baby. He stops briefly to rub a foot print off the paper and pin it back up, putting in an extra pushpin to hold the photo in place. He likes the corner picture best, the baby (or beast) staring straight at the camera with a hollow-eyed stare and mini-raptor's hungry grin. There was some celebrating among the staff after Aisha posted the photo. The cooks were all overly enthusiastic, patting Charlie on the back and grinning at him like goons with that hopeful look he recognized as an expectation of free beer. Rose looked horrified and wished Aisha luck. Susan pulled two slim cigarillos out of the glass case on the bar and she and Charlie smoked them out back beside the dumpsters so their strong smell wouldn't find its way into the restaurant.

"A father, eh!" Susan said, shaking her head and letting the smoke drift from her open mouth.

"Yep." Charlie took note of his posture: taller, chest expanded, sturdy, reliable.

"My father was a fucking imbecile." She laughed with that raspy tickle that unsettled him. He felt his body slacken under her words, his belly protruding to its natural state. He remembered what she was wearing that day: a tight-fitting white suit that glowed against the dirty grey of the back alley. She shone like a lesbian Madonna. He felt blinded by her truth—it was painful to the eyes. "You'll be fine," she said. "You'll be better than him, at least."

When Aisha told him she was pregnant he walked right out the door, down the hall, down the stairs, along the banks of English Bay, up the steep hill on Davie, into his favourite French bistro, and back down the hill on Davie before going home. He ate a piece of Alsatian pie at the bistro and felt miserable afterwards—he hated eating alone. In that entire length of time Aisha's position on the couch and the expression on her face had not changed. She was gazing ecstatically into the maple tree outside their window when he left and she was gazing at the damn tree when he returned. Somehow he knew this meant she would not be leaving. It felt too easy; there was no discussion, no decision to be something new together. Their lives were running parallel and then all of a sudden they found themselves joined, two random atoms suddenly fused by a magnetic force.

AS CLOUDS AMASS, ROLLING in from the east, the sun is beginning its descent toward the ocean, shooting angles of light into the restaurant that reveal every single dust particle in the room. The windows were cleaned during lunch service and now someone's poor job is illuminated, even streaks running the length of every window. Rose is carrying around a napkin and a steaming mug of hot water to buff the wine glasses on the tables. Martin wheels in a shopping cart full of booze and starts arranging the wine bottles and stocking the beer cooler. While he unloads the cart, he chats with Topher, the head chef of Adagio, an Italian fine-dining restaurant across the street. Charlie walks over to the bar as Martin uncorks a bottle of wine and pours him a generous taster. "Here, try this. I'm thinking of adding it to the list." Martin's face is shiny after a fresh shave. There's a nick above his lip that's bleeding.

"Quiet in here today," Topher says, as Charlie tips back his wine glass. A taster is not a drink; a taster is part of the job. Many years ago, before Charlie's father had a heart attack, he employed Topher at his restaurant, Le Carré. Topher knew Charlie as a fat little boy who stood quietly, like a ghost, in the corner of the kitchen. "Tu es un fantôme, tu n'es pas ici," his father would say. *You are not here.* When his father drank too much, Topher drove him home, and on those nights Charlie would wake to his father singing over the stove, swigging straight from a bottle of wine on the counter. "Viens. Viens ma petite bête. Mange avec moi." Charlie *was* a little beast — a chubby, acne-pocked little beast. His father would stuff his face with cream-drenched noodles, layers of fatty meat, salty fries. He'd eat anything brought to his mouth: liver, blue cheese, tripe. At the age of eight, he already knew the difference between a béchamel and a velouté.

"Tell me what you think," Martin says, as he pours a taster for Topher as well. Topher sips the wine and swishes it around before swallowing and making some light smacking sounds on the roof of his mouth. He comes to Marinacove in the afternoon between lunch and dinner service on a regular basis to drink and to poach the wait staff. He doesn't believe in drinking in his own establishment. Charlie doesn't care about that kind of thing. The result is the same: they are both well on their way to being sloshed in time for the dinner rush. "Acidic," Topher pronounces. "Notes of blackcurrant and raspberry."

"Tastes like toilet water," Charlie says, slurping up the last dregs of wine and pushing his glass back at Martin. There's suddenly a lightness in his brain: the thick, stagnant chaos that filled his head this morning is dissipating with the tickle of alcohol.

"How about this one?" Martin joins them in the tasting.

They work their way through most of the wines on the list, even the ones they've carried for years, until the charade runs its course and Martin finally cuts to the chase and pours Charlie a long Crown and Coke. Charlie counts the pour — one, two, three, four — giving Martin a grim but approving nod. It's rude to refuse a drink from a friend and Martin is his good friend. He notices Martin already has his own hidden below the bar in the well. He sets Charlie's drink on the counter with a clink and a tinkle that makes Charlie smile. "For courage," Martin says.

"I don't need it," Charlie says. "But I'll drink anyway."

"He's asking for a raise today," Martin explains to Topher.

Charlie shakes the ice cubes in his glass feeling annoyed. "You're bleeding." Charlie motions to Martin's lip. "Right here."

Martin grabs a bar napkin and dabs at the cut.

"I'll join you in that drink, then," Topher says. There's a twinkle in his eye Charlie doesn't appreciate. Martin pours another Crown and the three men *cheers* awkwardly, an unexpected air of camaraderie — a brief entente among alcoholics. "How's your mother?" Topher asks, giving his drink a gentle stir with his swizzle stick. Many years after his father died, his mother went into the care centre, and for years Topher was the only person other than Charlie who ever dropped in to see her. He suspects there may have been something going on between them, probably long before his father's death. He wonders how much Topher knows, if his mother ever confided in him or spoke of the late-night cooking sessions at home, his father spinning like a whirling dervish in nothing but boxers, his clothing in a pile in the hallway, piping sausages hopping out of the skillet, skidding across the floor as his father chased after them with a fork, shouting, *Watch out! Maudit!* Plates were smashed; a bottle of olive oil shattered into a million bright gold pieces across the floor; the blood-red brilliance from a smashed glass of wine looked like evidence from a crime scene. His bleary-eyed mother would stumble out of the bedroom, but the only thing she ever said was *don't forget to turn off the stove.* She lived in constant fear of his father burning down the house, but she never told him to go to bed or to quit drinking.

Even though her mind is fading, his mother still talks about that one time Topher brought flowers to the care centre — white begonias. It's as though she's forgotten that Topher had vied constantly for Charlie's father's job, waiting for the opportunity that eventually presented itself.

"So they can afford to hand out raises here?" Topher says, glancing around the empty restaurant. Outside the clouds have darkened and the ocean is threatening the seawall, menacing the last few hardcore joggers on their afternoon runs.

"Who eats in the middle of the afternoon?" Charlie wants the words to sound tart, but instead they get lost in a yawn and end up sounding lazy.

"Ah." Topher smirks and takes a sip of his drink. "I'm just giving you a hard time, Charlie." He runs his finger through a patch of dust on the bar. "What were your numbers like this week?" Charlie shrugs and takes a gulp. He'd rather concentrate on finding the bottom of his glass as quickly as possible than acknowledge Topher's smug smile. "We did fifty," Topher says. "Not our best, but better than last year." He leans back and rubs his belly as if it were a piggy bank. Martin whisks away his empty glass and replaces it without exchanging a word, a fresh napkin placed under the drink. They did less than half that number last week.

"We're doing fine," Charlie says. He fudged the books to make up for twenty pounds of lobster for a seafood risotto that never sold. Actually, he has massaged the numbers several times over the past few months, something that becomes easier the more often you do it. Charlie jiggles the ice in his glass, hoping Martin will get the message and replenish his drink too.

"I don't know. I've been making fuck all," Martin says, picking at the congealed blood sealing his cut.

"November is a quiet month," Charlie says, jiggling his glass harder, sending ice across the bar floor. Martin misses his signal. "We're going to be booked solid for the holidays."

"Really?" Martin does a poor job of hiding his surprise. He walks over to the hostess stand and flips through weeks in the reservation book.

"They're not all in there yet," Charlie calls to him. "I haven't had time to enter all the big parties." He has one

Post-it note in the back with *Williams, party of seven, Dec 12th* scrawled on it.

"Sure, you'll be busy, man of your talents. Your father would be proud," Topher says. The comment is insincere. An acrid smell is wafting from the open kitchen. From the bar, Charlie can see Rich, James, and Tara working at their individual stations.

"Do you smell something burning?" Topher says.

Charlie pours the drink himself. "Still bleeding," he says to Martin, pointing at his lip, before turning to make his way to the kitchen. Outside the waves have overtaken the seawall and the joggers have all gone home.

To Topher, Charlie's father was the pinnacle of success. But Topher never saw the man on the couch at four in the morning, bathed in the blue glow from infomercials on the boob tube, stuffing his fat son. It was at that late hour that Charlie learned the art of eating—how to hold his knife with the handle in his palm, and his fork with the tines pointed downward; how to tip his bowl and take the soup from the side of the spoon, how to tear his bun into bite-sized pieces before bringing it to his lips, how to pour first for his father then for himself. Charlie would lie in bed afterward, wide awake, rubbing his near-bursting belly. He'd listen to his father snoring on the couch, and as he watched the night sky turn cerulean he'd savour the flavours still lingering on his tongue.

After years of this ritual, Charlie's teeth turned to chalk; the acid from his midnight meals ate away at the enamel until there was nothing left to protect them. His teeth became soft and useless. It cost his parents a small fortune to repair them.

IN THE KITCHEN, CHARLIE assesses the chaos he knew he would find. People think kitchens are clean places. Their food arrives, the presentation is beautiful, the flavours harmonizing like a barbershop quartet. But no one considers the mess—the anger, the sweat, the bedlam, the burns and cuts and stings it takes to achieve the perfection of those delicate slices of rose-shaped cucumber balanced on the edge of their plate. James is standing at the cold line, his back to Charlie, julienning vegetables, a hand through the flop of bangs across his forehead every ten seconds. A carrot top falls to the floor and he gives it a gentle nudge under the counter. People don't think about what's hiding in the cracks of the linoleum. They don't think about the stinking mop that wipes the floors every night and smells like death. Charlie crosses his arms and waits for someone to notice him standing there. The smoke filling the kitchen offends his nose. Rich is bent over the stove stirring a pot of demi-glace, bouncing to the faint beats floating from the ghetto blaster in the dish pit, the frosted tips of his spiky hair dangerously close to the salamander. On the memo board in the back hall there's a picture of him from New Year's, bare-chested, head thrown back, chugging from a bottle of cheap champagne with his hands tied behind his back. His ability to metabolize alcohol is legendary. Charlie has witnessed the mythos on several occasions. Rich's expression in the photo can only be described as one of pure delight. In fact, exuberance seems to be Rich's natural condition.

"I feel like shit," Tara says, hunched over her rolling pin, a tray of cheese crisps in front of her, ready for the oven. "Fucking Finlandia. I don't want to be here. I would rather be anywhere than here. I would rather be dead than here."

People don't think about the hungover baker with nicotine-stained fingers setting those dainty mint leaves on their dessert. People believe when they pay good money for their food, it is made with passion and love. Love!

Charlie throws open the oven door, revealing a tray of blackened parmesan crisps. "These done?" Charlie barks. Tara jumps, noticing him for the first time, and yanks the tray out of the oven.

"Shit," she says, throwing the tray on the counter with a clatter.

"They're supposed to look like this," Charlie says, pulling one of the paper-thin parmesan crisps out of an insert. It looks like dead skin and trembles between his fingers. "They should be done by now. You should be making salad dressing."

"I was busy this morning." She's scraping the burnt crisps into the garbage.

"But why aren't they done?" Charlie expects to feel agitated, but the alcohol has roused a pleasant hum in his body. It's making him sleepy—he has to work to maintain his level of anger.

"They take time." Tara was banging the tray against the garbage can to free the worst victims.

"No they don't. They're easy. You roll them out." Charlie wields the rolling pin, pounding the cheese into the tray. "Throw them in the oven and they're done. Easy." Topher is leaning sideways in his seat to get a better look at what's going on in the kitchen.

"Yes, Chef," she says. He can see the mental flow of obscenities behind her eyes and this gives him a feeling of satisfaction. "Speed it up." He tries to snap his fingers, but they feel thick and doughy. "Rich, how's your mise-en-place?"

Rich looks up at him, a wide grin revealing his tiny Chiclet teeth. Charlie is fairly sure he's stoned. "How you's, Chef?" Rich uses a knuckle to test a chicken breast sizzling in a pan. Charlie walks over to the cold line, where James is still chopping, and picks up the stock bucket. "Why the fuck is this empty?" James and Tara stare blankly while Rich sings a little ditty and caresses his demi with a spatula. "Look at this," Charlie says, reaching into the garbage and pulling out potato ends and celery stalks, chucking them on the floor, "Perfectly good, perfectly good." His shouts ring pleasingly inside his head as he holds up each rejected vegetable part as though it were solid gold. "Money in my garbage," Charlie grumbles, lowering his voice so it won't reach Topher's ears. Charlie digs deeper through the trash can. There's a crudeness to kitchens that's never bothered him but would bother anyone else. Rotting garbage doesn't bother him. Mould doesn't bother him. Soured dairy doesn't bother him. He'll take a solid whiff of any of those things without hesitation. Sometimes he feels the world's no better off now than it was during the Middle Ages, when everyone threw their piss and shit into the streets. To him, some days, it feels no different. "What the—" Charlie pulls out a handful of burnt pancetta from the garbage can. The numbers will have to be cooked again this week. "Can someone tell me why there's twenty dollars' worth of burnt pancetta crisps in here? Rich?"

"Yo," Rich says, looking up and grinning like a fool. "You look good, Big Chef." Charlie has always assumed Rich was misusing the word *big*, meaning instead great or powerful or almighty, but lately he's not so sure. He has a feeling Rich may be calling him fat.

"Jesus Christ." Charlie rubs away the sheen of sweat that's suddenly sprouted across his brow and sets himself up at his station, leaning into the counter and letting it support most of his body weight. "We have an hour to be ready for dinner service, got that?" He blinks heavily. The pleasurable buzz has turned into a heaviness of the head. He needs another drink. Then he remembers he has one waiting right in front of him. He takes a gulp.

"I think it was one of the day people who burned the pancetta," Tara says, crouched down at the stove, watching her parmesan wafers. Charlie flaps a hand at her, meaning *shut up, pretty please*, and begins prepping the chicken breasts, scraping the cartilage off the bone with his paring knife. He finds the work satisfying after dealing with all this incompetence.

An elderly woman wobbles into the empty restaurant in a bright red rain slicker with matching hat and gazes around, glassy-eyed. She turns to make sure Charlie notices her, raising a hand in acknowledgment as high as it will go—about mid-waist—before hobbling to a dirty table Rose still hasn't cleaned because she's too busy smoking or ridiculing or doing whatever takes her so goddamn long. The old woman sits down and begins to gently move the plates of congealed food away from her. While Charlie wraps the chicken in thin slices of pancetta, he watches her pick a crumpled napkin up off the table, using it to sweep the crumbs to the floor and then blow her nose. A shiver runs down his spine and bile sloshes around his stomach. He takes a large swig of his drink, diluting the acid threatening his gut. Charlie hates to watch people eat alone. Food is meant to be shared, joined by atmosphere and conversation and good drink. Food is more than sustenance.

Food is more than necessity. To him eating a beautiful meal alone is akin to buying your own birthday cake and blowing out candles you lit yourself in your own lonely living room. What's the point? There are other things that get to him: someone walking alone down the street, indulging in an ice cream cone; or the lonely crinkle of an unwrapped chocolate bar at the bus stop. Anything processed with cheesy strings that hang from the lips makes him shudder. People are careless when they eat alone, more carnal, animal-like. They are more likely to smack their lips, pick their teeth, dribble down their chins, stuff their cheeks, chew with their mouths open. He once broke up with a girl after watching her eat a giant fajita alone at her kitchen table, stuffing in the last bite using each and every finger of both hands to tuck all the corners into her mouth. And he once retched when he came upon the sight of Martin crouched in the back on an overturned bucket a few feet from the dish pit, which was stacked to the ceiling with dirty dishes, shovelling his staff-discounted food down his yap because he had only five miserable minutes between clearing the appetizers off one table and bringing out the entrees to another. Why bother? To Charlie it was unconscionable behaviour. After vomiting into the garbage can, Charlie had tried to kick the bucket out from underneath Martin, but he managed to leap away, saving his dish just in time. "I was hungry," he explained. He was hungry! For a few weeks there was a ban on staff eating anywhere in Charlie's sightlines, but eventually Susan vetoed the rule, saying it was unreasonable and potentially in violation of labour laws.

What really gets him, though, are these old ladies. They come for their dinner alone around four o'clock, when no one is around to greet them at the door because all the staff have loped off to eat in the back or smoke in the alley. The ladies either seat themselves or they come over to him and peer up over the pass-bar, always saying something he can't hear. They all order the same three things on the menu: the crab cakes or the clam chowder or the shrimp salad sandwich. They sit at a window with a view. He can't watch them gaze at the ocean and then absent-mindedly turn back to their food, select another bite, chew, gaze, chew, gaze. They demand a senior's discount and pull out their bags of loose change. Rose is always nice to them, stooping to chat, bringing them free coffee, never letting their magenta-lipstick-marked cups find their bottom. There's always a neat row of dimes, nickels, and pennies left for a tip that clang around in Rose's apron the rest of the night.

The ladies remind him of his mother. A sharp tickle of bile rises in his throat again. He makes sure to never visit the care centre at mealtime, but there are always remnants: lunch carts of half-eaten gelatinous tapioca, smells (culinary and bodily) lingering in the hallways, splatters across Maman's shirt. He finds it hard to go often. When his father was ill and in the hospital his mother would go dutifully every day to visit him for exactly forty-five minutes, not a minute more. It was only after his father's death that his mother started complaining about the drinking, about the long hours he worked, complaining about the fact that she never had a holiday, about the things he broke in the house. Only after his death did she start missing the china bowl from her mother and the ceramic dog with the wet-looking eyes that her godmother had given to her on the day of her birth. A month after his father's death, she took a week-long vacation in Havana. Those were the pictures she had on the wall beside her bed in the care centre. Not pictures of her husband or son, but pictures of her sipping a Cuba Libra in the shade of an umbrella.

The last time he was at the care centre, he decided to mention the baby. She seemed lucid enough to give it a try. He set a takeout container in front of her and planted a plastic fork in the middle of the dish, waiting for the aromas of basil and cream to reach her nose before he told her the news. She fumbled for the fork and ate hurriedly like a person starved. He waited patiently, letting her enjoy the food in peace. The nurses had mentioned that she no longer ate her meals. They'd been giving her supplement shakes a shade of pink that reminded him of Pepto-Bismol or death. He pushed the takeout container closer to her. "C'est bon, Maman?"

"Oui." It was a dish his father used to make for them at home, something simple he could whip up with very few ingredients at his disposal.

"It's me, Charlie," he said loudly into her ear.

"I know. I know," she said, laughing and patting his hand, her once-perfect English thickened with the French accent from her childhood.

"That's right, Maman," he said, "it's Charlie."

"I know." She laughed again. She was meticulously scraping the sides of the container to make sure she got every last scrap.

"Aisha is having a baby." The way he said it made it sound as though he wasn't part of the equation. His mother didn't even know who Aisha was. "Maman, can you hear me?" He leaned in close, letting his lips graze her ear. "A baby." She looked down at her comforter with an absent smile, her eyes losing their focus in the garden print, a world of gardenias and roses and beautiful coloured birds.

CHARLIE THROWS OPEN THE back door and finds Rose holding a newspaper over her head while smoking furiously, fat raindrops falling from the sky. "It's fucking raining," she says, stating the obvious. A raindrop hits Charlie on the forehead and trickles down the bridge of his nose. He ducks under the newspaper. "Would you believe there is a hundred-year-old lady in there sitting at a dirty table looking around for something? I imagine she's looking for food. I know that's hard to believe, this being a restaurant and all." The tip of his nose is no more than an inch away from the tip of hers, his eyes bulging, warning her that if his head does explode, he will make sure it explodes all over her. "Why do I often find myself out here, reminding you of your job?"

Rose smiles sweetly and takes a last drag on her cigarette. She turns her head politely so the smoke doesn't hit his face. "All this nervous tension, Charlie." She pulls her bleached hair into a tight ponytail that reveals the acne along her hairline. "You'll give yourself an incurable disease." She carefully butts her cigarette and then gives his shoulder an irritating rub before sauntering inside. She pains him. Oh God, she pains him.

"There are other restaurants in this neighbourhood," Charlie shouts at the back of her head as he follows her down the hall. Her tattoos wrap around her bony arms like octopus tentacles. She is so skinny Charlie can't imagine how all of her organs fit into her torso. He wants to pick her up and plunk her headfirst into one of the garbage cans. "Topher's here," he yells. "I'm sure he'd be happy to give you a job." His voice carries out across the mostly empty dining room. The elderly woman looks up, startled. Topher and Martin are drinking martinis at the bar. Charlie storms into the office and slams the door behind him. "I'd like that insolent little girl fired."

"Who?" Susan says, glancing up briefly before going back to her work on the computer. There's an ugly bruise around her left eye, the lid swollen and red.

"What happened to your face?" He knows the answer to the question; she's been fighting with her wife for weeks.

"Oh," Susan waves his words away while scanning her computer screen. She types the way she eats—efficient as a robot. If he lingers in the office long enough, Charlie knows he'll get the full story. There's a curiosity nagging at him, but he's not sure he cares enough to go through what has the potential to be an hour-long introspection. The staff have been getting regular updates on the abuse Susan suffers at the hands of her wife. She'll come to work visibly upset, tight-lipped, begging everyone to leave her alone, but by the end of the night the entire story will have trickled out and suddenly you're standing in a puddle of her gloom. Charlie saw Susan's wife at the coffee shop last week, her arm in a sling. He's guessing the punches are thrown from both sides. He's expecting a divorce announcement any day now. "Sorry," she says, turning in her swivel chair to face him, "who do you want fired?"

"Rose. Rose, once again. I wanted her fired last week and last month and last year." The phone rings and Susan answers,

"Marinacove, Susan speaking." After a string of pleasantries she hands the phone to Charlie. "It's Aisha." Charlie grabs the phone, his foot already tapping impatiently. He doesn't like calls at work. "What's up?"

"Oh, not much." Aisha's voice floats through the line, high and soft, like a balloon disappearing in a blue sky. "Just called to say hi."

"Aisha." Charlie's voice is a pin poised to deflate. "I'm in the middle of dinner prep."

"Well, I was just feeling, oh, I don't know…" She lists off a string of aches and pains, to which Charlie makes all the appropriate hums and grunts. "You're pregnant," he says finally, "you're not supposed to feel well."

"She okay?" Susan says, after he's hung up the phone.

"She's fickle right now. She's all over the place. She's driving me nuts." Charlie leans back in his chair and rubs his temples. "I'm fucking tired."

"She's the one making the baby," Susan says, angling her chair back and examining him. "You don't even understand tired." The fluorescent lights give her bruise a purplish sheen. The ugly eye, the office clutter, the bad lighting—it all makes Charlie suddenly feel a dark sadness, a wrench in his gut that makes him want to crawl back into bed and forget his life. He's not in the mood for one of Susan's lectures. What does Susan know? She's never had a baby. He thinks about his beverage sitting above the pass-bar in the kitchen. He hasn't figured out how to drink in front of her yet. She's always sniffing around.

"There's no firing today. I called everyone else off because of the storm." The window behind Susan's head is being pelted with rain and beyond the window the ocean lashes the beach and pier. Charlie can barely see the lights of the Lions Gate Bridge through the weather. "Unless you want to put on an apron tonight?"

"Do you think people want to look at this while they eat?" Charlie says, motioning from his sweaty brow down to his rotting shoes.

"No," she says, giving him a stony once-over. He waits for her to laugh, but her gaze remains level. "Did you think I was serious?"

"Tomorrow then, immediately," he says, stretching his neck from side to side, releasing a series of loud cracks. He indulges in an impressive yawn, loud and wide-mouthed, and thumbs one of his cookbooks, rubbing at sticky spots along the way. The staff are always in here, loitering, stealing pencils, gumming up things with their dirty fingers. He pinches his arm, using the pain to keep his eyes open. "Rose refuses to call me Chef, you know," he adds, to strengthen his case. Sleep is trying to take over his body—it talks to him, tells him things like it's okay to curl up in a corner under the desk, tells him no one will notice if he sleeps in his car for a half hour before the dinner service. He keeps asserting to himself that no, it is not okay, but his resolve is waning. Sleep may have a point.

"It looks bad, doesn't it?" Susan says, fussing with her hair as though that will somehow take the swelling away from her eye. He's been staring at it without realizing. He may have been sleeping with his eyes open.

"I'd give you a steak to put on it, but our food costs—"

"That's why I don't have a kid," she says, examining her eye in the reflection off the computer screen. "She'd fuck it up.

Do you worry about that, about fucking up this little person?"

"I don't think about it much," Charlie says, skimming a recipe for Bayonne ham with petits pois, allowing another exaggerated yawn.

"Don't," Susan says, gripping Charlie's chair and swivelling it so they face each other, "fuck up your kid." Charlie's head swings around on his limp neck. "Christ, Susan." He treads at the floor to try and release his chair from her grip, but she hangs on. The eye is worse up close, bloodshot and weepy. It shocks him out of his lethargy for a brief moment, the pain inching up his sternum once again, throbbing like a bad memory. He taps his index finger at the recipe, as though he's found the answer to both of their problems. It's right there in the Dijon mustard sauce. "I think I'll do ham for a Christmas feature this year."

Rose pops her head into the office. "I have one bloody table. All she wants is coffee and the entire cream shipment is spoiled. She's banging her mug on the table."

Susan releases Charlie's chair and gets up to leave.

"I want to talk before dinner service begins," he says. She's going to make him wait for their sit-down. It's probably part of her negotiating strategy. The longer she makes him wait, the happier he'll be with anything, but he knows that game and he has a number in mind and nothing is going to convince him otherwise.

"Let me deal with this first," she says, as she trots out the door.

Charlie lays his head down on the desk and lets his eyes blur. The wind howls outside. He pretends the wail is one of his mother's French lullabies singing him into a deep sleep. Did she ever sing him lullabies? He can't remember. His father would sing him French drinking songs but always got the words mixed up. The fatigue is worse today. Lately Charlie has been having trouble sleeping at night. He dreams of his teeth chipping, crumbling, falling out. Last night, as he got into bed at four in the morning, Aisha pulled his hand to her belly. He imagined a tiny, sharp-toothed raptor delicately clawing at the lining of her womb, plotting its escape. "Stay still. Pay attention," she said, as though the fetus was about to deliver an astounding recital from her belly. She gripped his hand and moved it around, trying to anticipate the spot where a kick or punch might land, but he didn't feel a thing. He told himself it was the baby's cautious respect of his authority. "Do you want something to eat?" he said, getting out of bed.

"You have to be patient, Charlie," she said, poking at her belly to try and wake the beast.

"There's smoked duck with egg noodles in the fridge." She had wanted duck for an entire week: confit, à l'orange, red-wine braised, seared with cherries and port sauce. "No duck," she said. She stretched and gazed up at the ceiling, telepathizing with the barnacle. It was as though she was talking across worlds to the dead, the intensity she summoned to choose her next meal. "Pasta." She untied and retied the bun on top of her head. "Something creamy. No tomatoes."

"Pasta. Creamy," he muttered, as he made his way into the kitchen.

They sat in bed to eat with linen napkins on their laps. He cradled the bowl, twirling the fork in the noodles and placing a generous bite in her sweet, pink mouth. Nothing rivalled the approval of a pregnant woman—if he got it right she bathed him in praise. "Oh, oh, oh." She closed her eyes and sank back on the pillow. She was not difficult to please. She grabbed the bowl from him, balancing it on her belly. "You don't want any," she said, offering him a spoonful.

"No." He sat back, feeling, for once in a long time, satisfied. He watched her eat in silence, each spin of her fork, each dart of her tongue along her lips.

"Charlie," Aisha said, putting down her fork. "We're having a baby." She had never admitted this fact before—*we*, his responsibility. "I'm scared."

He got out of bed and left her lying there alone with her noodles.

"Where are you going now?" she said, sitting up and pushing the bowl aside.

"You need parmesan," he said, rushing to the kitchen.

"But I'm almost done," she called after him.

He got distracted once he left the room. The dishwasher needed to be loaded. There was a recipe he wanted to check. He played some online poker. When he got back to the bedroom with the parmesan, Aisha was asleep, the bowl of pasta cold on the bedside table.

Crumbling teeth are a symbol: someone told him that once, a few years ago now, at an underground dinner party in the West End. The soirée was hosted by a Michelin-star-lauded chef, something overpriced and overrated, and very private and very chic. There was a secret word for the buzz code—chateauneuf or kumquat or bluefin. Basically it was a hundred and twenty dollars to sit on tasselled cushions around an egomaniacal asshole's coffee table and sample "epicurean delights" as described by said asshole. Charlie wore his most ironic T-shirt.

The conversation that night was appropriately diaphanous. Between the foie gras toasts and the beef tartare, talk turned to worst fears. A woman with impossibly long hair had him wedged into a corner between a sofa and an armchair; the hair tumbled in dark waves nearly to her waist and he could smell her sweat under the citrus of her shampoo. Usually he hated the intimacy of small spaces and discussions like this one, but after five grapefruit soju cocktails he was working on a decent buzz with a freshly cracked beer in hand he'd found hiding at the back of the fridge.

The group wouldn't accept his first answer: he had no fears. "Everyone has a fear, Charlie," the host said, stepping out from his kitchen lair. "Charlie," he said slyly, pointing a wine glass at him, accidentally emptying the last droplets of red onto the white-tiled floor, "come on now, Charlie. What about fear of failure? What about fear of an empty restaurant, Charlie?" Charlie had just started working at Marinacove. He wanted the host to stop taking digs, so he told them about his teeth. The long-haired woman was the only one concerned for him. She was still asking for specifics and inspecting his mouth long after everyone else had moved on to the man who was terrified of Canada geese. "It means something," she said, flipping her hair importantly from one shoulder to the other. Tiny beads of sweat sprouted on her upper lip. Her mane was like a black cloak around her shoulders. "But what?" he howled, "What does it mean?" The alcohol and the woman's beautiful hair were causing him to overreact. Later, she played the piano with everyone gathered around like a

Christmas cliché, but Charlie felt he was the only other one there—just him, bowed beside Aisha at the keys.

He's never bothered to look up the meaning of the recurring nightmare, but he is still filled with dread and a sense of suffocation whenever he wakes up searching for his teeth in the sheets. Last night when he came to bed, he fell asleep immediately and had the worst nightmare yet. He kept drifting back to sleep only to be startled awake again and again. In this dream, all his teeth were gone and Rose was sitting across from him, spooning a salmon-coloured purée into his mouth, her tattoos slithering around her skinny arms. He woke in a cold sweat, still able to taste the fishiness, feel the texture in his mouth, the motion of his gums and tongue masticating the thick substance, trying to ease it down his throat. He was beginning to think he may have other fears, ones that were lying dormant and were stirring now, stretching their spindly arms and yawning.

Long after Aisha had fallen asleep Charlie lay wide awake, his hand on her belly while she snored peacefully beside him. The long-armed maple tapped at their window—a warning of the storm to come. A sharp wind off the ocean cut past the apartment buildings and rattled the branches, sending orange showers of leaves to the ground and ushering them down the street like a bunch of boisterous schoolchildren on a field trip. Charlie lay there listening to the scratching along the pavement, his mind a hot element fuelled by the day at the restaurant and by Aisha, her fear, the barnacle. He tried to let his mind cool, thinking of his body in the icemaker at work, chunks of ice clunking him in the forehead. *Sleep will come. Clunk. Sleep will come. Clunk.* He no longer wanted to close his eyes because of the pink purée nightmare. When the sun rose his eyes would shut. He had his father to thank for that.

In the dark, he stared at Aisha, his hand still resting on her belly. Who was this woman? How did she get there beside him? How was it that some of his DNA was now furiously multiplying inside her body? How could he explain to Aisha that it was all up to her, that no one had taught him how to be a father? He had been taught how to be a ghost, a spectre in the back kitchen. He felt a strong kick and jumped, his hand shooting into the air.

The maple tree outside the window tapped out answers in undecipherable Morse code. As he waited for the first whispers of sun, he imagined buying a chainsaw and climbing up into that goddamn maple tree to get rid of that tap, tap, tapping for good.

CHARLIE LIFTS HIS HEAD off the desk and looks out the window. Sinister grey waves are rising from the surface of the water, taking their time, anticipating their own destruction once they reach their destination. Pain splinters through Charlie's head. He fell into a deep, dream-saddled sleep—how long was he out for? When he staggers out of the office Topher is gone. Martin is polishing glasses and chatting with Susan. Rich, Tara, and James are cleaning the forgotten corners of the kitchen. The elderly woman is still there, with Rose sitting across from her. Their table is clean and fresh cups of steaming coffee sit in front of them. They're both staring at the rolling ocean. Charlie can't even look at them. He busies himself on the line, knocking back the rest of his drink and prepping the sweet garlic purée for tonight's roast chicken. When Rose walks by he rattles his empty cup at her and before long there is a fresh drink in front of him. He takes a swallow: strong— Rose is trying to push him over the edge. At this point in the evening the restaurant is usually bustling, but tonight a dreary hush floats over the near-empty dining room.

"Tara," he says, "you can go home." Her apron is off before he's even finished the sentence. Out of the corner of his eye he watches Rich and James for any mistakes while they're cooking. "Vinegar rag that plate, James. I can see your greasy fingertips all over the rim."

Customers begin to trickle in looking wet and wind-haggard, shaking out their coats and umbrellas. Aged parents with their sullen teenagers, eager-eyed tourists hungry from their day of sightseeing, girlfriends with arms linked in preparation to hunker down for a couple good hours of gossip; everyone wants to sit at the windows for a better view of the storm. Charlie glares at Susan's back while she jabbers with Martin, trying to burn two perfect circles through her shiny suit jacket. An older couple walks into the restaurant and Charlie can tell by the way they survey the room — disinterest and mild disgust — that they have money. Rose takes them to a quiet corner table, performing the little bows she reserves for the wealthy.

"Coulis," Charlie snaps at James, watching him plate a raspberry chocolate mousse. He's forgotten the dot of mango sauce that cheers the presentation. Charlie slices green onions, the blade blurring under his fingertips.

"Watch your—" James stops himself before he can finish his sentence. He's watching Charlie's knife with apprehension.

"Are you telling me how to cut onions?" Charlie snaps, laying his knife down on the cutting board.

"No, Chef," James says, bowing his head. Charlie goes back to his slicing and looks up to see Susan smiling at him. "Almost forgot," she says. "Let's take a seat at table thirty-nine." Salary negotiations are always conducted in public places where witnesses are present.

Their table is near the back of the restaurant, away from the smattering of customers and out of staff earshot. Susan sits across from Charlie, pausing to carefully shuffle in all the corners of her papers before looking up and shining a beatific smile at him. It sends a sharp stab through Charlie's liver. "First and foremost, Charlie, the Logan Group wants me to tell you they appreciate everything you've done for this restaurant." Charlie sits back with a nod, folding his arms across his chest, ready to accept the short soliloquy of praise with a firm and dignified handshake. He'll even forget the comment about fucking up the barnacle. Susan talks for several minutes, extolling his virtues, pointing out instances where he was vital to the restaurant's success, before laying her hands flat on the table, palms up, and bowing her head in concession. "But at this point the Logan Group cannot increase your remuneration."

Charlie sits stunned for a moment, staring at the bright pink lipstick Susan's slathered on to distract from her eye. He leans forward and turns her papers toward him. "Are you reading that from a script? Speak English, Susan."

"I think you know what I'm saying." She holds his gaze. He can see a hint of pleasure in her good eye. Blood runs hot up his neck and boils in his cheeks. He wonders if all the whiskey he's consumed this afternoon has made him more flammable. "Don't bullshit me, Susan. I've been waiting a long time for this."

"Charlie," she says, yanking her papers back and covering them with her arm. "Don't shoot the messenger."

"What the fuck, Susan? I'm going to be a father."

"Oh God, Charlie," Susan says, rubbing her forehead and looking around the restaurant to see if anyone's heard him. "I'm getting a migraine."

"A migraine?" Charlie says, raising his voice. "Right, because this is about you right now."

"Listen," she says, gesturing to the mostly empty dining room, "You know what *they* are like." When she says *they* she means millionaires. People assumed that wealthy clientele made for booming business, but in fact there was a reason they were rich: the servers pried each and every loonie from their tightly clenched fists. "We're a few bad months away from sticking someone on the street corner in a salmon suit with a sign advertising half-priced lunch entrees."

"I know how much *you* make. I've seen your paystubs."

"Food costs, Charlie?" A little vein is beginning to bulge in Susan's forehead. "Duck? Seven days of duck? If it weren't for my Wine and Jazz Wednesdays we wouldn't even be covering costs."

"Right, or maybe it was those flowers you planted." Last week she was out front in her suit jacket and miniskirt, bent over the wine barrel planters with a trowel. The week prior she strung twinkly lights around the entrance that blinked at seizure-inducing speeds. "No, Susan, it's the goddamn food. People come to a restaurant to eat."

"Maybe if you started paying for all the booze you drink

here." Her voice has turned nasty. "You're drunk right now, for Christ's sake."

"Why did you let me walk around all afternoon like an ass-hole?" he says, ignoring her comment. His fists are clenched under the table and even with concentration he can't seem to loosen them. He's suddenly aware of the nothingness they're strangling in their grip. Open or closed, they're still empty.

"This isn't French fine dining, Charlie. It's not Le Carré." His fists release, lay limp in his lap. It takes him a second to regain control of his limbs. He's never mentioned his father's restaurant to Susan.

"Well, this went well," she says, shuffling her papers together and standing up. "Six months and we'll take an-other look."

He stands quickly with a grunt. He doesn't appreciate her getting up first, leaving him alone at the table staring up at her; she should have given him some kind of warning so they could stand together. He watches her walk across the dining room, straightening wine glasses as she goes along. James and Rich are trying desperately not to look at him. Six months will drag like a ship anchor weighed down by five hundred pairs of crab cakes eaten by the same five old biddies on rotation.

"Incompetent," Charlie mutters back in the kitchen, push-ing Rich out of the way. "I'll do this one," he says, ripping the chit and rubbing salt and pepper into a bright red hunk of meat. He pushes his cup at Rose as she walks by, "I need another." The anger begins to sizzle all over his skin, his vision blurring. He throws the steak on the grill and sees his father standing by the prep counter, twirling in a maddened rage, throwing handfuls of limp spaghettini at the wall. No, this is not Le Carré — that message was clearly delivered by a birthday card peacock this morning. Rose pushes a drink at him. None of them understands how lucky they are to have him sweating in this restaurant. Their pockets would be fat with moths instead of bills if it weren't for him. He brushes the steak with generous layers of butter and watches the juices drawn out of the flesh spit as they drop into the fire. "Are you watching, Rich?" Charlie turns the steak once and admires its grill marks. "You don't turn it and turn it," he says to James, motioning to the meat. "Don't say you don't do that, because I've seen you. Goddammit. Too slow." He grabs the bowl of potatoes from James and whips them himself, creating thick white peaks. "Creative license," he shouts at Rich, pulling several spices down from the rack and sprinkling them liberally. He brings his nose down to plate level, flourishing the garnish before setting it delicately over the whipped potatoes and drizzling the leftover juice from the steak over the vegetables. "Let go, just let go" Charlie says, slapping measuring spoons out of James' hand. They go clattering across the kitchen tiles. "There," Charlie says, plating the steak and kissing the tips of his fingers. "Parfait!" He throws the plate onto the pass-bar. "Runner!"

There are only a few tables of customers left. Two West Vancouver cougars on their second bottle of rosé laugh together — probably about their husbands' shortcomings, Charlie guesses. A young couple shares dessert at the other end of the restaurant, the guy texting on his phone as the girl concentrates on gathering up every last remaining drop of chocolate raspberry coulis on the plate. The well-heeled salt-and-pepper boomer and his portly wife taste wine while Rose stands dutifully by their table, presenting the bottle.

Charlie carries his drink to the back stairs for a cigarette. A carved pumpkin from last week's Halloween decorations has been left out here to rot, its sad, sunken face glaring at him. He glares back. It grimaces. He grimaces. It mocks him and he picks up the fool thing, its softened features sinking further into themselves, and bunts it down the flight of concrete stairs, watching it come apart with soft, wet squelches, a ring of pumpkin stuck around his shoe. He knocks back his drink and bends over to scrape off the pumpkin guts, almost tipping over—he's drunker than he thought. The rain suddenly comes down harder, stinging his head, and he steadies himself against the railing before heading back into the restaurant. "Cleanup on aisle four."

"Huh?" The waterlogged dish boy looks stunned that Charlie is actually speaking to him.

"Clean up the back stairs before someone cracks their skull," Charlie says, slurping his drink. The boy drops his rag and slinks out the back hall.

"Charlie?" Susan's head pops around the corner. "It's Aisha again."

"No time. Tell her to call after the dinner rush."

Heavy metal music thumps from the small stereo next to the dishwasher. Charlie yanks the cord out of the wall and carries the stereo to the back steps, launching it into the dumpster next to the dish boy, who is picking bits of obliterated pumpkin up off the concrete. The stereo lands with a soft thud on a pile of mouldy hamburger buns and vegetable peelings. Dish Boy stares wide-eyed for only a moment and then pretends not to notice his stereo in the garbage as he walks back up the steps into the restaurant. Charlie is impressed with the boy's recovery. He pulls out another cigarette and smokes it in the doorway, watching the rain shoot down from the sky. When he comes back inside, Dish Boy is quietly staring at the dishwater.

"Like this," Charlie says, pushing him aside and furiously scrubbing at the pans collecting in a teetering pile on the counter, sending dishwater on the floor. "Do it like this." He heaps scrubbed bowls and ladles and cutting boards with a clang and then shoves them so they go skidding along the soapy surface of the metal counter and come crashing onto the floor. "Like that," he says, chucking the dishrag into the sink.

Charlie stalks back into the kitchen and dices an onion so he can feel the sting in his eyes. Rose pushes a plate with the steak half-eaten back across the pass-bar. "Overdone," she says. "Inedible, supposedly," she shrugs. "Not my words."

"Bullshit." Charlie pokes the hunk of meat and holds it up to the light, turning it this way and that, before throwing it back on the plate. "You tell him that steak is cooked exactly the way he ordered it."

"Okay." She shrugs again, taking a detour into the office with the plate before heading back to the table. Susan comes out of the office and surveys the dining room. Before Rose even reaches the table, the well-heeled boomer wags his finger as though he is scolding a small child.

"He wants to talk to you," Rose says, dropping the plate on the pass-bar with a clatter.

"Charlie," Susan warns, as he strides past her with the plate, the steak sliding around dangerously, nearly becoming airborne several times. Martin has detected the tension mounting in the dining room, his eyes darting from the dissatisfied table to Charlie to Susan while he picks at the scab above his lip.

"Good evening, sir," Charlie says, flourishing the plate before lowering it to float right under the boomer's nose. Rose runs a wet rag over the tabletops while Martin jerks around the room throwing down fresh cutlery on the empty place settings, both of them attempting to get close to the action in anticipation of the drama about to unfold. "Perhaps in this dim light it's difficult to see, but I can assure you your steak is cooked to your specifications."

"I already told the waitress I won't be paying for it." When the boomer speaks he does so without looking at Charlie and gazes at his wife instead, a calm, satisfied smile on his face. "And honestly, my wife's meal isn't very good either."

"We simply won't come back," the wife says, limply dangling her fork over the food. The man seems relaxed, as though he weren't that hungry to begin with. Charlie studies his profile for a minute and recognizes him instantly as his Chef de Partie from Le Remoulade, a slightly older, more distinguished looking version. When Charlie first started there as a Third Cook, the man took him under his wing, helped him advance all the way to First Cook.

"Do you know who I am?" Charlie says looking into the man's face.

"Should I?" The man smirks, misunderstanding, ready for a game. The wife crumples her napkin and places it definitively on top of her seafood risotto. "We won't come back," she says again.

Charlie stares at the man, giving him a chance to let his features register, but the man shrugs, bored of the game already. "I give up. Who are you?"

A snort escapes Charlie's nose as he drops the plate on the table. "No one." He turns to head back to the kitchen, but his legs fail to communicate with his torso. "I'm a ghost." His last words are lost in the clatter as he falls over one of the empty tables. Suddenly Rose is under one of his arms and Susan the other. A shattered wine glass twinkles in the carpet. "Okay, Charlie." He can't tell who the words come from, but they are gentle.

"Thank you," he says, shaking the women off of him. The gratitude is tinged with both sincerity and reproach. "Give your steak to your dog for all I care," he shouts over his shoulder at the man and his wife. Charlie walks to the bar and motions to the glorious bottles of liquor behind Martin.

"Why don't you take a breather," Martin says, stacking pint glasses.

"I'm not looking for anything," Charlie says. He'll make his own drink, he just needs Martin out of the bar. "Get those people a doggie bag."

But instead of walking behind the bar something draws him away toward the windows. In the reflection of the glass he can see Susan and Rose placating the wife, her bangs floating up from her forehead with each angry puff. Her husband is already out the door. Anyone left in the restaurant is making a hasty exit now, pulling wallets out of their pockets, sliding visas in billfolds. The storm has taken on a new dimension, one Charlie has never seen before. Below he watches the boomer lean into the gusts of wind as his wife scurries to catch up to him. The ocean looks as though it is reaching out, trying to take the restaurant into its insatiable belly. He stands close enough to the window to feel a chill over his face. The wind is buffeting the glass, trying to find any crack where it can sneak in. The pane rattles a few milli-metres from his nose. "Charlie." Susan's voice floats some-where behind him. "Phone for you." He doesn't move. The rattling is a distraction. He snaps out of his daze and saunters over to the phone, swaying slightly. When he picks up the receiver, he expects to hear his father on the other line: "Ça va, mon petit fantôme?"

AS SOON AS HE opens the back door of the restaurant, Charlie hears the ocean. The wind whips around his head and he pulls his toque low over his ears, making a dash for his car. The Douglas spruce towering overhead dips unnaturally, creak-ing and groaning as though it might come crashing down on his head. He watches it cautiously for a moment before climb-ing into the front seat. Down the way, one of the binners that frequent the alley behind the restaurant weaves between the garbage cans and falls on his knees in a large puddle, his hair a tornado above his head. The evergreen branches scrape across the roof of the car. "Shit," Charlie says, putting the car in gear and peeling out of the spot. He slows down as he approaches the homeless man, worried he'll roll into the middle of the road or leap in front of the car. As he passes, the man looks up at Charlie, and it's Topher on his knees, his eyes dark and menacing with booze. Charlie only considers stop-ping for a moment.

As he drives down the empty streets strewn with tree detritus, Charlie can see the waves pounding the shore. The road swims in front of his eyes. How much did he have to drink tonight? More than usual—seven, eight, maybe nine drinks? Could've been more, he wasn't exactly counting. Less than Topher, for sure. *Baby's early, Charlie.* It had been Aisha's sister on the line, her disembodied voice cutting through the telephone.

Charlie can see the generators exploding in the distance, bursts of cartoon-radiation green. The lights are out around the bridge and in the city, a gaping void where there should be the glittering of illuminated towers. The causeway through Stanley Park is covered with a blanket of broken branches, the trees swaying like pendulums. Charlie comes around a bend and slams on the brakes, the car skidding perpendicular to the road. A massive pine is down, blocking the entire causeway.

Rain pelts the car, a constant barrage sliding down the windshield. Charlie pulls off his toque and blinks at the tree, rubbing his head as if trying to conjure an intelligent thought. He searches his pockets for his phone before seeing it in his mind's eye, sitting on the prep counter next to the cutting board. He forgot it in his rush to get out the door. Out of the car, the rain pours over him like a cold shower. The street is deserted. Fear nestles deep into his belly, lifting the haze of alcohol he's been swimming through the entire evening. In the distance, Charlie can hear the sound of sirens, the sound of waves crashing, the sound of someone yelling at him, *You're awake, Charlie. You are wide awake.* It's not like a light bulb illuminating his brain, it's the kind of frickin' bolt of white-hot lighting that brings Frankenstein's monster to life. Charlie scrambles over the tree and starts to run.

~

THE CBC IS REPORTING that a red cedar estimated to be over a thousand years old was felled by last night's winds. The largest of its kind in the world, the reporter says, now lying prostrate on the forest floor. Charlie can't imagine something of that size, something that had survived hundreds and hundreds of years, uprooted and toppled in the dead of night. The tree must have made a terrible noise as it came down, shuddering and groaning with Godzillian force, a mythic reptile slain.

The ocean is dead calm now, cool, steely, shimmering in the early morning light, circling the tall, shut-eyed buildings of the city like a sheltered lake, without a hint of the rage from the night before. Charlie stands in the middle of the empty restaurant looking out across the mouth of Burrard Inlet at what is left of Stanley Park. The entire west side has been ravaged by last night's storm. When he drove through the causeway on his way to work this morning, the forest was noticeably thinner, ocean appearing where trees once grew tall and dense. He sips his scalding coffee and surveys the altered landscape. He has a headache from his hangover, but it feels far away, like an afterthought. The fire hasn't been started in the oven and the restaurant is cold. He can see his breath. Martin is sleeping on the leather couch in the lounge, snoring lightly, one of the patio blankets pulled up under his chin. Charlie lets him sleep and walks out back to collect the firewood. The winds have piled garbage into one corner of the parking lot and seagulls are pecking away happily at a loose scattering of soggy french fries. He piles a few logs into his arms and trudges back up the steps to start the fire.

Once the fire starts glowing good and hot, Charlie turns on one of the burners and heats some butter in a pan for eggs. He throws back two aspirin, crunching the pills into bitter powder and letting them melt down his throat like an acidic regurgitation. He feels hollowed and equates that with hunger, a need to be filled. Two eggs over easy. The yolk breaks on the second one and ruins the egg, but Charlie will eat it anyway. James calls to say he'll be late — things are a mess in Lions Bay. Charlie grabs a place setting from one of the empty tables and sits at the pass-bar, angling his plate and straightening his knife and fork. He takes a bite and the silence in the restaurant grows deeper.

Last night, when he arrived drenched and breathless at the hospital, a nurse helped him into a yellow gown and cap. In the delivery room he headed straight for the baby without realizing where he was going. There was a crowd of people working around the baby, grabbing tubes and vials, their hands on the tiny body, which was blue-skinned, not his, not of this world. He wanted to push past all of them so that he could stand above the baby, inert, and stare. All he could think was: *People get things they don't deserve all the time, so why can't I have this?*

"You look cheery in yellow," Aisha said, as he brought his face close to hers. Her eyes were swollen from crying. "It's a girl," she said. "Go with her." He followed the baby out of the room and waited on the outskirts of the neonatal unit. Doctors and nurses asked him questions, but he didn't hear much. He and Aisha hadn't talked about anything yet. The barnacle was here and she didn't even have a name. Every time he tried to think of one, lists of food whirled in his head. You couldn't call a child Dijon or Scallop or Frissé. Through the viewing window all he could see was one of her tiny hands, delicate as a sugary roll of tuile. The rest of her was obscured by tubes and tape and machines. "Every hour she remains stable is a good sign," was all anyone could tell them. One of the nurses pulled Charlie into the room and encouraged him toward the little plastic portal of the incubator. "It's good for them," she said, patting his shoulder. "They want to know you right away, the second they enter the world." He scrubbed his hands three times before putting on gloves and reaching into the incubator to run the tip of his finger over her forehead and along the ridge of her tiny nose. His hands still didn't seem clean enough.

ROSE COMES IN LOOKING tired, like she had no sleep. She walks right by him and goes straight for the coffee machine. Her hair is pulled into a messy loop at the crown of her head and she's wearing the same top from service last night, with a food stain on the sleeve. She stands at the back sink and tries to rub it out before sitting in front of him with her cup of coffee and taking out her scratch pad. She searches through her apron for a pen that works, squiggling invisible lines down the top page.

"You're here early," he says, measuring oil for a vinaigrette. Charlie's not sure why, but he needs her to look at him, and she does, but blankly, and then she looks back down at her pen. She shakes it vigorously and sucks on the tip, trying to encourage the ink to the nib, her cheeks hollowing in a way that makes her look gaunt, but pretty. She tries the pen again and the ink flows freely.

"Where's the fresh sheet?" she says, focusing on the little X's she's drawing at the top of her pad. There's a spot of ink in the middle of her lip.

"Hungry?" Charlie has a glob of egg stuck somewhere far down, where he feels dry and raw.

"This is my breakfast," Rose says, holding up her cup of coffee and giving him a look hairy with suspicion.

Ever since he touched the baby last night, he can't stop looking at his hands. For the first time he notices how ugly they are, covered in scars from burns and slips of the knife. He had tucked his index finger into the baby's palm, which was pure and untouched by the world. A baby's palm is as simple as it gets — it was the most delicate thing he'd ever felt in his life. Aisha was sleeping when he left the hospital. He left a note on top of a turkey sandwich wrapped in cellophane that he had bought from the vending machine: *Be back after the brunch rush*. He tries to dispel the image of Aisha sitting alone in her hospital room, eating the sandwich. She won't be alone, her sister will be there fussing and clucking and making enough noise for a roomful of people.

Rose pushes away from the counter and picks up a dish-rag. He knows he should tell her about the baby's birth, but there's something stopping him, as though the words are buried in the deep layers of fat in his gut. He'd need a shovel to dig them out.

"You might want to wake up Martin," he says instead. "He's passed out on the couch."

Rose rolls her eyes, indifferent. "No one's going to come in today anyway."

ROSE IS WRONG. MORE than half the North Shore is without power from last night's storm. People's homes are cold. No one can turn on their ovens or coffee pots this morning. Trees came crashing through front living rooms last night, leaving sopping messes of the carpets. The lineup goes out the door of the restaurant, along the sidewalk, and into the alley. Susan has to put on an apron and relive her serving days. She keeps sloshing coffee all over her tray. She and Rose dance around the room in an elaborately choreographed ballet. The bills come into the kitchen in a continuous stream— *chk, chk, chk*—long floating ribbons Charlie flourishes in the air, singing *eggs benny, French toast, florentine, side of sausage, side of bacon, hash browns, hold the hollandaise*. Charlie slides plates onto the pass-bar one after the other, lining them up, and Tara starts throwing down melon wedges. The din in the dining room makes it impossible to hear and Charlie has to shout his call times. "How long on fourteen?" Charlie mops his forehead with his sleeve as sweat pours off his brow.

"Minute left over-easy," Rich says, fondling a couple of eggs. Charlie can see him starting to panic.

"Rich, where's my bacon benny?" Tara shouts across the kitchen. "My crab cakes are up. I need it now."

Rich stands frozen in the middle of the chaos, rubbing his chin. It's something Charlie has never seen him do before. "What that?"

"The benny, Rich." Tara's voice is getting shrill.

Rich grabs a couple of English muffins and fumbles, almost dropping them on the floor. He grabs a ladleful of hollandaise and just as the golden liquid hits the eggs, Tara shouts, "On the side. Hollandaise on the side, dammit."

"Aw, fuck it," Rich says, throwing the ladle down and storming out of the kitchen.

Charlie follows him and finds him sitting on an overturned bucket beside the refrigerator, crying. There are new knuckle indentations, four perfect circles, in the fridge's door. Several matching impressions adorn the stainless steel surface.

"I buried so deep," Rich says, hiding his face in the crook of his arm.

"Come on, Rich," Charlie says. A separation occurs in his brain; the response he expects from himself—shouts, expletives, threats—doesn't materialize. His blood bubbles through his veins normally, his heart rate remains steady, his breathing calm. He grabs Rich under the armpits and yanks him upright the way you would a child who refuses to leave the birthday party. "We need you out there now," he says, but his voice is gentle.

"Deep, Chef," Rich says, tears wetting his cheeks. "I deep in shit. No way out."

"Come on," Charlie says. "We'll get you out. You're good," he says, patting him on the back as he shuffles him back toward the kitchen. "You're good."

Rich turns to look at him, blinking a little in disbelief. "Thanks, Big Chef."

Charlie and Rich stand side by side on the hot line and as the minutes tick by the streamer of bills gets shorter. Sweat is pouring off Rich's brow and his normally gravity-defying hair is limp and plastered against his forehead, but his eyes are sparkling now and he's slapping the English muffins on the plates with gusto. Charlie's singing and Rich joins in and James keeps saying it's the end of the world.

Despite the disaster, the feeling in the air is almost festive. The noise of people's voices, the clank of cutlery, the dishwasher going in the back. He can hear the dish boy — Tim, it suddenly dawns on Charlie, Tim is his name — singing along to Metallica. Which means if he can hear the new stereo, it's too loud — but for some reason this morning he doesn't care. He pulls a bewildered Tim into the kitchen to make salads. Everything comes together inside the restaurant in a way that is purposeful and meaningful. The food looks more colourful and smells better. There are many mouths to feed. It's their busiest brunch of the year, and for this Charlie feels happy.

As soon as the last plate goes out, Charlie takes off his apron and heads for the door. In the back hallway, he interrupts something between Rose and Susan as he rounds the corner, the two standing close with a crate of empty bottles at their feet. "Good work this morning, ladies," he says cheerfully, bustling through them and enjoying their confounded looks.

He sits in his car for a minute and watches Rose skip down the steps carrying the milk crate of empty bottles, which she dumps in the recycling bin with a loud clatter. He rolls down his window and calls after her as she goes back up, taking the steps two at a time. She stops in her tracks and turns, squinting in his direction with a hand on her hip. "What is it? I've got a table."

"Aisha had a girl."

"Oh!" He can see by the way she moves down one step that she wants to approach him, extend a hand or a hug, but she stops herself. "Well, congratulations," she calls out. "What's her name?"

"I don't know."

"Why are you here?" she says, shooing him, her arms batting the air. "Get going!"

"I'm outta here," he says, starting the car's engine. But once she's up the stairs and back into the restaurant, he lets the car idle. The motor's vibrations surround him and his face feels tight with dried sweat. He stares at his empty hands in his lap, strange in their stillness. He rubs the thick callus on his right-hand index, where the edge of the knife's blade creates friction. Even if he gives up cooking, the callus is something that will be with him for a while, maybe even forever.

Over the ocean, the sun is breaking up the clouds and he blinks back the bright light. He pulls down the visor and the yellow envelope falls in his lap. After a moment of turning it this way and that, he rolls down his window and chucks it into the dumpster, sending a seagull into the air. "Take it with you," he yells at the bird.

He pulls out of the restaurant parking lot and heads for the hospital—the barnacle needs a name.

THANKS TO CARIN

I EXPECT MY SISTER, Carin, to look surprised when I walk into the restaurant, but when she sees me she just smiles, almost wickedly, like *you're in for some trouble now.* For a split second I want to leave, drive back down to the coast and my routine. It's the same feeling I used to get when we were children and our desire for mischief became overbearing. I knew if I didn't go play by myself, Carin and I would soon be covered in permanent marker or picking gravel out of our knees or lighting our dolls' hair on fire. Retribution was always swift in our house, as Mom was on her own. Sitting on a straight-backed kitchen chair, I'd get the lecture—the one about being older and more responsible—until the tears ran down my cheeks and I got my back rub and glass of milk. Carin, in her defiance, always got the worse punishment.

I sit at a table near a window while Carin moves around the room, chatting up customers, dropping off beers for the afternoon drinkers. She makes waitressing look like fun, like a good career move, something you could be happy doing for the rest of your life. She glides by my table to set down a colourful drink and I get a whiff and glimpse of hair from her armpit — still a hippie. "I'll be off in fifteen," she says. "And by the way, June, what the fuck are you doing here?"

I smile and take a sip of my drink. It tastes like booze and strawberries. Out on the strip the squat motels sit up and down the sand-swept road, trapped forever in peach or sea-green paint. Nothing ever changes here. Mom is gone now, but otherwise everything is exactly the same, as though I've stepped into one of our round-cornered photos from the seventies, all the colours tinted gold-brown. The only new addition is a huge inflatable plastic mountain floating in the lake with kids scrambling and falling off the sides into the water. It looks so temporary, like it could disappear with the prick of a pin.

Carin comes out from the back room, her apron gone, a big bag slung over her shoulder, and steps behind the bar to pull a six-pack of coolers out of the fridge. The bartender cocks an eyebrow and she flashes him a grin. "I'll get you back."

"Sure you will," he says, rolling his eyes.

Carin comes around to pull me close in a hug. I stiffen involuntarily, the smell of her sweat sweet like overripe fruit. "She's getting married," Carin declares to the bartender, who shrugs with indifference. "Not for a couple of months," I say. The bartender has already turned his back to slice limes.

"Is it that soon?" Carin gives me a rough kiss on the cheek near my mouth.

"You look good," I try, giving her an approving nod.

"You hesitated." Arms akimbo, she takes a moment to look me over before batting a hand at me and laughing her way out the door. I fall in step beside her as we head down the strip. Teenagers hold hands along the promenade, and on the beach kids sit at their parents' feet, digging holes in the sand. Every second storefront is selling ice cream or sunscreen or bikinis. Carin holds her bronzed arm next to my pale one. "Don't you get any sunshine in the city?" She throws her arm around my shoulder, the way she used to when we were kids. "Are you checking up on me?" she says, squeezing me around the neck, and then without waiting for my answer, "Did you bring a bathing suit?"

ONLY SIX HOURS AGO I was in the city with Anton, standing on the street in front of our condo, trying to explain the reason for my impromptu trip to visit Carin. Along Davie, businesses were setting up for the day; the window seats in the coffee shops full; The Elbow Room packed, a single frazzled waiter buzzing among the tables; the salespeople pulling and tugging at the mannequins in the boutique windows. Earlier this morning, between showering and breakfast, I was struck with an urge beyond reason to see Carin. It was impossible to wait; I had to see her this very day. So I called in sick to the insurance office where I worked and packed a small bag.

"Doesn't your sister live in a shack with hippies?" Anton asked. He was sitting on the hood of my car as I searched for my keys, his eyebrows stitched with worry.

"She lives in a trailer," I said. "She's sick. The flu. She doesn't have anyone there."

In fact, I hadn't talked to Carin in months, so for all I knew there was nothing wrong with her. I kissed Anton's hand and put the car in drive, sending a resolute wave out the window as I drove away, a gesture that said: I have a job to do. But in all honesty, I have no idea why I was so desperate to drive five hours through the mountains to see my sister. A tension had been building inside me for a while now, but it was only last weekend at my own shower that I realized something was wrong. I wasn't the only one getting married—in fact, it seemed all of our friends were. For the past several months my calendar had been packed; I was organizing engagement parties and showers, attending weddings. I was thirty years old—it was that time in our lives. But on the day of my shower nothing felt right. The backyard garden looked trapped in the aggressive hands of a five-year-old girl: pink napkins spread out on knees, rose petal plates, miniature food, and heart-shaped balloons. It all left me feeling nauseous. I was alarmed by the sight of a cluster of women (my friends) gathered around a large sheet of paper fastened to a tree with several loops of masking tape. Each one of them, armed with a crayon, added lewd details to an anatomically incorrect life-size male (my husband). One of them waved a long, skinny balloon in my face. "Who's pinning the first penis on Anton?" I was alarmed, but the strange thing was, I had organized parties exactly like this one.

Over the past few weeks, thoughts—random things like the dry cleaning, upcoming dinner parties, the wedding invitations—had been accumulating in my mind, teetering as I balanced them one by one, and once Carin popped into my head, I couldn't rid myself of her. The thought of her was throwing the tower off kilter. I suppose I could have sent her an email or picked up the phone. But even if she was not

actually sick, there was always something awry in Carin's life,
and so in that way the lie wasn't really a lie at all.

And now, as I float beneath an unrelenting blue sky, I'm
already reconsidering my decision to visit. Whenever I'm
around my sister it feels as though someone has tightened a
bunch of screws in my head. Carin is stretched out on an air
mattress the size of a queen bed, looking sphinx-like, her long
dark hair parted in the middle. I am in the inner tube, limbs
jutting from the donut hole, floating like an upturned beetle
down the channel.

"I never get sick of this," Carin says, reaching for two coolers from the six-pack at her feet. She opens one, flicks the
bottle cap onto her mattress, and takes a gulp before opening
mine. "The last time we did this I was dating that guy with
the Supra." She snaps her fingers. "What was his name?"

"Something with a *K*. Kyle, Kurt—I don't know," I say,
rubbing my temples.

"Man, I loved that car." Carin passes me the bottle and
thinks. "That was almost two years ago."

"Has it been that long?" I sip at the fluorescent cooler and
then hold up the bottle to squint at the label: Limelicious
Hard Punch. "I think this stuff is giving me a headache."

"Oh, just drink it," Carin says, flexing her toes and adjusting her bikini. "You're so picky." She's gained weight since I last
saw her, the bathing suit bottom digging into the extra flesh
around her waist. Pudge, Carin says. Something to hang onto.

"And the hubby?" She sends a kick of cold water at me and
I splash her back, but her mattress is so large the water barely
reaches her. "Anton's fine," I say. "He just started his residency
at St. Paul's, so he's pretty busy."

"I always knew you'd end up with someone like that," Carin says, sitting up to dangle her legs in the water.

"Like what?"

"Lawyer, doctor, that type."

As we pass under the first bridge, I sink further into the donut hole, my legs sticking up in the air, icy water over my midriff. The channel widens and deepens so that we're barely moving and we float along lazily. "Don't you think it's a little strange?" Carin asks, slipping off her mat into the channel. "You dropping in like this."

"Is it?"

"This is not exactly how I pictured my day going," Carin treads water in front of me.

"I can't visit my sister? See how things are coming along."

"Coming along?" Carin raises her eyebrows and then disappears under the water. I brace myself, expecting to have my tube flipped, but instead she swims away from me, back toward the bridge, against the current. When she finally surfaces she's several metres away. "How's the planning going?" she shouts and starts a dog-paddle in my direction.

"Fine," I shrug.

"A wedding seems like so much work." Carin has reached my tube and is hanging off the side, breathing heavily. "You should just elope. I've never been to Mexico."

"I have a wedding planner to help." I close my eyes and try to relax my jaw muscles. Sue Clarkson, wedding planner, with her curlicue handwriting. She is in the habit of couriering samples, which could easily be sent by email, to the insurance office, stamping URGENT across the manila envelope. Sue has two stamps, the other being IMPORTANT. At some point, I began filing the envelopes, unopened, along with all the other mail. Pictures of towering fondant cakes and bouquets accented with sprigs of baby's breath; sparkling cocktail recipes. The guest list is several pages long. Anton has invited his entire extended family of sixty-three people; I have Carin. "The girls at the office threw me a shower last week," I say.

"No one told me." Carin pushes away to climb back onto her mattress.

"You would have hated it."

"How do you know that?"

"There were balloon penises."

Clouds appear behind the hills, a breeze picking them up and stretching them across the sky. Carin opens another bottle. Her empty rolls off the air mattress and drops into the channel. I fish it out and plunk it into the half-empty pack. "Slow down," I say.

"You have a maid of honour?" Carin asks, dipping her head back into the water as though she doesn't really care what my answer is. I wait until she surfaces before answering no. I was hoping Carin wouldn't ask, but I knew she would. I know so many other women, responsible women, punctual women, women who wash their hair more than twice a week. There are certain expectations. Carin doesn't say anything. She smirks and looks down the length of the channel. Her expression reminds me of her younger self, the one who would stick out her chin stubbornly or kick you in the shins if she felt she wasn't getting fair treatment. "Am I gonna get to meet him one day," she says, after some time.

"Anton?" The tube has spun around so I'm looking at

Carin's feet. She is lying on her stomach now with her legs splayed open.

"Don't I need to give my approval?"

"You'll meet him at the wedding."

"Oh, sure."

We float in silence past a dinghy full of kids. One of them must have lost something, because they're all quiet, staring intently at the water.

"I guess I should be helping," Carin says.

"With what?" I can't stop a laugh.

"I don't know, pluck petals off roses or something," she says, finishing her cooler. "Do you need a flower girl?"

I laugh a little harder and Carin joins in.

"Just show up."

"We're getting to the gross part," Carin says and I lift my feet out of the water as we pass the underwater pipe. Thin, feathery weeds choke up the channel. Carin shivers, still haunted by her childhood phobia of waterweeds. I catch one on my toe and kick it at her. We laugh some more and when I float by her, I grab her hand and rest my heels on her air mattress. It does feel good to be with her again. When we're apart I always forget I miss her. And then when I'm with her I'm suddenly hit with these horrible pangs of yearning for her company, even though at that moment she is right there in front of me. Usually I have to leave soon after that because something she's said makes me want to strangle her. She's always known how to push my buttons.

Carin lifts one of my heels. "You have claws."

With my feet on display, I suddenly realize they have gone untouched for months, calloused and rough, the toenails curling over fleshy tips. How can someone forget their own feet? I am careful, always, with hygiene; I use grooming to assess a person's competency. Carin, with the armpits, tends to rate very low on that scale. Instinctively, I dip my toes back into the water and then feel stupid for being so obviously self-conscious. "Aren't we getting off soon?" I say, quickly finishing the rest of my cooler.

Up ahead I can see the end point, the concrete stairs leading out of the water and the big blue-and-red school bus waiting to take all the drifters back to the town. Above the gas station a large banner reads *Relvis and Hot Dogs* and a man in a white sequined Elvis outfit sings "In the Ghetto" on a makeshift platform in the parking lot. Carin hops out of the water and pulls her air mattress up the concrete stairs and over to the gravel driveway. I hoist the inner tube onto my shoulder and while we wait in line to get on the bus we push the air out of the mattress. Carin is distracted by a large group of raucous men standing in front of us, drinking beer. They board the bus and pay their fare and we follow them on. I hand the bus driver our money, but he waves it away and with a gesture toward the drunk men, says, "They took care of you." I roll my eyes, but Carin struts over to thank them, grinning widely.

The only seats left surround the group of drunkards. I take one in front of them and focus out the window as the bus pulls away. I suddenly feel completely out of place in my hometown, out of place on this bus next to my own sister. Everything feels wrong; my bare feet on the dirty floor, my head nearly touching the ceiling, the friction of my wet bathing suit on the vinyl seat. I miss the cool white walls of my eleventh-story condo. Watching Carin I see everything I'm not. She's already made a friend, chatting up one of the better-looking guys in the group. He opens a beer and hands it to her and she slides in beside him. She tells a loud dirty joke and the back of the bus erupts in laughter, but when she looks over at me I find it hard to even smile.

CARIN AND I NEARLY died on the channel one year and to this day she still refuses to take responsibility. We used to float down weekly, Mom piling us into the pickup with our inner tubes tied down in the truck's bed. It was a great way for her to get rid of us for a couple of hours, dumping us into the channel at the Okanagan end and picking us up later in the parking lot across from Skaha.

One afternoon, standing side by side on the banks, Carin wanted to tie our two inner tubes together with rope so we wouldn't float apart. The channel was high and fast that year, water licking at the edges, pulling along rocks and clumps of grass, and Carin was scared. With my legs braced against the icy water and my inner tube bouncing around my waist in anticipation, I shouted at Carin to hurry up and get in. She was going through a phase where she never wanted to be more than arm's reach from me. "She'll grow out of it," my mother kept repeating. "One day she won't want to have any-thing to do with you." When I started to lose feeling in my toes from the freezing water, I finally agreed to let Carin tie the tubes together, but I made her promise not to talk to me if she was going to be clinging for the entire ride.

The first bridge the channel passes under is bisected by a

large concrete support wall, and even from a distance I could see the water breaking around the pillar, creating a foaming mouth that wrapped around either side of the cement wall. When we reached the bridge Carin went on one side and I went on the other, the rope holding in the middle, balancing our equal weights. I clung to the wet rubber tube, afraid to let go and be sucked underwater by the strong current, my legs battering helplessly against the concrete as water poured over my head. Part of the rope wrapped around my calf and I kicked wildly to stay afloat, fumbling with the twine that linked our tubes, but the knot was on Carin's side. I screamed at her. "Carin, untie us! Carin, you dingbat!" It was hard to hear her over the roar of the water, but she kept calling my name and I could hear her sobbing. Every time I screamed at her, I swallowed a mouthful of water. "It's your fault! Carin! Your fault!"

The man came from my side of the channel. I hadn't noticed him sitting there in the dark angle of the bridge, watching me hang on for dear life. He was standing up the bank a ways, making swimming motions with his arms, but I ignored him. His scraggly hair reached down past his shoulders and he wore dirty jeans and an unbuttoned shirt that displayed a hairy, tattooed chest. He fit the description of men our mother warned us not to trust. I watched him walk up the bank a bit further, take off his shirt and his crummy boots, and wade into the water. He fought the current out to the middle of the channel and then floated placidly toward us like some sort of grizzled river nymph. He straddled the concrete wall and pulled a knife out of nowhere as the water swelled around him. With one quick flick of the blade he slit the rope and set us both free. I floated away so serenely that for a moment the whole thing seemed like a dream, but when Carin's inner tube drifted toward me without her, my heart stopped. Still on my tube, I tried to paddle upstream to find her, but the current was too strong. Finally I spotted her coming out from under the bridge, flailing through the water. I kicked downstream where it was shallower to catch her tube, and then stood to watch her thrash messily until she was practically under my nose. Her eyes were puffy and red from crying. "You can touch, dummy." Those were the only words I said to her for the rest of the ride. The incident was another point of proof toward everything I already knew — that Carin was my responsibility, that I would always be watching out for her and she would be hanging on tight, like that rope around my ankle.

THE BUS DEPOSITS US right in front of the Sunnyside trailer park and we pad barefoot across the hot asphalt into the cool shade of the willows that line the road. Carin has a lot near the channel, close enough that the ducks wander over for bread crusts and if you look hard you can get a glimpse of the water sparkling between the trees. "Want a tour?" Carin says, hopping up the little steps to the trailer.

"I've been in there before." I drop into one of her lawn chairs.

"I've upgraded," Carin says, disappearing inside.

"Where's Mom's truck?" The hitch trailer is noticeably missing our Mom's white Dodge. We made the long drive to the coast every summer in that truck to go to the PNE fair. Weeks before we left, it was all I could talk about — the rides

I was going to go on, the carnival games I was going to win. As we followed the highway through the mountains, I would get lighter and lighter until I was bouncing around the cab.

"I sold it," Carin says, from a little window above my head. She was always stunned by the entire trip to Vancouver. She played along, but I don't think she ever liked going to the city. I had to drag her onto all the rides at the fair. She missed the ducks. She missed the lake.

"Never used the truck anyway," Carin says, coming back down the little trailer stairs with two bottles of beer.

"I would've bought it from you."

"What do you need a truck for in the city?"

"That's not the point." All the coolness from the channel ride has left my body and I feel overheated and annoyed.

"Would've been a bitch to park downtown," Carin says, taking a drink from her beer.

"Doesn't it seem pointless to have a hitch you can't actually hitch to anything?"

"Where would I go, anyway?"

"I don't feel like beer," I say, heading into the trailer to find something else to drink. The living area with the kitchen and fold-down dining table are the same, except for the new flatscreen in the corner. There are clothes scattered across the black leather couch and breakfast dishes on the table. I open the fridge—it's mostly empty and smells of sour milk. To get to the bed, Carin has to climb past the breakfast benches. There's a little tan-coloured curtain for privacy.

"I would've cleaned up if I knew you were coming," Carin says when I come back down the steps with a glass of water.

"You don't have a phone," I sigh.

Two ducks waddle onto the lot expectantly. I reach out to the one closest and it snaps at my finger.

"Yeah, he's a nasty one," Carin says. She goes back into the trailer and comes out with a bag of bread, pulling out a slice and throwing the entire thing at the duck's head. He snatches it and drags it behind a tree, flapping at the other ducks approaching him. "Don't take it personally."

"Do you have power?" I ask, pulling my phone and charger from my bag.

"Of course. Didn't you see my TV?"

"So you can afford cable, but no phone." I unload a tent from the back of the car and begin arranging the poles by size on the gravel.

"The phone is more of a lifestyle choice."

"Hm."

"You want some help with that?" I take one look at Carin lounging in her chair with the half-finished beer and know she'll get in the way more than she'll help. "You can sleep in the bed with me if you want," she says.

"No, that's okay."

"I can make room inside. It'll get hot out here in the morning. Sun beats down." Carin grins and watches me struggle with the tent poles.

"I'd rather sleep outside," I say pointedly.

"I'll leave the door unlocked so you can use the washroom."

After staring at the inside of the refrigerator, Carin orders pizza for dinner. We eat at her dinette, the pizza box covering the entire table. Later I sit in one of the lawn chairs outside. Carin's watching TV inside and it's quiet, but for the occasional bug frying in the massive zapper she has hung from a tree beside the trailer. The contraption looks large enough to kill a small bird. A moth flutters around its fluorescent green light and gets nuked by an electrical current that lights up the patio. I stare for a while at the phone cradled in my lap and then call Anton. His voice is tired. "Were you sleeping? I guess it's kind of late." I say, checking my watch.

"I just finished my shift. How's your sister?"

"Fine, same old."

"She recovered quickly from her flu." Something in his voice tells me he knows I lied.

"I guess. Her place is a mess," I say. "She sold Mom's truck. I wish she'd get her life together."

"People do things at their own pace."

"She's twenty-eight, Anton. She's going to be a waitress for life." Another electric current lights up the patio.

"Maybe she likes waitressing."

"Come on." I slump back in the lawn chair and look out at the sky. I suddenly miss the feeling of Anton's arms draped over me. "Why am I here?"

"Beats me. You probably needed to know she's okay."

"Who actually likes waitressing?"

"Maybe Carin does."

IN THE MORNING I wake up disoriented, the air in the tent solid with heat. Sometime during the night I got turned around and I claw at the vinyl sides, kneeling on my glasses in the process as I blindly try to find the opening. The zipper comes into focus. With what feels like a gasp from both myself and the tent, I tumble out onto the gravel. Carin stands a few feet away with the ducks, a steaming cup of coffee in her hand. "I was wondering when you'd wake up."

"What time is it?"

"Almost eleven."

"What?" Across the street I can hear people unloading from the channel bus. "Why didn't you wake me up?"

"You were snoring."

"So?"

"So, you sounded tired."

I climb into the trailer, looking for something to drink, and end up with my head under the kitchen tap. "I think I'll sleep inside tonight," I call out the window.

The rest of the morning I lounge in the shade of the trailer, reading magazines and clipping my toenails. I look for nail polish in Carin's bathroom, but can only find an old tube of mashed lipstick and tanning oil. There's still no food in the fridge (I ate stale Ritz crackers for breakfast) and Carin's back in her bikini, sunbathing on a lounger, a huge glass of lemonade sweating in her hand.

"I'm going for a run," I say, lacing up my sneakers.

"You're on holiday," she says, swatting the air. "Relax."

"That *is* what I do to relax." I stand to stretch my legs, leaning up against the trailer to flex my calf muscles. "I run every day."

"Where?"

"What do you mean, where? Around." I pull my arms across my chest. "Don't you have work today?"

"No." She licks at some condensation running down the side of her glass. "It's a part-time gig, for right now."

"What else do you do?"

"I relax."

"You're good at that," I say, jogging on the spot.

"Sun's different here," Carin says, flipping onto her stomach. "Don't stay out too long."

I pad out of the trailer park and run along the channel, following the path that banks its edge. The heat hangs in the valley, stretches from mountain to mountain, sagging under its own weight as my feet raise clouds of dust. I enjoy the push against the swelter, the tightening of my leg muscles propelling me forward. It makes me feel capable, as strong as the channel rushing against the muddy banks. I take a detour into our old neighborhood, running past our childhood home, a split-level rancher with a wide green lawn and two-car garage. The new owners have changed the siding and planted some rhododendrons under the living room window, but otherwise the house looks as I remember. I run past the community centre where we took swimming lessons, the A&W where I had my first job, our old high school.

It was when Carin dropped out six credits shy of graduating that I decided to move to Vancouver. There wasn't much left for me in the Okanagan, just motorboats and drunk driving, and I couldn't stand to watch Carin fritter her life away. She never seemed to care, didn't dream about anything beyond Penticton. When people used to ask her what she wanted to be, she'd make up a ridiculous profession, a monkey trainer or jellybean taster.

Mom died a few years after I moved to the coast. I thought the shock might spark something in Carin, but she stayed almost stubbornly the same. The small inheritance she was given was piddled away slowly, weekend after weekend.

Somehow, being far away from her made me certain I wasn't going to become her. Penticton became a reminder of all the things I missed about my mother, but Carin still ate at the little café near the beach where she and Mom used to go on a lazy weekend; she'd tell me about it as if it was nothing. "Went into Jenny's today, had the best fucking bowl of soup."

As I run along the bridge and onto the side of the highway, I try to draw deep breaths, but my throat feels raw from the dry air. Cars whip past me as I try to keep up my pace, but I've lost the rhythm. I stop and bend over, hands on my knees, and feel a wave of nausea pass through my body. I hear hoots behind me, a loud honk, and a whoosh of dusty baked air. The blue-and-red school bus drives by with several drunken knuckleheads hollering out the windows. I straighten and give them the finger — something Carin would do, but it feels good. "Morons," I gasp, trying to catch my breath. Wishing I'd brought water, I start walking down the side of the highway, the ground shifting under my feet like a heat mirage. There's another honk and a spray of gravel. I turn, ready to flip off the next bunch of assholes, but it's my own car on the side of the highway. Carin sticks her head out the window. "Need a ride?"

Without saying anything I walk over and get in.

"You don't mind?" she says, checking the mirrors and pulling back onto the highway. "I borrowed it. The keys were right on the counter. I needed some booze."

I roll down the window and lean my face into the breeze.

"You're red!" Carin says, looking over at me.

"I was running."

"You okay?"

"I'm fine," I say, closing my eyes.

"It's just—you're sweating a lot."

"Just drive my goddamn car."

"Well, I won't say I told you so."

"Don't start." I squint at her.

"You're lucky I found you," Carin says, swerving into the fast lane and cutting off another car. The highway swims in front of me. I've lost some small anchor.

"Fine, Carin. Thank you, okay? You were right." I'm drifting.

"Is that why I'm getting the attitude?"

I brace my hands against the dashboard and lean forward.

"I *can* be right too sometimes," she says.

Drops of sweat drip off my nose and onto the floor of the car.

"You're the oldest." Carin flourishes a hand. "I'd bow down, but I'm driving."

"Carin, pull the car over."

"What?" She looks over at me confused.

"Pull it over."

She crosses three lanes of traffic to the side of the road and I swing open the door and stumble to the ditch. I bend down, resting my elbows on my knees, and throw up all over the grass. Everything comes up and when it's all out, I dry heave. Once I've finally stopped, I feel Carin's gentle hand on the small of my back. Cars speed past us on the highway. She hands me a bottle of water and I take a swig, spitting it out on the ground. I take another swig and swallow. The water is warm and metallic from sitting in the heat of the car. It's days old. I get back inside and we drive the rest of the way home in silence.

CARIN HAS CLEARED THE trailer floor of clothes and laid a foamy down with a neatly tucked pink-and-blue flowered bedsheet and matching floral pillow. They're Mom's old linens. I don't know why, but the whole scene makes me feel lonely. I can hear Carin outside laughing with someone as I go to get a glass of water. She opens the trailer door and pokes her head in. "Do you want to come out with us tonight?"

"I'm still feeling sick." I pour myself a tall glass of water.

"Heat stroke?"

"I guess."

We stare at each other a moment, the refrigerator humming in the background.

"Okay," Carin shrugs. "I guess I'll see you in the morning, then."

"Sure." I head back into the living room as Carin, drunk, struggles to close the door. She lets out a giggle and then opens it again. "June?"

When I turn back the look of sadness in her face surprises me. "Yeah?"

"Are you mad at me or something?"

"Why would I be mad at you?"

"Just checking," she says, shrugging again and ducking out the door. From the window I watch her and some guy traipse out to the street, Carin's hand tucked in the back pocket of his jeans.

I slide into the cool sheets, trying not to disturb Carin's tucking job. Beside the foamy she's placed a thick manila envelope addressed to me. I tear it open and papers fall out everywhere—pink cakes with white flowers, white cakes with pink flowers, white cakes with white flowers. Out flutters a handwritten note from Sue Clarkson: *Pick one you love. Love, Sue.* Love Sue? I shove the envelope of pictures as far under the couch as I can reach and flip off the table lamp. In the dark I squint at a corkboard Carin has propped up against the wall with pictures pinned all over it of her with a variety of guys I don't recognize. In the middle of them all there's an old picture of Mom. I reach out and unpin it from the corkboard. It's from the early seventies, her hair parted in the middle, her eyes thick with liner. The expression on her face is typical Carin: cool deadpan. She was probably the same age as me in that photo or close anyway. I realize looking at the picture what different paths our lives took and that maybe if we'd met at that age, as strangers on the street or in a bar, maybe we wouldn't have been friends or even spoken to one another.

WHEN I OPEN MY eyes the photo of my mother is a few inches from my nose. I put it back on the corkboard and hope Carin hasn't noticed I moved it. Outside Carin is sprawled on her back on her air mattress in the gravel, her head fallen partially onto the ground, her neck at an awkward angle. I walk down the three trailer steps and look around. There are beer bottles all over the patio table and an overflowing ashtray by Carin's head. Near her feet there's also a pair of large men's sneakers, but I don't see the possible owner anywhere. I place my foot near her head on the air mattress and give it a good bounce.

Carin groans and rolls over onto the gravel. "What?" Bleary-eyed, she tries to focus on me and then dismisses me with a limp wave.

"It's going to rain," I say, before heading back into the trailer.

She spends the rest of the day in her bedroom with the curtain drawn, coming out only once to make fried eggs. While the rain comes down outside, I wander around, bored, tidying up the trailer, wiping down the inside of the empty fridge, and flipping through cheap gossip magazines, the only reading material I can find. I call Anton and tell him I'll be coming back by tomorrow evening.

By late afternoon the rain has stopped and the sun comes out and burns away the clouds. I take a walk along the beach and eat a hot dog for dinner, sitting on the promenade watching couples, families, and groups of friends go by. A limousine drives slowly down the strip, honking, with grads waving out the sunroof. I go back to the trailer but don't head inside, instead dragging one of the patio chairs to the channel, where I can watch the sunset. Carin comes out with her own chair and we sit together in silence for a while. The sun has just finished dropping behind the mountains, pulling with it a shade of darkening blue. Across the way, a teenage couple is standing on the edge of the channel with a dinghy, testing the water with their toes. I shiver at the thought of floating down in the dark. "Feeling better?" Carin asks eventually.

"I am. I'm going home tomorrow morning," I say. The couple is in the water now, drifting under the first bridge. "How are you feeling?"

"Great." As if to demonstrate, Carin stands up and touches her toes a couple times before bending into a yoga pose. "So, let's go out tonight."

"I don't think so," I say, shaking my head. "I have a long drive tomorrow."

"Come on. Can't we have one fun night?"

"I thought we were having fun."

"Right," Carin says, rolling her eyes and stifling a yawn.

"I'm not in the mood."

"I want you to meet someone. Remember that guy on the bus?" She smiles brightly and I figure it's probably easier to say yes then to say no at this point. "One drink."

AS WE WALK ALONG the crowded promenade, I pull self-consciously at the hem of the denim skirt Carin has lent me and try not to worry about how or if I will sit down. I picture seams split wide open, leaving me exposed in the middle of the bar. The strip radiates in the glow from the hotel casino. Tricked out lowriders and muscle trucks cruise the street as competing hip hop *boom boom booms* from their open windows. Carin leads us through the patio jammed with tables full of people to the back of the restaurant, where the bar is just as packed. I ease myself—minding the skirt—onto a stool at the edge of the bar, Top 40 blasting from speakers in the ceiling above us. Carin waves at one of the bartenders, trying to order us drinks overtop a row of people seated along the bar. He pulls down two tall glasses and several bottles of colourful booze. I recognize the bartender now. He was on the channel bus and he was also the guy Carin was with last night. He's not as good-looking as I remember. It must have been the wet hair, now a fuzzy mess of blond curls around his head, like he's attempting cherubic but failing miserably. He sets two drinks in front of us. "You found me," he says, grinning at Carin and bobbing his head.

"This is my sister, June," Carin says. "June, meet Jet."

"From the bus, right?" he says, shaking my hand. I press my lips together, suppressing a smirk. His hands are wet from working behind the bar—ice, beer, and mixers. Idiot boyfriend number... oh, I've lost count.

"I brought your sneakers," Carin says, pulling them out of her bag.

"Awesome." Jet pours a round of pink shooters for all three of us and we touch shot glasses and down them. He pours another round and I push mine toward Carin. "Come on," she laughs. "We're just getting started."

"My shift is almost over," Jet yells over the music. "I'll come hang."

"Great," I say, sarcasm lost in the bass thumping from the speakers. I take the shot and throw it back. "Happy?" I say to Carin.

"Be nice," Carin hisses in my ear.

We barely interact the rest of the evening. Carin sits with her back to me, bowed deep in conversation with Jet. Every time I get to the last inch of my drink, Jet's friend behind the bar whisks it out of my hand and gives me a new one. For that reason, at least, I always have something to do. At some point during the evening, my neighbour turns on his barstool and takes interest in me. He's of the gelled crunchy-hair variety with a tight T-shirt sporting the lettering "Wingman" across the chest. He spends most of the night talking about his speedboat. I must look bored, because Carin taps me on the shoulder and asks me if I want to leave.

"This is my sister," I tell Wingman, motioning to Carin with a floppy hand. I can't remember his name, so I don't introduce him.

"I'm trying to get your sister to come out on my boat," he says, squaring his shoulders and drinking from his pint.

"Fat chance," Carin laughs, thumbing in my direction. "Queen Prudent over here."

"Her?" Wingman rests a meaty hand on my shoulder and gives me a shake as if he's known me for years. "No way."

I grab his wrist and remove his hand, shooting Carin a look that says, *keep going and die.*

"A dinghy, maybe," Carin says, cracking herself up and spilling some of her drink on my skirt.

"All right," I say, dabbing at the wet spot with a bar napkin. "That's enough."

"She'd mess up her hair," Carin says, raising the pitch of her voice a squeaky octave. She hoots and slaps Wingman on the back.

"Fine," I say, finishing my drink in two large gulps. Carin's eyes widen and I smile at her. "Let's go for a boat ride."

CARIN STANDS AT THE edge of the dock shaking her head and for a quick second looks disturbingly like our mother. Wingman turns on the boat and drowns out whatever Carin is shouting at me. The night is warm and star-speckled, and as Wingman unties the moorings I wave goodbye to Carin again. "Don't wait up," I call to her. Just as the boat pulls away, she jumps in and sits down beside me. "Because you're drunk I feel I should tell you, you're acting like an idiot," she shouts into my ear over the noise of the outboard motor.

"I'm having fun." I trail my fingers through the water and flick the droplets in Carin's face. "Isn't this what you want?"

The lights along the strip shimmer and warp as the boat cuts through the water. We turn away from the beach and pick up speed, Wingman grinning back at us. Within minutes we're surrounded by darkness, black sky and water. I can barely see Carin sitting next to me. The desert hills stretch around us, sucking the moisture from the night air. Above, stars spin shapes across the sky. Wingman's laughing; the boat skips and accelerates. "He's wasted," Carin yells.

"Faster." I shout the word several times at Wingman's back. Carin digs her nails into my arm, but I push her hand away and stand up, letting the dry air rush past my limbs and through my hair. With the speed of the boat it's easy to let go of everything—the flower arrangements and seating plans and balloon penises. Carin stands and grabs my shoulders, trying to force me back into the chair. "What?" I say. The word is lost, the wind whipping my hair around my face. The boat carves the water and we stumble, trying to regain our balance. "Sit down, you idiot," Carin shouts, grabbing at me again.

"Get over yourself," I shout back, shaking her off. "This is you," I say, pointing to myself. "This is what you look like."

The boat takes a sharp curve and rocks to one side. In one quick flip Carin is in the water. The spray from her splash hits my face and then the darkness eats her up. The boat keeps going, Wingman not realizing he's dropped her, and I lurch up to the front screaming at him to stop the boat. He cuts the motor and the whole lake is swallowed in silence.

"You asshole." I peer over the edge of the boat and call out for Carin. "You were going too fast." Wingman passes me a flashlight to shine into the water, but all that's reflected back is more darkness.

"You were the one that wanted to go faster," Wingman says, looking over the other side of the boat.

I turn around and kick him in the leg. "Shut up." I lean out and scream Carin's name. After a moment and from what sounds like a great distance, I hear the *slap slap* rhythm of messy strokes and call out again. I see the white of her shirt first. She swims slowly and steadily to the boat, climbing the ladder, her clothes sticking to her and draining water over the deck floor. Without pause, she clomps heavily right up to me and punches me square on the chin. I lunge at her and we roll around in the boat, pulling each other's hair and slapping. Carin bites my shoulder and I twist her arm. *Bitch! Cow!* Eventually we tire ourselves out and sit in the dark, panting on opposite sides of the boat. The lap of water against the hull and the illusion of the stars fixed in space make me feel a bit better. Blood thumps through my temples and I start to laugh, tears rolling down my face. Wingman's disembodied voice comes from somewhere in the dark. "Do you girls want me to take you back to the dock?"

CARIN LEAVES A TRAIL of water behind her as we walk back to the trailer park. She's soaked, hair dripping and mascara running, her favourite white slingbacks floating somewhere in the lake. I walk several paces behind her. When I ask her if she wants to wear my flip-flops she doesn't even turn around.

We cross over the dam that feeds the channel. Orange floodlights illuminate the bridge, casting a light thick with winged insects. Papery moth bodies brush against my bare limbs. When we get to the other side, I try to catch up. "Carin?" She quickens her pace. "Come on. Slow down."

Carin spins around suddenly and I almost bump into her. "You could've got us hurt. I could've drowned."

"I'm sorry." I shrug my shoulders, surprised at how good it feels, how freeing to be helplessly wrong.

"Sometimes sorry is not what someone needs to hear," she says, turning and walking away from me.

"Carin, I'm really sorry," I say. My giggles return and I try to choke them back. I try to make them sound like tears.

She whips around with her hands on her hips. "Are you laughing?"

"No," I choke, laughing hysterically now, doubled-over with the effort of trying to conceal it.

"You're the one who's crazy." Carin yells at me and stomps off down the dark street in the direction of Sunnyside. My laughing fit settles into gentle hiccups. All I can hear now is the gravel under the slap of my flip-flops.

THOUGH I'VE NEVER TOLD her, I was thankful for Carin that day on the channel when we were kids and we tied our inner tubes together. As we floated, a storm was building off Skaha Lake and the clouds were blowing in fast. We were tired from the ordeal under the bridge and shivering from the cold, so we decided to get out of the water to find a payphone and call Mom to pick us up early. Grabbing onto the long grasses edging the channel, we hauled ourselves up onto the steep bank. I ran up the incline, dragging my inner tube behind me, determined to leave Carin to chase after me. The grasses grazed our thighs, and the rocks and prickly weeds bit at our bare feet, but Carin never whimpered, scurrying to keep up with me.

When she suddenly dropped her inner tube and grabbed my arm, I turned and slapped her. It was quick and instinctual. She didn't flinch. Her eyes remained focused beyond me on the ground, the insistence of her hand enough to keep me still. A few inches from my feet, a large rattlesnake rested, wrapped in a fat, lazy spiral. Another step would have landed my foot in the middle of its coil. My stomach shot into my throat and for that moment while Carin's hand gripped my arm, I felt our hearts racing together. She guided me as we slowly crept around the snake, and back on the path we walked side by side to the gas station. We didn't speak a word to each other, but I could feel Carin's pride, her delight at having saved me.

We never told Mom anything about what happened that day — the tubes tied together, the bridge, the man, the knife, the snake — and now that she's gone it bothers me. I'm not sure why we never told her that story. I guess we thought — the way kids always do — we'd be in trouble.

IT'S ONLY NINE O'CLOCK, but the trailer is already stifled with morning heat. I pull back the little curtain to Carin's bedroom, where she's sleeping with her mouth hanging open, a small puddle of drool on her pillow. Sometime during the night she kicked off all her covers in what looks to me like a violent rejection, her arms still a frozen flail above her head and her legs stalled mid-kick. I pull the curtain shut quietly and walk back outside.

The car is sweltering and I roll down all the windows while I load my bag into the trunk. As I pull out of the trailer park, I catch sight of Carin in the rearview mirror, stumbling from the trailer in her pajamas, her hair a rat's nest on top of her head. I pause for a moment and then reverse, putting the car in park and leaving the engine running. Carin leans into the window. "Here." She reveals two sweaty aspirin from the clutch of her palm. "Thought you might need these."

"Thanks."

"You were a mess last night." Carin grins at me. "It was hilarious."

"I'm sure it was very funny for you." Sitting, looking up at Carin, it's the first time I feel like the younger sister.

"Get home safe." Carin is still chuckling as I start to drive away. "Mexico," she yells, as I roll through the trailer park.

I stick my head out the car window. "I'll think about it."

Carin follows the car to the edge of the road and as I drive away, she hops across the hot concrete in her bare feet, waving at me in her goofy way. I reach my arm out the window and wave back before pulling out onto the highway and following the snaking road through the arid hills and up into the green mountains. The air turns cool on my skin, sending a shiver of goose bumps up my arms.

Deep into the mountains everything thins: the trees, the air, the clouds. I'm not sure if this mountain highway is actually the highest I've been above sea level, but it feels that way. Every time I drive it, I feel like I can see great distances. The forest stretches and spills off the sides of the Earth. I reach the highway's crest and then I'm descending again. Everything from here on is closer to the coast. It's here, at this height, that it hits me: a pang of missing that catches like a stone in the softness of my throat and settles somewhere in my stomach. I finally miss her at the right time. She is my childhood. She's the part of me that has passed and I miss her.

THE SPIDER IN THE JAR

AFTER COLLECTING THE BEER bottles from the bunkhouses at the sawmill, the brothers headed into the forest behind their house to eat wild blackberries until their bellies were rotten with them and their fingertips were stained purple.

"Lookit." Ben crouched on one knee, shaped his hand into a gun and took aim at a sparrow perched on a branch. "Bam!" The bird took flight through the trees. When the boys were in the forest, Ben spent a lot of time talking about BB guns.

"Don't scare them," Henry said. Their Mama kept three birdcages in the kitchen — one with finches, one with budgies and one with an African Grey — and Henry liked to stick a finger through the cages to rub their bellies or feel the curt jabs from their beaks. Every morning, it seemed to Henry, they tried to escape. At first light, he could hear them flapping around, screeching and knocking against the metal cages. By lunch they quieted, and by evening they slept. There was always a racket in the kitchen in the morning with the birds and the coffee machine and the brothers.

"It's not real," Ben said. He stood right in front of Henry and aimed his weapon at Henry's black eye. "Bang!"

Henry flinched then looked away.

"Pantywaist," Ben said. It was what their father called men he didn't respect. Whenever Henry heard the word he thought of their mother's underwear, the caramel-coloured ones that reached up past the belly button. Ben picked up two sticks and twirled them between his fingers like nunchucks, spinning his legs around with circular kicks. He pointed a stick at Henry's swollen eye. "Does it still hurt?" It was the first time Ben said anything about it.

"No," Henry lied. The area around the eye was a deep shade of purple, and this morning when Henry looked in the mirror and pried open the lid, there was a bloody spiderweb across his cornea. That day Ben had stood on the other side of the school's chain-link fence, watching as the boys yelled *faggot* and chased Henry across the field toward the trees. Henry thought there would be lots of places to hide in the forest. Part of him had believed that once he hit the treeline, he would disappear or swoop high up into the branches of the evergreens like a winged creature.

"It's this way," Ben said when they reached a fork in the path. They were looking for a cave they found yesterday, past the clearing and past the creek. Henry wasn't allowed to cross the water because he wasn't a strong swimmer, but Ben had a way of making him do things, like sticking six peanuts up his nose. Henry had snorted most of them out, but he had to go to the emergency clinic for the last two.

This time they had matches with them, pilfered from the glove compartment of their mother's car. The cave had been pitch black and Henry had ripped his favorite T-shirt scrambling from it after Ben let out a scream that made his eardrums go fuzzy. Ben was only teasing him, but in the total darkness of the cave Henry had imagined a bear's coarse fur brushing against his cheek.

The creek came into view now, twisting through trees dripping with moss, and Ben ran ahead, wading through the water and coming out the other side soaking wet. He took off his shirt, wringing it out before putting it back on, smoothing the wrinkled cotton over his chest. "We need a torch," he shouted across the water, picking up bits of dried grass and twigs from the ground. Henry scanned the length of the creek, trying to find a safe place to cross. The water was deep in parts, swirling gently where the rocks created whirlpools. Henry crossed along a line of large boulders, taking his steps carefully on the slimy green rocks. He tried not to think about being swept into the water and dragged all the way to the ocean. Every summer on their first day at the lake, their father would check his wristwatch and time Ben as he swam the length of the shore. He'd compare the result to last year's time and then enter the numbers in a small booklet that fit in his shirt pocket. Henry would stand on the shore and watch, leaning against their father's leg and letting his body go limp, his limbs hanging as though he were sick or very tired. When Ben came to shore, their father would pull out a stub of pencil for recording and give him claps on the back as Henry shrugged off the water drops that fell on him.

By the time Henry reached the entrance to the cave, Ben was on his hands and knees, already half inside, the unlit torch under one arm. Henry rushed to follow behind him, accidently bumping into his behind. "Give me some room, would ya?" Ben said, kicking at him. One of his kicks got Henry on the nose, making him sneeze and sending a spasm of pain through his eye.

The tunnel leading into the cave was narrow and as they crawled through, their bodies sealed off any light from outside.

"What about bears?" Henry said, feeling phantom bristles along his skin.

"The hole's too small, dummy." Ben's voice was muffled.

The damp rock hugged the brothers as they squeezed blindly through the passageway, and then all of a sudden the cold walls were gone. The air became verdant, cool and wide. Henry reached out into the dark space and felt nothing. They sat silently in the void for a minute, close together, their knees touching. Henry tried to quiet his breathing so it sounded normal—the cave exaggerated every small noise. Ben lit a match, the delicate glow flickering, barely lighting the small circle between them. He held the match to the torch and the flame stirred before fizzling out. He lit a second match and the torch ignited, flaring brightly and filling the space with a smoke that smelled of burning hay.

"Holy crap." Ben's face warped in the fire's weird light as he stood and swung the torch around. "This is awesome."

The cave was almost a perfect circle of smooth rock walls with a dusty, pit-marked floor.

"Awesome," Henry said, but the knot in his stomach was still there as he watched the sharp shadows move across Ben's face.

A couple metres away from the brothers, something fell from the ceiling and landed near their feet. They stepped closer, peering down at the dark lump before looking up to find a black quivering carpet above them. Before Henry's brain could make sense of the sight, Ben dropped the torch and darted out of the cave. In the now-total darkness, the impression hit Henry like a knee to the stomach — the cave's ceiling was thick with large black spiders. Henry scampered back through the tunnel, but no light appeared before him. For a second, he wondered if he'd gotten turned around and was actually going deeper into the cave. His arms shook as he clawed at the darkness, trying to get his bearings. He hit something soft, reached out, and felt the stiff fabric of Ben's jean jacket, his bony shoulder blades. Henry pushed at his brother's back, but Ben had dug in his heels, sealing the exit with his own body. Henry's throat tightened and from him came a strangled moan — an animal-like noise. "Benny, let me out." Henry's entire body trembled now, tears streaming down his cheeks. "Please." His screams became frantic shrieks, echoing around the cave until they no longer seemed like his own. He thrashed around like one of the caged birds at daybreak. And then, all of a sudden, everything gave way — light poured around Henry's body and he burst from the tunnel's mouth, sprawling in the dirt, arms flailing over his body.

"Get them off me," Henry shrieked. "Get them off."

"There's nothing there," Ben said, doubled over, laughing so hard he was crying. He wiped at the tears streaking his cheeks, his dirty hands leaving behind bands of warrior dirt across his face. Even though Henry knew he was unharmed, he couldn't stop screaming, his eyes wild and wide to the forest around them. Ben grabbed his shoulders and shook him.

"Shut up, already." But Henry couldn't stop. "Shut up. Shut up, you pantywaist," Ben said, shoving Henry to the ground.

Henry sat in the dirt and tasted blood on his tongue. "You're supposed to protect me," Henry said, trying to swallow his sobs.

"You should learn to protect yourself," Ben said. "Otherwise people are always going to say stuff about you."

Henry was quiet after that and Ben left him sitting on the ground to walk home alone.

DURING DINNER BEN FIDGETED in his chair, almost knocking it over twice, until their father asked him if he had to go to the bathroom and their mother slammed her fork down on the table, making their baby brother, Eli, laugh. Ben then blurted out their discovery of the cave in great detail—how he had found the hidden tunnel, how he had fashioned the torch, how he had burned some of the giant spiders. He left out the part where Henry cried. In fact, he told the story as though Henry wasn't even there and Henry had to yell over everyone's voices, "I was there too, ya know." Henry got a spanking for crossing the creek and Ben got one too for letting him cross. The next day their father asked Ben to show him where the spiders' cave was, but Henry had to stay at home to wait as punishment. He sat at the window all afternoon watching the edge of the forest turn to shadows.

They brought one of the dead spiders back in a pickle jar. Their father said he'd never seen anything like it before, and the brothers fought over the jar all night, turning it round and round, pressing their noses to the glass, examining the bristles on the spider's crooked legs, its leathery body, its wolf-ish eyes.

"It's my specimen," Ben said. "I collected it."

"It doesn't belong to you," Henry said.

"Who does it belong to, then?"

"God," Henry said.

Their mother wouldn't let them keep the jar on the table while they ate dinner. "It's a hideous thing," she said.

After their meal, Ben brought out his magnifying glass and an encyclopedia from the set their father had given them. He made a drawing of the spider, labelling its parts — *ceph-alothorax, pedipalps, chelicerae*. At the top of the page he wrote *ARACHNID* in big, bold letters. Ben kept a protective arm around the drawing so Henry had to crane his neck to see anything. Eli pulled himself up and hung onto Henry's chair, his chubby legs bouncing rhythmically while he sucked on Henry's knee. Henry grabbed the spider jar and thrust it in his face, twisting his mouth and roaring at him. "I need to see it," Ben said, grabbing the jar back and setting it carefully in front of his drawing. Henry watched Eli for a moment before reaching down to pinch the soft fold of skin behind one of his knees. When the baby cried and fell to the floor, their mother stuck her head out of the kitchen. "What happened?"

"I don't know," Henry said, stroking the fine hair on Eli's head. "It's okay, baby. It's okay."

Later that night, Henry locked the bathroom door and took off all his clothes. In front of the mirror, he brushed his teeth vigorously until a thick froth poured from his mouth onto the counter. With his black eye he looked like a hideous thing. He snarled like a rabid dog then spit the toothpaste into the sink. He ran his hands over his skinny arms and legs and along the ribs jutting out from his chest, whispering *cephalo-thorax, pedipalps, chelicerae.*

There was a bang at the bathroom door. "Get out," Ben yelled.

After Ben finished his drawing and the brothers were in their pajamas, they watched as their father packed the spider jar in a box and sealed it with loops of masking tape. Tomorrow morning first thing, he would send it off to a lab in Victoria for analysis. He posted Ben's drawing on the fridge.

Later that night, Eli cried and slept in their parents' bed, and Henry had nightmares, but he didn't tell anyone.

WHEN HENRY WOKE THE next morning his first thought was, *Today is Ben's birthday.* He kicked off the sheets but lay in bed watching the patterns from the curtain roll across the ceiling. The shapes morphed from fat triangles to skinny diamonds to long spears and then disappeared. Henry decided he would change himself today. He'd tried it before, but it never worked. By the time he was back in bed that night, he'd realize he was exactly the same. He was determined this morning, though, not to be the same old Henry. He combed his hair straight back instead of parting it in the middle and practiced speaking with the British accent he'd heard on the radio the other day.

The birthday party was at the lake and the day was sunny, but a cool wind skipped across the water, stirring up waves that lashed the shore. Fat picture-book clouds glided across the sky, trailed by dark shadows over the lake's surface. Henry helped his mother tie blue balloons to the picnic tables, where they whipped around in the wind, competing for attention. Ben and his friends gathered to eat hot dogs then open presents. Henry's father pulled the last gift out from under the picnic table, and in the frenzy Henry helped Ben rip open the package. Ben held the brand new BB gun—a pump-action Daisy Red Ryder with a solid wood buttstock—high above his head and everyone cheered, even Henry, because he was different today. After the gifts, all the boys went into the lake. Henry stood beside the shore at his father's side for only a moment before running full tilt toward the water.

"Be careful, Henry. You can't go in over your head," his mother called after him.

"Be careful, Henry," one of the boys mocked.

Henry bellyflopped into the lake, the cold sending prickles over his flesh and knocking out his breath. He thrashed his arms and kicked his legs, scraping his feet on the rocks in the shallow water and gasping as waves hit him in the face. He wanted to turn back to the shore's safety, but after a minute he realized his feet could still touch the lake's bottom and he could bob along easily, only pretending to swim like the other boys. If he found himself too far, losing the feeling of sand between his toes, he simply paddled himself around and went back. The water was no longer cold but felt pleasant and Henry began to feel as calm as the pure, fluffy clouds drifting overhead. Shouts and laughter bounced over the water as he buoyed himself along. "Ello," he said in his cheerful British accent to any boy who crossed his path. "Ello, ello." The water was clear, his pale toes wiggling like creatures among the glittering rocks on the lake bottom. The boys splashed one another, sending droplets through the air that hit Henry's smiling face. He drifted over to the dock, where Ben and some friends were doing cannonballs into the water, and he floated underneath, weightless between the cobwebbed pillars. Through the slats he watched the boys' bare feet slap along the dock; occasionally he poked a finger up and tickled their soles. "Quit it, Henry," Ben shouted from somewhere above. His head appeared, hanging over the end of the dock, "I see you."

As Henry drifted back out into the open, someone jumping from the dock landed on him, sending him under. Henry swallowed a large gulp of lake water, panic springing through his body as he flailed to get to the surface. A foot hit him in the side of the head. He reached out to grasp onto something and felt a body in front of him. His fingers clutched at the loose cloth of a pair of swimming trunks that floated around someone's skinny legs. Henry yanked on them to pull himself out of the water, but the shorts came down, so he grabbed at one of the arms pushing at him and brought himself to the surface, gasping and rubbing the water out of his eyes.

"You pulled my shorts off," the boy screamed, shoving Henry back under the water.

When Henry surfaced again, all the boys were screaming and swimming away from him farther out into the lake or climbing up onto the dock. The boy scowled at Henry as he climbed up the ladder, hanging onto the back of his swimming trunks as though Henry might try to pull them off again. Henry sunk down until only his nose was above the surface. "Sorry," he said, but the word was trapped underwater. He could hear the syllables lose themselves in the bubbles. His father glided through the water and scooped him up over his shoulder, the way he used to when Henry was little, carrying him back to the picnic tables. As they walked across the sand, Henry heard someone say *pantywaist*. At first he thought the word came from his father, but then he realized it was only his mind playing tricks on him. By the time he was back sitting at the picnic tables, the boys were all standing in a line again at the end of the dock, taking turns doing cannonballs.

IN THE KITCHEN, THE moonlight came slanting through the window and made the countertops glow. Henry drank a glass of water, sitting cross-legged on the table in case the spider came alive and escaped its jar, but then he remembered the spider was in Victoria. On the fridge, the white page burned around the lines of Ben's drawing. Henry stared at the picture of the spider until his eyes started to wobble and its legs started to move.

Earlier that evening, Henry and Ben were brushing their teeth together at the sink when Ben spat and turned to Henry and said, "All my friends think you're weird." Henry shrugged and then, with his mouth still rabid with foamy toothpaste, bit Ben on the shoulder.

Eli cried again that night and kept Henry awake. Henry wanted to be in bed with his parents, but he couldn't ask because their father was angry at him for biting Ben. Instead he hung over the top bunk, watching Ben sleep and thinking about the cave. He thought about how it would be a good place for hiding, how if it was sealed properly nothing could get in.

THE NEXT DAY WAS Sunday, so Henry and Ben headed down to the bunkhouses. They collected bottles at the mill every Sunday and Thursday, storing them in crates under the cabins. Every two weeks they loaded the empties onto the Uchuck that arrived in Tahsis to drop off produce and other supplies. They would receive a cheque made out to their father that he would cash and divide between the two of them. On a good week they made four dollars each. Usually it took them the whole afternoon, because they liked to peer in the windows at the kitchenettes and the beds with untucked blankets. If they were lucky there were dirty clothes on the floor or food left on the tables — egg shells or half-eaten crusts sticky with jam — that hinted to what kind of person might live there. When they had time, they looked in the garbage bins for anything interesting, but today Ben moved quickly, the crate of bottles rattling as he jogged from porch to porch.

"Why are you going so fast?" Henry said.

"I have target practice."

"With who?"

"The birds."

At the next cabin something made Ben slow his pace. He bent down and pulled a magazine from the garbage can and tucked it into the back of his pants. Henry followed him around the back of the bunkhouse and they sat side by side on a log. Ben pulled out the magazine. "Wanna see something?"

"Yeah," Henry said.

Ben turned the colour pages slowly, each one with a naked woman, sometimes several naked women crouching or snarling like animals.

"Which one do you like best?" Ben said.

"I don't know."

"You have to pick one." Ben handed him the magazine.

Henry flipped through the pages until they were a pink blur. "I can't."

Ben rolled his eyes and grabbed the magazine out of Henry's hands.

"What are you going to do with it?" Henry said.

"Keep it." Ben rolled it up and stuck it back in his pants. "You don't even know what it is, so what do you care."

"I know what it is."

When they got back to the house, Ben ran up the steps and came back out with his BB gun. "Can I come?" Henry called after him. Ben strutted right by Henry and headed for the trees. Henry walked back into the house, letting the screen door slam, and went to the washroom to look at himself in the mirror. His eye was getting better, the edges of the bruise yellowing like an overripe pear. He walked around the house listlessly for half an hour then headed outside.

The forest was alive with noise, sun streaming straight down through the arms of the trees and heating the forest floor, making the air smell green and lush. The birds talked to Henry in such loud chatter, he felt confused about the direction of the cave and kept stopping to wonder if Ben was behind a tree up ahead, aiming the BB gun in his direction.

Henry had a can of gasoline from the garage and under Ben's bed he had found the matches they'd stolen. The creek bubbled around the stones as Henry crossed to the other side. He knew the gasoline had to be poured in the middle of the cave for the fire to get big enough. He got down on his hands and knees and crawled slowly through the tunnel so he wouldn't drop the can. His nose filled with the mossy smell of the rock as the cave opened around him and the temperature dropped. He held his breath and kept his head lowered, not wanting to glimpse the hundreds of sleeping bodies above him. Everything was still—the only sound came from the gentle slosh of gasoline in the metal can and soon that stopped too. All the urgency drained from his body and his muscles went slack the way they did when he stood at the edge of a lake. He sat cross-legged in the centre of the cave and after a while he felt peaceful. The spiders minded their own business and nothing bothered him. His arms and legs took a sharp-angled shape and the hair along the nape of his neck stood up in rows of bristles. His fingertips tingled with imaginary gossamer threads.

He tipped the can and the sweet metallic smell spilled out over the cave floor. The sound made everything come to life, a thousand legs rustling above his head. He scurried out, leaving a trail as the can clanged between his knees, the smell following him into the overwhelming green. He shook the can to make sure it was empty and tilted the spout to sprinkle the remaining drops around his feet. The knees of his pants were soaked in gasoline. He pulled out the box of matches with the wild red bird on the front and got down on his belly to better judge the snaking wet trajectory across the dirt, and the distance between himself and the cave entrance. Wiggling backwards on his stomach like a lizard, he sniffed at the ground. His fingers fiddled with the matches, a few spilling before he managed to strike one and light the line. The trail sparked and he leapt to his feet.

When the fire hit the cave a boom pushed the air out of his lungs and sucked the sound out of the world around him.

He hit the ground, sunlight through the trees blinding him briefly before a thud of darkness swallowed him.

When he opened his eyes Ben was there, his mouth wide open like a fish gasping at the bottom of a boat. Face wild with delight, he danced around Henry's head before yanking him up and slapping the dirt off his back. The blast had thrown Henry several feet. A grin spread across Henry's face and Ben laughed even harder, the muted sound reaching Henry's ears as though he were approaching the surface of a lake from a great depth. He could hear Ben's muffled voice repeating over and over, "You're okay." On the way home, Ben leaned toward him, an arm around his shoulder and yelled into Henry's ear, "You flew like a bird."

THE ENTIRE TOWN HEARD the explosion. It woke Eli from his nap and sent their mother running down the front steps. It made windows shake all over the neighborhood and shot birds into the air. In town, people froze in intersections, covered their heads, or looked skyward. Everyone wondered where the blast had come from. Henry's mother and father discussed it over dinner while Ben and Henry kept their eyes on their plates and ate quietly.

A letter came from Victoria, but the jar was never returned. They classified the spider as a common house spider, or *Parasteatoda tepidariorum*. Ben turned the uninhabited cave into a fort with a canvas door and camping lanterns lighting its insides. Henry almost never went back to the cave and when he did he felt uneasy there, as though he didn't belong. He thought about the explosion often though, but only at night when he was alone in bed. Sometimes he'd see a trail of fire coming from his fingertips and radiating out into the world. Sometimes he'd hear Ben's voice saying *you're okay. You're okay.*

CLEAR SKIES, NO WIND, 100% VISIBILITY

WHEN THE MAYDAY COMES over the radio, my mind is else-where and in a distant enough place—up the trail that leads to the telecommunications tower, where the hawk perched on the steel lattice watches over the entire Kamloops valley—that it takes me seconds longer than it should to respond to the emergency call.

Temperatures were hitting the high thirties when I drove to the station earlier in the afternoon, leaving Angie sprawled out in a cool bath with the baby, a glass of red wine with an ice cube floating in it sitting on the edge of tub. Other than the heat, everything else about my day has been normal the way normal should be, routine leading me through another shift lost in small individual tasks—weather briefings, setting up voice switches, organizing flight management systems— the kind of duties you've forgotten before they've even been accomplished, the mind see-sawing away on that silky edge of boredom. Time has a strange way of unfolding in a dark room of blue monitors and blinking lights, a roomful of dead-eyed drones watching the sky on screens, the fickleness of clouds, the unpredictability of wind and electricity. Weather data is transfigured into notifications disseminated back into the sky, anything pertinent to an airman's safe travel: turbulence, icing, lines of thunderstorms, wind shear, funnel clouds, fireworks displays, mine blasts, avalanche artillery. Information endlessly reviewed.

On winter days when storms keep the planes grounded, we pass the time between weather updates reading, doing crosswords, arguing current events that seem worlds away. No cellphones, no laptops or electronic distractions of any kind allowed on the Floor. It's the idleness that gets me agitated and picking at my thumb cuticles while others around here delight in the boredom, tilt their chairs back, kick their feet up and brush the potato chip crumbs off their shirts, enjoying the blur around the margins of their lives. It's no exaggeration to say I work with some lazy slugs. John breathes through his mouth for Christ's sake, like a sick person. When I pack my bag for the day I don't stuff it with car magazines or fishing tackle catalogues or porn. (I've seen John with the porn.) I'm not about to let my brain go to mush, all that brilliant fatty matter oozing out of my ears onto this glowing console. When I pack my bag I throw in some Chaucer, I stuff it with some Kant or Thoreau or some dry history shit from my student days, the thick annals of lives lived, the stuff Thom and I used to deliberate sitting under autumn maples on the frigid stone walls of the university campus. I let all that language rattle around in there while I wait on the glowing buttons and

flickering screens of shifting stats that—if you allow them—
get abstract real quick. I let the words percolate and it makes
me feel good. It makes me feel better, at least.

"They could switch it up, put in something new," John
says, coming back from the row of vending machines.

"I don't know, John. I don't eat that shit."

John plops down on his chair and wheels himself over to
my desk as I issue squawk codes that transform into flashing dots as the radar sweeps past. Today is the last of a five-
day run of graveyard shifts and I've lost track of time. John
forces us to keep the heavy grey blinds drawn because of his
"migraines" and the only hint of early evening is the bright
sliver of light fighting through the edge of the window. I feel
tired in a way I don't trust, as though the lack of sleep has split
my mind from its body; I've abandoned ship to watch over my
physical self like watching over an irresponsible sibling.

"Something healthy." John says as he paws through a bag
of potato chips like he's searching for a carrot stick in there.
"Like popcorn."

The hawk is an exercise of sorts, a meditation—something I've been trying more and more frequently—to take
me out of this creaky swivel chair and away from the stuffy
control room. My supervisor walks past in a polo shirt and
black slacks cinched tight with a belt below the bulge of his
waistline. I nod hello. I think about heart attacks. Their sud-
denness. The *thump, whir* of the struggling air conditioner.
Back to the hawk. Sleep deprivation has a way of making you
think in circles. John keeps distracting me by brushing crumbs
off his belly, and I have to refocus—wingspan, hooked beak,
talons—before he finds another scattering somewhere on his

body and I have to start all over again. Sometimes I have the urge to pound John on the chest, right in the left quadrant, see what'll happen, get a little colour into those cheeks. The truth is, at the moment when the hawk takes flight into the grey sky, gliding down the mountain above the treetops, I realize that I've never seen anything quite like this bird's trajectory, and what a damn shame that is, and how nice it is to see something like this alone and from a great height.

And it's at this exact moment the call comes in from the water bomber.

"Golf Foxtrot Victor Bravo. Mayday, mayday, mayday."

I'm aware of the pause — a mere second and a half — even as I'm responding to the mayday. The lapse is a weakness I didn't realize I had in me. Static fills my head as my heart starts to pump faster.

"Golf Foxtrot Victor Bravo." I say, "Pacific Radio received mayday, state the nature of your emergency."

John slides the binder with our emergency protocol across the desk toward me and I begin flipping through the pages. Suddenly I feel wide awake, my heart a stopwatch tick-tocking and the air rushing through my chest. Voice procedure shrinks the Floor to an airless box: language reduced until there is no room for interpretation. There are very specific things I need to say and do written in clear detail on the pages of this binder. All I need to do is follow them in a straight line, top of the page to bottom.

"We're losing fuel fast." The pilot's words escape between short gasps of breath. "We need to land now."

"Can you give me your position?" Beside me John is mobilizing everyone: ambulance, RCMP, JRCC. I watch him move across the room to let the supervisor know I have an emergency.

I've spoken to this pilot once already today, earlier in my shift. The recollection comes back all at once: The pilot reporting an engine indication, a small leak in the gas tank he attributed to a possible rupture after picking up his load. He told me he planned to drop the water before heading back to the airport. I wished him safe travels, stepped away from procedure and let my voice drop like a newscaster from the fifties. It was a small indulgence. A lapse caused by boredom.

"We are…We are currently fifteen kilometres west of Fintry Park." The pilot's voice has changed since the first call. When I spoke to him earlier he sounded confident. Now his voice is whittled to a thin edge. "We need crash and fire rescue."

"Roger." My finger scans lines in the binder. "What are your intentions?" I know the question is meant to shift the pilot's state of mind. It's one of the most important lines we learn during voice procedure training. It's like hitting a reset button—it reminds the pilot he's the only one in control of the aircraft.

"My intentions?" I can hear the strain in his voice as he tries to handle the plane.

"Crash and fire are on their way."

"There's nothing but trees out here. I need a beach, a highway, something." His voice splits, comes unravelled like the end of a frayed rope. "We're dropping. Jesus Christ."

At the back of my mind, beyond the static, the hawk is still soaring, nothing but wings and air—the quietest descent. The radio goes dark.

"Golf Foxtrot Victor Bravo, this is Pacific Radio. Do you copy?"

A heavy blanket of electricity is filling the room, storm clouds piling. All the slugs are coming to life—animating— no longer slumped over their consoles staring into middle space. John is watching me carefully, but I won't look over at him.

"Golf Foxtrot Victor Bravo, this is Pacific Radio. Do you copy?"

There are several more moments of silence before the high pitched tone of the emergency transmitter comes whining through the 121.5.

"Shit." I slam my hand flat on the desk. Seconds later the radio fills with other pilots in the area calling to report the crash. The language is like a force field helping me keep my distance from all the voices. There's panic in all of them, but most keep it controlled well enough that I can understand what they're saying, well enough that I can call them professionals.

"Golf Foxtrot Zulu Whiskey. Mayday, mayday, mayday."

"...into the side of the mountain."

"...huge fireball west of Fintry Provincial Park."

When the calls stop I get up and walk around the room, snapping the blinds one by one, yanking the thin little cords and sending them up so fast they crash and rattle into the tall windows. "I want to be able to see what's going on out there," I shout at no one in particular, to the whole room, launching my arm in a wide arc to account for every single one of them. "What the hell do we have windows for?" No one in particular looks in my direction. "And if it bothers you, John, wear some fucking sunglasses." I slam the door and head for the vending machine glow at the end of the hallway. John follows me and at first I think he's going to start complaining about the blinds again, but his approach is too slow, too careful. When he gets to me he stretches and his back cracks. "You good?" he says, without looking over, drumming a finger down the machine choices.

"Fine, yeah," I say, fishing in my pockets for change.

"First one, eh?"

I look over at John, but he's tapping his foot and staring at the vending machine, nodding his head as though it's emitting some kind of musical beat.

"Well," John says, considering the coins in his hand. "You're part of the club now."

"What club?"

A few months ago in a conference hall for a seminar on flow and capacity management, I sat in silence — the only person under fifty in the room — and sipped my acrid coffee, letting it burn my lips while I listened to all those grey-hairs add up their years to retirement. When I was asked to introduce myself, I stood and said, "My name is Wes Harris and I have thirty-three years until retirement." The room thundered with laughter, all these rip-roaring red faces going berserk at the thought of thirty-three more years. They laughed so hard they cried, grown men wiping tears from their jiggling cheeks. I meant it as a joke, but for some reason I couldn't laugh along with them. I sat back down in my seat. Sipped my coffee. They all looked the same to me, inside and out. It was the pallor of their skin, that waxy sheen and puffiness around the eyes after years on the job — the signs of a dull heart. I check my reflection in the screen for those signs. Pull down my bottom eyelids. So far I see nothing of the sort.

"Some guys go their entire careers without a call like that. Now look at you." John slaps my shoulder. "Not even a year in and you've had your first."

"Guess so." I go to put a coin in, but John gets there first. "Is that something to be proud of?" I ask him.

"Had my first, oh, almost ten years ago now." He takes his time choosing his pop. "My only, actually. Pleasure pilot with his wife. Oil pressure problem. Found the plane half-submerged, tail up near the beach. Just a few feet of water, but they both drowned. Mountain'd be quicker."

"Sure would." When I reach out to put my coins in I notice my hand is shaking.

"Why's that grizzly sleeping on a cloud, right?" John chuckles, cracking open the can and taking a long sip. "Heard that one?"

"Nope." I shove money into the machine.

"When'd they raise the prices on this thing, anyway?" He takes another sip and gives the machine a jab. "Another quarter and still the piss-poor selection."

I punch random buttons. A can drops into the slot and I grab it and leave John standing at the machine talking to himself. When Angie was two months pregnant I flew to the other side of the country to train for this job, a year in a program with a 3% success rate—flashcards, mnemonic devices, simulators—studying day and night in a dorm room in Cornwall that smelled of feet (could've been my own feet.) But I ate it without complaints. Forget the fact that I could knock off a paper on the Islamic Golden Age over an all-nighter while half in the bag. I may have had a future on one of those leafy campuses, but instead I became a human mainframe for weather and word patterns. *Alpha, Bravo, Charlie, Delta, Echo, Foxtrot, Golf, Hotel, India.* That's the versatility of the human brain.

Back at my desk the screens are winking and the condensation drips down the sides of the can, pooling at its base. After the sugar, my hands have steadied themselves, but my heart is still pounding in my chest, like waking up from a bad dream you can only remember the outline of. Sometimes you need some fire and brimstone to wake you up. I guess that's where I am now, awake in front of all these buttons telling me things, giving me the answers. All I have to do is record and repeat. But the fire and the brimstone aren't here, far from it. And in a funny way I feel nothing. After all that, I am still sitting at my desk, tapping my fingers on the particleboard. That's what the training is for. The shaking is a symptom of the adrenaline. *Juliet, Kilo, Lima, Mike, November, Oscar, Papa, Quebec, Romeo.* I'll get a phone call soon. I start to prepare the package. Everything that is recorded is kept, sealed, mailed, analyzed, investigated by the Transportation Safety Board. I pick up scraps of paper where I had scribbled details and set them aside to be included in the envelope. With the blinds pulled up the entire room looks different. John's back at his desk rubbing his temples, making a real show of it. I take in the view from the windows: Cinnamon Ridge, the golden hoodoos under clear blue skies. No wind. Perfect visibility. A good day for flying. A host of sparrows lifts from the line of windbreak birches south of the tarmac, swooping in two giant arcs before settling back again among the branches.

The phone is ringing at my desk and I have a hand on it, but there's that pause again—one second and a half. *Sierra, Tango, Uniform, Victor, Whiskey, X-ray, Yankee, Zulu.* On the tarmac a shimmer of heat blurs the ground and far in the distance—far as one can get it seems—off on the other side of those great blue mountains, smoke.

"LOOKS LIKE A HAWK," Angie said, one slender hand shielding her eyes, the other resting on the baby nestled against her chest in the carrier. Sophie was four months old and it was late October, the air brisk and needles on the path, sticky with resin. The hike was a way to avoid the boxes stacked to the ceiling in our living room. NAV Canada had placed me in Kamloops and we'd just moved into a split-level rancher twice the size and half the price of what we would've found in Vancouver. We didn't know anyone in the city. Everything was new and it was easy to be busy and happy.

"I'm going up," I said, arms crossed over my heaving chest. I coughed and spit into the dirt.

"No," Angie smirked, "you're not."

"I am." My knee was throbbing and I stooped to rub it. I'd broken it several years ago when I fell out of a second-story window during a game of indoor paintball, and every so often after exercise or strange weather it would start to act up.

"Sore?" She smiled at me and bounced the baby from side to side. "Why don't you catch your breath?"

"I'm fine." I said, shrugging her off. We had reached our goal: the telecommunications tower up the mountain behind our house, the one whose red spire blinked above the tree line. The path snaked up the mountainside, keeping its grade gentle, but the distance was enough to get me huffing the cold air as I tried to keep up with Angie. Even with a baby strapped to her chest she was faster than me. I could tell she was staying ahead on purpose, trying to make it look easy, but there was a shimmer of sweat on her upper lip. On the way up, we'd talked about ways in which to build a new life. It was difficult to say who had asked more from the other coming here— Angie, giving up the possibility of returning to her counselling job, or me, venturing into a whole new career. On any given day it felt different.

I bent down and took a few deep breaths.

"You know, it isn't a race," Angie said, sitting on an old rotted-out log covered in moss.

"Sure it is." I winked at her and climbed the first rung, feeling the joints of my bum knee grinding together. The hawk was perched about halfway up the tower.

"You're an idiot."

"Well, you married me," I said, adjusting my hands to get a better grip, "so what does that make you?"

"A charitable soul." She sounded tired even though I'd let her sleep through the night and well into the morning. "Please don't kill yourself to impress me."

"Oh, I know little I do will impress *you*." I took another step up. The rungs were far apart and it took a bit of a push to get up to the next one.

"I can tell from here it's a Harlan's hawk." She leaned back on the log and tilted her head to the sky.

"Well," I said, looking down at her. "That, from a city girl, does impress me."

"I know some things." She got up from the log and brushed off her bum. "Okay, Wes. Let's go. You've had your fun. I'm ready for some lunch."

I ignored her and kept climbing.

"Wes! For real now. I'm not kidding around."

I'm not sure what sent me up that tower. It was the hawk, at first, and curiosity, but once I started climbing there was an excitement and an anxiousness that kept me going. With each step my limbs felt more capable and my heart felt larger. I had an ear-to-ear grin that usually only struck me after beer number seven. I figured out a system to scale the tower using the diagonal red lattices to boost myself, and climbed to its mid-point quickly, waving down at Angie every few minutes. She didn't wave back, but stood on the log, hands on hips, looking pissed. I knew what she was thinking: *stupid little boy*. And I grinned that ear-to-ear smile down at her exactly like a stupid little boy would.

As I got closer to the hawk I slowed down, remaining still for several moments before ascending the next section. The hawk didn't move. Its brown feathers glinted with flecks of gold as it scanned the valley, head turning slowly from side to side. I'd taken one step closer to the bird, watching it from little more than a foot away, when it launched itself into the sky. I could hear the click of its talons and feel the wind from the beat of its wings as it set in motion. As the hawk glided down the mountain above the treetops, I took in the entire expanse of the valley—like a dark green bowl turning on a table top. Angie was pacing below the tower now, yelling obscenities and waving her arms, but I was conceivably high enough to be out of earshot. Tilting my head back, I hooted like a pimply-pocked teen out a car window, and even from that height I could tell Angie was rolling her eyes. I leaned out from the tower, brandishing one arm and one leg through the air, and called down to her, "I can see our house."

The bird was almost out of sight when my knee gave out. All the words I was hurling were suddenly trapped in my throat and every cell in my body focused on the one hand that gripped the cold steel. It happened so quickly Angie didn't even notice. I waited for a shriek or some kind of commotion from below, but all I could hear was my own panicked breathing. The contents of breakfast, scrambled eggs and buttered toast, sloshed around my stomach. I flailed until I found footing and my other hand found a grip. I closed my eyes against the valley and breathed deeply as I steadied myself, the hawk the only image gliding through my brain. My sweaty hand could have lost its grip and I could have ended up a crumpled mess of bloody bones at Angie's feet, but what I saw was freedom, the hawk vanished into the vast envelope of trees.

I started down slowly. Every few minutes Angie would call up to me:

"It's starting to rain."

"Harder coming down than going up, eh, smart ass?"

"Sophie's waking up."

"It's going to pour soon, I think."

Later that night on the Floor I had my first urge for a taste of that freedom. I was two months into my new job and I'd memorized the dates of every holiday for the rest of the year.

I didn't realize how close I was to the ground until I felt Angie's hand.

"Don't worry, I got you," she said.

"I'm fine." I shook her hand off my ankle.

"I got you."

"I don't need you to get me."

OUTSIDE THE WINDOW THERE'S a black sky and evergreens even blacker beyond the perimeter of the backyard fence. The trees surround the valley; the city feels insignificant, almost unwanted. I feel unwanted. None of it holds a thing for me, not a memory or a future, and it's peaceful in its emptiness. *What are your intentions?* The question comes from some dark corner of Sophie's bedroom. Even with the fan whirring in the corner, the air in the room is oppressive. I close my eyes and hold Sophie against my chest, rest my chin on her damp head. In the baby's room during the blackest hours of the night I can breathe, stare out the window, smell her hair, and let my mind bottom out. It's like turning down the static on a radio.

"What are you doing?" Angie's standing in the doorway naked, her head a mess of dark curls.

"Didn't you hear her?"

"I heard you." She crosses her arms and leans to take a look at the monitor.

"She was crying," I whisper overtop the baby's head.

"I didn't hear her." There's skepticism in her voice. I'm almost always the one to get up with Sophie in the night. It's my way of making up for those four lost months while I was away at training, but for whatever reason Angie doesn't trust my effort. She's told me none of the other dads are so willing. She feels the need to lie to the other parents and feign exhaustion. She gets a solid eight hours every night but still guzzles coffee all day long.

"Sh!" I hold a finger to my lips.

"I must be wiped out." She tousles her thick dark curls until they nearly stand up on end. "How was work?"

"I'll tell you later. You're naked."

"It's hot."

"Go back to sleep."

Out the bedroom window, the apex of the spire has a blinking red light. *What are your intentions?* I've barely thought about the pilot since sealing the envelope of data for the TSB, but now the question is nagging me. I hear my own voice, cold and flat as the computer teller at an automated check-out. The crews probably won't have had time to recover the plane tonight. The valley isn't easily accessible and there are spot fires all over the region, making a recovery dangerous. It could be days or weeks before they find anything, depending on the fire's temperament. When I was a kid we used to watch the bombers flying low over the Okanagan Lake. They travelled narrow valleys other aircraft never flew, their planes heavy with cherry-red chemical water, flying through thick smoke at treetop level and dropping their payloads right over the tips of the burning evergreens, then suddenly rose — lightened and askew — toward the sky. Some summers the edge of the mountain was like one long flickering orange ember at night. I met a few of those guys going through orientation. The pilots accepted the dangers of their job and some of them lived for it. Some of them would pray for a fire so they could bomb. Otherwise, it was sitting around twiddling thumbs. Rapping their knuckles on particleboard desks, waiting for something to happen. It's not that they wanted the forest to burn, but there was an itch there they couldn't ignore.

I put Sophie down and head into the living room. Angie has fans in every corner of the house, a small one spinning on the kitchen counter and a standup pointing out one of the open living room windows, sucking the hot air out of the house. The only movement in the room comes from the propellers and the screen saver on the laptop, a twirling planet in a black cyber sky. I sit down at the computer and find a new message from Thom headed: *The Useless Bungling of Wes' Own Ineffectual Life.*

The new message reads: *Dear Asshole, have you ever considered the fact that my very purpose in life is to be the existential thorn in your side? You left me with no choice since the day you cut off your own balls and became a so-called reasonable adult.*

For the past week, he's been trying to convince me to call in sick so we can meet up in Osoyoos a day early. The lake cabin has been a summer ritual since we met in first year. The message goes on to question, for the hundredth time, my decision to flee Vancouver for Kamloops and leave him to drink cases of beer all by himself. He blames me for the broken coffee table and overflowing recycle bin.

I reply: *Dear A-hole, have you ever wondered if the reason you seek my company is that you cannot, for even a single moment, stand yourself?* This is the nature of our relationship.

When I met Thom we were both first-year students at the University of British Columbia. After our English classes we'd end up at the same pub and eventually we ended up at the same table. I was with him the night he met Veronica at an art show in the student union gallery. She was showing some photographs and we had stumbled in at the sight of free food on our way back from the pub. Thom spent the entire night standing at a table stuffing his mouth with spinach phyllo pastries and drinking glass after glass of cheap red wine in plastic cups, wine he knew would make him angry enough to kick over every garbage can he spotted on the way back to his place. Veronica went home with him despite it all. She says she likes to photograph his tragic face. When they say goodbye, she grabs him by the chin and pushes his lips into a pucker she kisses. Mornings she wakes him up by straddling him and taking his portrait. "For a project I'm building," she says. Twice he's had to shell out a considerable amount of money for broken lenses after he wacked the camera out of her hands in a groggy, flash-stunned confusion. It was Veronica who introduced me to Angie, made her appear at our table one night as if by magic. She said, "Wes, this is my friend Angie. You don't want to fuck this up."

Mostly Thom is happiest lying on the rotten sofa on their front porch, smoking weed and reading. The two of us never talk about work or offer details of our day to day, and in that way we can exist together in a world separate, a world per-haps a bit loftier, a bit brighter than the one we live in, a life we would have dreamed up after a lecture in Comparative Literature and a row of pitchers at the pub. Occasionally — though I can't be sure — I think Thom forgets I have a child. He likes to talk about ideas. He likes to argue — is happiest, even, when arguing. He likes to remind me that I wasted my MA and subsequently my contemplative life. He likes to remind me that he can drink me under the table. This is the way I see Thom at this very moment: in his living room, pacing the creaking floorboards, practically climbing his bookshelves stacked with the Western canon, fist in the air for reasons fair or concocted, a neat row of beer bottles arranged in patterns along the coffee table, trying to engage in debate the figure of his girlfriend hunched over a computer, photo editing. He'll argue with himself, if no one else will listen.

The last time we were all at the lake cabin was almost two years ago. Angie was pregnant but not telling anyone yet. Thom and I spent the weekend getting absolutely bombed, drinking whiskey and coke out of plastic cups and barbecuing on the beach. I was feeling celebratory — in sharp contrast to Thom, who was bemoaning the fact that I was dropping out as an unclassified student and moving to Cornwall to start flight service training.

"What!" Thom had said, shaking his head. "What a waste! But marriage will do that to you."

"Thom, God! Please don't start," Veronica put her hand on Thom's neck. It was hard to tell if she was going to strangle him or give him a massage. "Can't we have a holiday without badgering? For once!"

"He's not even part of a program, Thom," Angie said. "Don't be sad because your friend's getting a life."

Angie had spent the day in the lake, swimming, while I watched her from the dock, drinking. She'd aim straight, swim far out to some hidden point on the horizon. Eventually I was drunk enough to follow her into the water, my messy hands slapping the water like dull blades. I played that game with her, grabbing her ankles underwater and pulling her under, the game she hates, putting those messy hands all over her body, the smooth skin over her shoulders and along her neck, her waist, her thighs, my fingers running under the edges of her swimsuit. Later she leaned against me, legs stretched out on a chair in front of her, hair still wet, my hand resting on the inside of her thigh and twitching to move farther up.

"Marriage will do *what* to you?" I said. I felt like humouring Thom. I felt better than him.

"Smarten you up. Smarten you silly, maybe." Thom smirked into his plastic cup. There wasn't much left but ice. "We won't be doing that song and dance."

"Marriage is hardly a song and dance," Angie laughed.

Veronica stretched her arms far above her head and yawned, making a point of being bored with Thom.

"Oh, it is. Mostly a dance, though." Thom stood up from the table, curtsied and did a lively soft-shoe.

"Sit down, you idiot," Veronica said, shaking her head.

"I think I'll have another," he said to himself as he opened the two-litre of coke with a hiss.

"Have a glass of water, Thom," Veronica said.

"It really has though. Changed your whole look. The look of you." Thom was staring at me across the table with disgust. "You're a different person."

"Fuck off." I was smiling.

I felt sorry for Thom that night, and for Veronica too, because of her association with him. My pity grew out of Thom's own pity, out of Angie's secret and our own happiness. The entire scope of our lives together stretched out before me that night, clear as a backyard surrounded by a blanket of trees and a sky full of stars. And that night, sitting across from Thom, my hand on Angie's thigh while she sipped her water with lime, I found it all incredibly funny.

I WAKE UP IN the chair in front of the computer and make my way through the dark house to the bedroom. Angie's set up a fan in this room too, pointing it at the bed so the breeze makes ripples across the sheets. She settles herself closer to me as I get in.

"What happened?" she mutters into the pillow.

"She went right to sleep."

"At work, I mean?" Angie raises her head and tries to find my eyes in the dark. She always seems to know when something is off. It will never be possible to lie to her.

"Water bomber crashed into the side of a mountain." I lock my hands behind my head and look over at her. She's in one of my threadbare shirts. It's worn soft, with holes in the sleeves.

"Jesus." Angie raises herself on an elbow. "Your call?"

"The whole thing was over in under a minute." I lift up the shirt and run my hand over her stomach.

"You want to talk about it?"

"No."

We have sex and we both come fast, which is the way it always is now, infrequent to the point of desperate mutual hunger. I come so hard it almost hurts, as though I'm being sucked right into her body, bound so tightly by her flesh I cease to exist. She asks me if it was good, better than any waitress I could get in town, and I laugh off the snarky comment. I tell her it was better than good.

Angie's up and into the bathroom immediately, because of her recurring bladder infections, trying to piss out any unfriendly bacteria that might be trying to climb up her urethra. Usually, by the time she gets back in beside me I'm fast asleep—and those are the only nights I sleep well. But tonight I'm still awake, eyes-closed-pretending as she slips quiet as a mouse across the carpeted floor, standing stark naked at the window awhile to look out at our neighbourhood, dawn light behind the mountains, her hand pressed to her mouth as though she's trying to stop something from escaping. When she eases herself back into our bed, I realize, for the first time, how careful she is not to wake me up.

THE LIGHT IS WHITE HOT through the curtains and the windows are closed against the noise of the neighborhood, but there are still reverberations—lawnmowers, motorcycles, children running down the sidewalk. The knock on the bedroom door is what woke me up and it comes again, louder this time. I sit up on the edge of the bed, groggy with sleep. The room is thick with heat, nearly airless. The fan is buzzing, jerking through its rotation. Angie pokes her head through the door with the baby on her hip and holds up the phone. She's wearing shorts and nothing but a sports bra on top. "Work," she mouths as I take it from her.

It's the Transportation Safety Board. "We had a few questions for you regarding yesterday's incident."

"The crash?" I run my hand over the bedsheet. It's damp. I feel over-rested, my mind in a fog. I try to rub my head out of its stupor. They're calling to go over the data: weather information for five hours prior and one hour after the crash, audio records of radio contact, records from the navigational aids and radar. There's someone else on the line, a voice that pipes in every once in a while to elaborate on a question or detail, someone's name I didn't catch. Everything they are checking is normal for any emergency, but now they're asking me for a chronicle of all previous shift activity and an account of my sleep patterns.

"My sleep?" My voice catches in my throat, dry from the hot bedroom.

"The details of your sleep schedule over the past week."

"Why?" I reach for a glass of water on the bedside table, take a sip.

"Have you been having any difficulty sleeping?"

"Sorry, am I being investigated for something?" Beside the water glass is a roll of antacids. I tear back the paper, pop a few in my mouth.

"These questions are procedural."

"Procedural?" I rub the tingle of sweat on the back of my neck along the hairline and pop the window open, the racket from the neighbour's mower flooding into the room.

"Normal for any investigation."

"Oh, normal." I take a deep breath out the window; the smell of cut grass. "All right."

"Mr. Harris, have you been unusually fatigued this week?" I can hear the other voice talking to someone in the background. Somewhere in the house Angie is singing rhyming songs.

"Fatigued? No." I crunch another antacid, chalky residue coating my tongue. "I sleep like the dead." The words are out before I take the time to consider them.

"Can you think of anything else, Mr. Harris, that might help us with our investigation?"

"Anything of importance was submitted to you in that envelope. You should have everything you need." I try to keep my tone even, but it comes off sharp and annoyed.

"If you think of anything else you can reach us at the office."

"I won't need to reach you." I push the drapes back and bright midday light pours through the window. What time is it? Suddenly, it occurs to me I might have slept for more than a night. Would Angie let me sleep for an entire day? Longer?

"Do you have any questions, Mr. Harris?"

"No," I say, pulling the drapes closed again, a draft sucking them against the open window. "Actually, yes. How old was the pilot?"

I can hear papers being shuffled through the phone line.

"He was thirty."

I thank them for their thoroughness and hang up the phone.

THERE'S ANOTHER CALL FROM the flight service station in the afternoon. Data that doesn't correspond to the timeline and catapults me off the couch to scramble through drawers all over the house searching for some paper and a pen, the baby howling, startled by my abruptness, and Angie running her outside to walk the yard and calm her down. I watch them from the window, Angie pinching a yellow honeysuckle bloom free from the vine, holding it up to tickle Sophie's nose. Everything right in the world. The supervisor must hear something in my voice, because he tells me—same as the TSB agent—this is standard protocol when a plane goes down. And why do they want my sleep account? He says the words again: standard protocol. He wants to know what kind of questions the TSB agent asked. I get him off the phone quickly without mentioning my worries, but there are things I've started thinking about ever since the call this morning. If

I had exercised caution during that first communication with the pilot, advised him to land instead of wishing him *safe travels* like a fool, things could have turned out differently. There's an empty aerodrome not too far from the crash site. There's a field next to a high school nearby. I had to look closely at a map, but they're there.

"Why do they keep calling?" The screen door slams as Angie comes back in with the baby, yellow pollen on her nose.

"I don't know." I rub my face in my hands. All day the extra sleep has hung over my head like the weight of a bottomless lake. "They're going over the data. It's standard protocol."

"But what are they looking for?"

"How would I know that, Ange?"

"Shouldn't you know?"

"I'm going for a walk."

I intend to head for the forested paths behind the house, but as soon as my feet hit the front walk I lose steam and end up sitting on the edge of our curb, the sun barrelling down my back. The neighborhood is buzzing in the late-afternoon August heat, tinder-dry, vulnerable to any kind of spark. There's been a water ban all summer and the lawns are brown and thirsty. There are thunderstorms in the forecast. From where I'm sitting I can hear the phone inside the house ringing.

IN THE MORNING WE prepare to leave for the cabin. On the radio they're calling for a high of thirty-nine degrees Celsius. "Hotter here than Kuwait today," I say, scanning the weather section of the newspaper.

"Maybe we should stay." Angie's leaning against the kitchen counter, arms crossed, holding her elbows the way she does when she's willing to have a long talk. The baby's in the playpen in the middle of the living room, ignoring us. She's been fussy all morning from the heat. Angie says babies are sensitive to changes in a house. Somehow we've lost most of the day. At this rate we won't reach Osoyoos until dinnertime.

"The car is packed." I brush past her to fill my travel mug with the leftover dregs of morning coffee, but the pot's empty. "Did you drink it all?"

"I'll make more," she says, without moving. "We can unpack the car."

"I'll make it." I measure off spoonfuls. Pour the water. "Are you going to put on a shirt?"

Angie looks down at her sports bra. "It's like a shirt."

"No, it's not."

Early this morning I got another call, this time someone from the Critical Incident Stress Management team. It was a woman on the other end of the line, one of my peers, but the call was anonymous. The program is made up of a group of volunteer counsellors, people who have gone through similar incidents. I recognized the woman's voice, but couldn't place her. I asked her what she wanted to know, but she said she didn't have any questions, just wanted to talk. I told her all I wanted to do was get a head start on my holiday.

"Why would we stay?" I ask Angie, folding the paper. The coffee machine starts spitting.

"Have you slept at all?"

"Yeah, I slept."

In fact, I waited until Angie was asleep to pull out the maps again and spread them all over the kitchen table. I pored over the data, checking and double-checking, reviewing everything I knew to be true. There is an edge of doubt that seems to be wedging itself further into me. "Thom and Veronica are expecting us," I say. "He barely leaves the house, you know."

"Maybe we don't need to be around that right now."

"What difference does it make?" I throw some T-shirts into the last bag by the door. "We're going to sit with our feet in the lake and drink beer."

"Exactly." She cracks a tray of ice and drops two cubes into her cup of coffee.

"Exactly?" I throw the duffel bag over my shoulder.

"I have a pretty clear idea of the way the entire weekend is going to go." Angie sits down at the table and unfolds the newspaper.

"I'm taking this out to the car."

THE HIGHWAY IS CONGESTED, cars packed to capacity, little faces pressed to back-seat windows, slack-faced boredom and wild eyes. In every car that passes I can see fights brewing like storm clouds sliding into a valley. When we got into the car the surfaces were so hot I could barely touch the steering wheel. Angie has been quiet since we left and just when I think she's sleeping again she turns to me and asks, "Why do we always have to go somewhere on the long weekend?"

"Why would we stay home?"

"I don't know." She closes her eyes and rests her head against the window.

"You're so tired all the time."

"Too much sleep." There's a note of hopelessness in her voice, something I've heard before. Lately answers have been different between us, a slight shift, enough tilt to make a pencil roll off a table top.

"Maybe you should get that checked," I say.

A few weeks ago Angie found a scrap of paper in my desk with the rough ideas for a poem sketched across it. It was something I'd done dead sober over a sleepless night, a few leftover thoughts from a poetry workshop I'd taken at university, scrawled so the words were barely legible. She was curious about it, excited by what she'd found, but for some reason seeing that paper in her hand made me feel shame. We had a huge fight. It was the white-paged honesty of it—the poem—that made me accuse her of being nosy, that made me say all sorts of insane things, that she was looking for girls' numbers, that she thought I was heading to the bar after work to fuck waitresses. I told her that if I was going to get so much grief for doing nothing wrong, I might as well be fucking waitresses. We were standing in the kitchen and I stuffed the piece of paper into the garburator, barely getting my hand out of the hole before flipping the switch and setting the blades in motion.

"Look," I say, checking Sophie in the rearview mirror. "She's sleeping already."

Angie's taken off her shoes and placed a rolled-up hoodie behind her neck in preparation for the long drive.

"Close your eyes and sleep," I say.

"I'm not going to sleep. I just don't feel like looking at everything."

After a while she asks me if I want to trade places.

"I'm fine." I look over at Angie, but she stares straight ahead at an empty length of highway as though she hasn't heard me. "I'm fine," I say again.

"I know you are," she says before closing her eyes.

THE LAST TIME WE saw Thom and Veronica was early spring. It was the first time they'd met Sophie—she was already nine months old—and Thom had looked stunned by her delicate hands and tiny teeth. He stuck a finger in her mouth and she bit him.

That night we drank until the sun came up. Thom and Veronica rent the main floor of a ramshackle house off Fraser Street in East Vancouver. Above them lives a Korean exchange student and below them a construction worker in his early twenties. The air is always thick with the smell of kimchi and weed, and whenever I smell those two things I have an overwhelming urge to drink a large amount of beer.

In the backyard, Thom had set up two folding chairs on the plywood flatbed of the construction worker's truck, with an overturned plastic bucket as a table between them. The girls stayed inside talking about whatever women talked about when there were no men around and Sophie was asleep on their bed, surrounded by a barricade of pillows.

"Your neighbour doesn't mind you drinking on his truck?" I'd said, taking a seat in one of the folding chairs. There were cup holders for the beer.

"I'm letting *him* park in *my* driveway," Thom said, passing me a can.

We settled back in our seats, the sounds of a city neighborhood around us, rush hour traffic down Fraser Street, ambulance sirens and the strains of Sepultura coming from the basement suite. I'd already grown accustomed to the quiet nights in Kamloops. Thom had dragged an extension cord through the yard and plugged in an electric campfire. It flickered as the night dimmed behind us.

"So, congratulations!" Thom raised his beer can. "To the wee one!"

We clinked cans.

"You need to get down here more often. Leave Ange and the kid. Come crash on our couch."

"It's not that easy," I said, smiling. Sitting on the flatbed, we could look down the yards of much of the street, take in people through the lit windows as they busied themselves inside their homes. "One day when you and Veronica have a kid you'll see what I mean."

"Who said I want any part in that?" Thom took out a pack of cigarettes and lit a smoke. "Ver been talking to you, or what?"

The construction worker came out to get his lighter from his truck and Thom tried to score some weed off the guy, but he said he didn't have any. My sense was maybe Thom asked him a little too often.

"If Ver wants a baby she'll need to find herself some other primo donor," Thom continued after the construction worker had gone back into the basement. "You can buy sperm on the internet now, can't you?"

"You try to be miserable."

"What do I have to offer? Look at me!" He took a drag on his cigarette and blew rings skyward. "I won't be paying for it either. She better start saving, 'cause that junk ain't cheap. 'Specially the 'intellectual' kind."

"It's self-sabotage."

"God!" He pointed his cigarette at me and shuddered. "What if it was one of my undergrad students? Jesus! She'd want the highfalutin literary stuff. And they're so hungry, I bet they're all selling their sperm. Jesus, that's going to be our world population right there. Oh, sure. I'm going to have to move north. Hey, maybe I'll come live with you in Kamloops."

"There is something wrong with you and we all know it, yet none of us are willing to help you. What does that say?" I finished my beer and dropped it at my feet, opening another can.

"I don't have your straight-and-narrow vision." There was a hint of a sneer at the corner of his lip. "My mind," he said, tapping his temple. He gave me a significant look and took a sip of beer.

"You're not making much sense tonight. And who says I'm on the straight and narrow?"

"Hah! You're as arrow-straight as they come. Are you kidding me?" Thom laughed long enough that I stopped smiling. "What I'm saying is," he said, drawing out the words, "my mind doesn't follow that trajectory—love, marriage, baby. I'd shrink into a little itty-bitty man. I'd become petite."

"So what do you see when you look at me?" I leered and waited, took a large gulp of beer.

"Atrophy." He wiggled a pinky at me and chuckled to himself.

"You bastard."

"Didn't you used to write little poems?" He was smiling now too, like a kid with a stick.

"You're basing your future on our sloppy pub-night pillow talk, both of us one wink away from passed out on the floor. It's pathetic."

"Hey, at least I still have a hope in hell of achieving enlightenment."

"They have you on the same circuit," I said, smirking into my beer. "Is a PhD so different? Don't you think I know they have a hamster wheel at that university built especially for you? You get on that campus and your little legs are going faster than mine, my friend."

"Yah, that may be. But didn't I tell you?" He pulled a thread of tobacco from his lip. "I'm planning on being a monk."

"No, you didn't tell me that." I laughed hard enough that I slopped beer down one pant leg. "You'd make a shitty monk."

"I'm going to live in a state of perfection." He tilted his can back and finished the beer, adding it carefully to a wobbly tower of cans next to his chair. "Nirvana."

"I thought you'd already achieved that." I smirked at him.

Thom laughed and made a weak attempt to disguise a belch.

"So where do you go to be a monk around here?"

"There's a place near Mission."

We talked well into the early morning, until the edges of the clouds turned pink and we were slumped over our chairs trying to grasp at a conversation slipping sideways toward total incoherence. We were talking about politics and great books and greater wars as though we knew anything about those subjects. Thom kept backing me into corners, pointing his finger in my face until I finally surrendered and stumbled up, knocking over my folding chair, and told him to fuck off. I don't think either of us knew what it was over, but we both knew we'd reached that point in the morning where we hated each other. I found Angie and Veronica inside on the couch under a pile of blankets, talking.

"Are you crying?" Angie said. An arm came up from under an afghan.

"They're just leaking," I said, waving her away. There were tears on my cheeks, but it was impossible to tell what from, the booze or the anger. Angie crawled out from beneath the blankets and peered out the window at Thom. "You guys have been drinking all night."

Veronica stood beside her. "Is he still out there?" She went about puttering in the kitchen and muttering to herself about the sorry mess in her backyard and the neighbourhood waking up to bear witness.

I leaned against the wall as I stumbled down the hallway to the bedroom. "If you wake her up I'll kill you," Angie called after me.

Sophie lay in the middle of the bed, chin tilted to the ceiling, mouth open, abandoned to sleep. There was something immensely pleasurable about staring at my sleeping daughter when I was drunk. "You're so beautiful," I said as the exquisite little breaths escaped from her mouth.

"Get out of here," Angie hissed. Her hand came out of the dark and pulled me down the hall.

"When are you guys going to learn you're not twenty anymore?" Veronica said from the kitchen. "Tea, Ange? What do you need, Wes? Some coffee?"

"He's a stubborn bastard," I said, wiping the back of my hand over my weepy eyes. It was certainly the booze.

"So he told you?" Veronica dipped the tea bag in and out of the hot water, steam drifting up around her face.

"Told me what?"

"That he dropped out of his PhD program," she said. "Hasn't left the house all week."

TRAFFIC IS PILED UP along the highway. Sophie is crying, has been crying on and off in howling fits for the past two hours. The wildfire has closed part of the road, with escorts taking convoys of cars down the mountain. No one has moved for twenty minutes. Angie's been halfway over the front seat, ass in the air, for most of the ride, and we silently agreed to stop talking to each other after the first half hour of arguing. *Maybe she's hot. Maybe she's bored. Maybe she wants us to stop yelling.* Kids hang limply out car windows. People walk along the edge of the highway, stretching their legs, taking their dogs for a piss, lifting their hands to shield their eyes as they stare down the long line of stationary cars. I've been sitting here fiddling with the air conditioning and thinking of alternate endings.

"Just leave it on one setting," Angie says. "Cold is cold."

I've been thinking of more possibilities in which the plane lands safely. And the hawk no longer seems to be serving its purpose. Instead of a weightless exhilaration, what I feel when I think of the hawk is dread, the kind of terror that ricochets through your insides when your foot slips off a steel rail, when you make that critical mistake. The feeling is enough to eject me from the car and out into the highway's swelter.

"I'm going to take a leak," I say, slamming the door behind me before I can hear Angie's reply. I walk quickly down the line of cars, heat hammering me from above, bouncing off the windshields and fenders so I have to squint, my sunglasses sitting useless on the car's dash, where I threw them after whipping them off to massage the ache gathering between my eyes. I leave the road and cut off into the brush along the side of the highway, wading through waist-high grass and jumping over a drainage ditch before hitting the trees. Pricks of sweat erupt across my forehead. *What are your intentions?* It's a question I thought I had the answer to. I wipe at my wet face. In the forest, I weave through the trees, my breath coming heavy after only a minute. I can feel something in my body, an ugly growth, an extra layer around the middle of something that might be insubstantial now, but is growing.

Once I'm hidden from the road I relieve myself, sending the stream over the side of a tree stump. In here the air is only hot, alive with the noise of insects and forest detritus crackling under my feet. Only now do I smell the fire. I picture the pilot climbing out of the wreck, walking through the burned-out forest back into town, how everything would smell better, taste better. He probably wouldn't notice the heat. The whole world would look different. What would he do first? Eat a hot dog. Wade out waist-deep into the lake. Would he go back to exactly the way things were? Did he have someone to love? Would he keep flying? Would he keep waiting for summer fires? I wonder if in thirty-three years I will still be that man standing on the highway, squinting at the traffic, badly needing to take a leak but holding it. Suddenly falling off the deep end seems attractive to me. If Thom can fall off the grid, lose his mind without consequence and sit around the house all day reading, then why can't I? I could go back to university, accomplish what Thom threw away. I've seen it happen: bursting into flames. Falling from great heights in a blazing ball of fire. Maybe Thom has it all figured out. When life gets too straight and narrow, throw a wrench into the mix. See what happens. What happens is everyone tiptoes around you, grabs you an extra beer from the fridge, says *poor Thom*, takes your picture, makes it part of a project.

Through the trees, tail lights brighten along the highway and car engines start at the head of the line. I jog down the middle of the road between the rows of cars, singles or families back in their seats staring straight ahead, hoping to move even if only by a few feet. By the time I reach the car, sweat is trickling down my back. The doors are open and I can hear the wailing before I even get close to the car. Angie is pink-faced in the back seat rocking the screaming child.

"You took the keys with you." She calls over Sophie's hoarse shrieking as I get into the front seat. I check my shorts and find them in one of the back pockets. It was autopilot: turning off the car, pocketing the keys as if I was alone. "Shit," I say, turning the ignition and cranking the air-conditioner. The seatbelt is burning hot. I can tell Angie has been crying. "Sorry, Ange. My head's not on straight."

"It's just Sophie." Angie fusses over the child, adjusting her clothing, smoothing the sweaty wisps of her hair. "I don't care about me."

"I'm not right today," I say, turning the dial higher, the frigid air making the sweat run cold along my hairline.

For a while, neither of us says anything. Angie's crying again in the back seat, but not for attention. As soon as a tear hits her cheek she wipes it away quickly with the back of her hand and looks out the window, jutting out her chin. I keep checking in the rearview mirror and the tears keep coming. The tail lights and car engines are a false hope—we haven't moved a foot. I sit like all the others in their cars, waiting blankly, staring straight ahead.

"We're not going to make it there before dark," Angie says.

Up ahead the tail lights glow again, a red wave of light coming down the rows. I put the car in drive. "Are you moving up?"

"I'll stay back here." Her head is back on the seat, her pink cheeks turned pale, the colouring of someone who has slept through a year. "I'm stroking her hair."

We wait another half hour before we are led down the mountain. Our car is near the back of a convoy of fifteen travelling along the highway, ushered by mountain patrol. The forest is charred, burned out like a war zone. Higher up and even through the thick smoke, I can see the bursts of bright flames climbing to crest the mountain peaks.

"Who was it who called this morning?" Angie says, as we round the corner and begin our descent. Her voice is fragile, nearly transparent. She's distracted by something out the window, the twisted remains of a forest.

"Oh, my supervisor. I'm in the clear." There's no reason for the lie. I fiddle with the air again. It's too cold now.

"That's a relief."

Sophie's calmed with Angie's fingers through her hair and I'm not hearing much of anything all of sudden, following the route down the side of the mountain, wheels rolling along the smooth pavement. Something switches over in my brain and everything goes quiet. Angie's stopped crying. All I have to do is follow the line and I'll find my way out.

THE MOTEL PARKING LOT borders the beach and when we pull into a spot the headlights stretch right across the sand into the water and the reflected neon of the vacancy sign.

"What are you doing?" Angie says, turning to look at me. "I'm too tired."

"Why don't I drive for a while? You can sleep on the way."

"I want to stay here tonight."

We unload, leaving Sophie in her seat to dream, making sure one of us is always on our way to or from the car so she's never alone. Angie sets out Sophie's pajamas on the floral bedspread, and the playpen next to her side of the bed. In the morning, when we step out of the motel room, the sun will blind us. We'll spend the day under the willow tree at the edge of the lake and we'll agree it was a good idea to change our plans.

"Everything in?" I say, poking my head in the door as Angie sets up a spot for diaper-changing. "I'll bring her in."

"Don't wake her up."

I lean over Sophie in the car, slide my hands beneath her and gently lift her out of the seat, her body drooping over my arms, face turned skyward, mouth hanging open, ready to drink down the night sky. Abandon. Angie stands in the door of the motel watching us, a broken shaft of light stretching across the concrete and hitting our feet. "Don't wake her up," she whispers across the parking lot.

"Tell them we're not coming," I say.

"Are you sure?"

"Call and tell them Sophie got sick."

Behind the curtains Angie is on the phone. The motel is illuminated under streetlights and neon, but when I turn toward the lake I'm surrounded by a darkness so immense I can't wrap my head around it. I tip my head back like Sophie, so far back my mouth hangs open under the black bowl of a bottomless sky, like the black water of a lake over our heads. Abandon. I spin her gently, dipping her head toward the warm sand and back up into the night, bringing her ear to my mouth and whispering, *baby, baby, baby.* The smell of her makes every minute of my life thus far—shitty or not—worth it.

The air is dry and I can feel my skin shrinking, pulling tight, the moisture sucked from my pores. Standing at the edge of the water, I worry about what's developing inside of me. Silver grasses along the edge of the highway hide crickets and the heat of the day still radiates, rising now from the concrete. There are remedies for a dull heart.

It takes time for my brain to make sense of the opposite of what it expects. It's the end of August, with temperatures the hottest anyone's ever seen and wildfires burning in the backcountry. During the day the mountains circling the lake are gold, tinder-dry, but at night beneath a clear sky and an almost-full moon, the entire valley is white. The mountains look like they're covered in snow, but the breeze smells like grass, green and sweet.

MOSQUITO CREEK

I CAN HEAR KATE. Her bare feet rubbing through the grass. Her lips leaving the rim of the bottle.

"You're getting warmer," she says. She's flicking her lighter. It won't catch.

I move slowly in the same direction, waiting for it—open air, tumbling space, anything.

Kate inhales. I can hear the smoke leave her lips. "You're hot," she says.

My left foot slides off an edge and I stop. Somewhere below, rocks spill and bounce away. I stand still as a rush of wind passes over me. My breathing comes heavy. I think *steady* as my hands work in and out of fists. I don't want Kate to see them shaking.

When I pull off the blindfold the entire inlet stretches out in front of me. Everything spills into it—the rivers, the forests, the suburbs, the city. The toes of my left foot hang out over the edge of the cliff. Below, the trains squeak and groan, barely moving along the tracks. Beside the tracks are the grain towers, ugly and grey, connected by pipes twisting like anatomy. The seagulls perch on the towers, fat and stupid and hungry.

I take a step back and turn to Kate. She's already up from the blanket, coming toward me all antsy with excitement. "My turn," she says, taking the blindfold and giving me the bottle of Malibu.

I don't know why we come here, but we've been doing it for a while. Kate invented the game. Sometimes we play, sometimes we don't. Sometimes we just smoke or talk or sleep.

The wind tangles Kate's hair in the blindfold and I pull the strands away to help her tie it around her head.

"How was it?" she asks, arms outstretched.

My heart is beating fast. I spin her once, twice, three times.

"I've never been that close," I say.

~

IN THE SUMMER LYNN CANYON is swamped with tourists. They come in by the busload, gathering white-knuckled on the suspension bridge with their cameras, clutching the rails as they try to get the ultimate shot of the falls. From the bridge it's a fifty-metre drop into a gorge of rocky ledges and tumbling water—head-splitting stuff, an instant death kinda deal. Standing in the middle of the bridge in flip-flops and a bikini, I let go of the railing and clasp my hands behind my back. A tour group in matching red baseball caps circles me as they angle their cameras, but I focus on the bottom of the canyon and start counting—it's a test of courage or faith or strength or something. The bridge swings and bounces as people nudge past on their way to the other side. We hucked a watermelon off the bridge once, watched it explode into a billion microscopic particles below. I get to twelve before I have to grip the rail.

Pushing my way through to the other end of the bridge, I follow hikers along paths that snake through the forest. Down toward the creek bed, I can hear water spilling over rocks and shouts bouncing through the canyon. *Jumping!* A second of silence followed by a splash. The creek spreads out in front of me through a break in the trees. There are at least forty kids hanging out on the rocks or sitting in teepees made with fallen branches. Clouds of pot smoke hang in the air. A group of guys sit together on a large boulder and scope the girls, who lie on towels spread out side by side. Yesterday was the last day of school—grade eight is over—and there's a vibe, jumpy and electric, running through the crowd of kids. Last summer, they wheeled one of the jumpers out of here on a stretcher—it happens more than you'd think. They put a brace around the kid's neck and wrapped him up in a silver shock blanket that looked like a giant piece of tinfoil. It took a while to carry him out on the trails, his friends queuing behind the paramedics to follow the stretcher out of the forest. Sometimes it's hard to judge the jumps when you're stoned out of your tree.

Jumping! Cheers and howls, another splash.

Kate's in a pink bikini, baking in the sun on a large, flat rock near the pools. She's undone the straps on her top and rolled down her bottoms to prevent tan lines. I can see the beginning of her bum crack. She's achieved that perfect cinnamon brown I can only wish for. She started at the beginning of May, before it was even warm out. After school she'd drag her comforter out onto her back porch and lie there in her bikini, teeth chattering. I'd sit beside her in a sweatshirt and jeans and we'd pretend to study. Her mother calls her a sun worshipper. It makes me laugh. I can't imagine Kate down on her knees in the chilly spring sun, her hands clasped, her head bowed. I can't imagine her praying for anything.

"You're so skinny it's gross," Kate says, squinting up at me from her towel as I hop over the rocks to reach her. "What took you so long?"

"Don't ask," I say, making a bored-to-tears face as I dip my toes into the freezing creek water. "I couldn't get a ride 'til my sister was ready. It's like she brushes each hair on her head individually."

"There's this thing called a bus," Kate says, sitting up and holding her bathing suit to her chest. I can see one of her nipples.

"You're flashing the whole world." I unroll my towel beside hers and flop back with a sigh.

"I don't care. Tie it, then," Kate says, turning her back to me. "Did you bring any food?"

"Nope." I pull the strings of her bikini top into a neat bow.

"Maybe I should get us some." Kate scans the forest like a 7-Eleven might be hiding behind the trees somewhere, and then lies back down, giving up. She pokes my ribs. "I can see your bones."

"What am I supposed to do about it?" I say, running my hands over my stomach.

"Eat."

"I eat all the time. I eat more than anyone I know." I push out my stomach and pat the bulge. "How's that?"

"I hate you," Kate says, rolling her eyes.

Another shout bursts through the air. *Jumping!* Above us, kids scramble up the boulders and dart in and out of the trees. In this part of the canyon there's a deep pool at the bottom of a narrow chasm—maybe ten feet across— where the water is seven shades, from turquoise to cobalt blue. From the cliff there are three different places to jump, the highest thirty feet, but most kids jump from the ten-foot boulder and a few from the fifteen. There's a lineup along the cliff, mostly guys, fidgeting while they wait, pulling on their bottom lips or scratching their heads. Some can't be more than ten or eleven. Sitting among them is Max, a guy from my grade, his long, skinny legs dangling over the edge. Whenever someone leaps from the rock, he tilts his chin to the sky and crows like a rooster. "What's he doing?" Kate says.

"I don't know," I say, watching him. He's wearing shorts with Doc Martens and the same Metallica T-shirt he wears at least once a week. Max and I went to elementary school together—back then he was the kid no one noticed until the teacher asked him a question he couldn't answer. Now he's the kid who doesn't care what people think. Last week instead of joining our usual gym class run to the top of Montroyal Boulevard, he stood three feet from school property and puffed on a smoke. There was no point in suspending him because school was practically over; our gym teacher, Ms. Carr, pretended not to see him.

"He's weird," Kate says. "Is he with Adrienne?"

"No. I hate that bitch."

Wet and shivering in a black bikini, Adrienne is standing next to Max. She is the only girl on the cliff. Her toes curl around the edge of the rock like she's a plump bird perched on a wire—a mean bird, a crow. For most of grade eight, she barked like a dog whenever I passed her in the hall at school. Why, I never figured out, but my guess was she didn't like my hair because it's wild and red and has a mind of its own. "Watch," I say. "She's gonna jump. She'll bellyflop."

"Maybe she'll explode," Kate says. Adrienne turns and disappears back into the forest. "Choke," Kate shrieks and I laugh pretty hard. Adrienne quit barking at me after Kate spread a nasty rumour about her, something about genital warts contracted over spring break. I'm still impressed Kate did that for me, because she could have got her ass kicked, but somehow Kate always manages to float above it all.

Another guy from our school climbs the rock face, moving quickly, finding steps where I can't see them, his friends hooting at him from the boulders at the base of the cliff. I can't remember his name, but he's a grade up from us and lives near the highway by Mosquito Creek. He was suspended for something this year—something to do with mouthing off or having weed in his locker. He passes the ten-foot mark, his skin translucent in the shadows of the trees, and disappears into the forest, coming out moments later to stand at the edge of the thirty-foot cliff. Beyond him the world is bleached, the sky burning white. He looks down, hands on his hips, to judge the landing, while his friends holler at him from below. People stand on the rocky shore, craning to get a better view; everyone watches when someone jumps from that height. Kate and I sit up, waiting to see if he'll do it.

He pauses long enough to take a breath. "Jumping!" He leaps from the rock into the air, legs scissoring before straightening. At first his fall is almost slow-motion—his body bow-shaped, muscles tense, ribs jutting. He drifts, floating like a slip of paper, soft-bellied with pointed toes. Then all at once, his milky skin moves fast as light, brightening the rocks with its radiance. The water swallows him—a small disappearance, no big splash. Standing up, it takes me a moment to spot him in the pool, glowing deep in the water like a rising moon. When he surfaces, he pushes his hair out of his eyes and swims over to the boulders, where his friends are calling out to him.

"Wanna go in?" Kate says after watching him for a minute.

"Nah, you go ahead," I say, lying back on my towel.

It takes the guy a while to notice her doing laps around him, but when he does they float off together, sitting on the rocks in a shallow part of the pool away from everyone. Joining them now would be too obvious. When they both look in my direction, I close my eyes and pretend not to notice.

I must have fallen asleep on the rocks, because next thing I know Kate is standing over me, breathless, dripping water all over my legs. "You know Elgin, right?" I squint into the sun bursting behind their heads. The guy is standing beside her, rubbing water out of his ears. "He goes to our school." He half waves, but looks past me which means he's only interested in Kate. "Come on," she says, taking my hand and pulling me up off the towel. "He knows a better place to go swimming."

WE WALK STRAIGHT DOWN the canyon, back toward the suspension bridge. In this part of the park the creek bed narrows and it's hard to hear over the roar of fast-moving water. Kate and Elgin are ahead, climbing over the rocks quick as mountain goats. Kate doesn't even bother to look back for me. Under the bridge are the falls where jumpers have died. Signs at the park entrance warn about the dangers with a diagram of a stick man twirling in a vortex. Jumpers have been sucked into whirlpools, trapped where no one can rescue them, their broken bodies drifting out eventually.

Elgin's standing at the edge of a natural waterslide carved into the rock. He sits in the bubbling stream before gliding down, dropping into the pool below. Kate follows him, descending less gracefully. "Let's go," Elgin yells at me over the rush of the creek. The water takes me quickly, the smooth rock like the porcelain of a bathtub, and then the rock is gone and the water hits me again, this time like a cold tile floor. My head goes under and I swallow a gulp of creek, my limbs scrambling around me. I break through the surface, gasping, "It's cold." Kate grabs my feet and pulls them into the air, sending my head under again. I spit water in her face and laugh so hard my ribs hurt. "That wasn't what I wanted to show you," Elgin says.

We hike further down the canyon, my skin tingling after the cold shock, shivers running down my limbs, everything heightened—glints of silver in the creek rapids, green-gold needles in the trees, prisms of light radiating through the branches. Around a bend I can see the tourists crossing the suspension bridge and Elgin stops, holding up his hand. "Wait a sec," he says. He peers over the edge of the glistening rocks before grinning, reaching an arm out to Kate. "You think you can handle this?" I don't like his grin or the way Kate's smiling at him. She takes his hand and looks down. "No way," she says, pulling back from him. Elgin's smile gets bigger. I walk right to the edge, standing beside them, and look over. The creek spills over the rocks, twisting into a huge waterfall, billows of mist swallowed into the dark water. "Yeah, right," I say, crossing my arms, waiting for Elgin's reaction. Kate puts her hand to her mouth, catching a burst of giggles which means she's nervous. He'll bluff until we beg him to stop, until we grab his hands and pull him away from the cliff, believing he's the bravest guy we know. "Go for it," I say, calling his game.

Elgin doesn't say a word, doesn't even look at me. He smiles at Kate again, then backs away from us quickly, breaking into a run. In one leap he's gone off the cliff. Not like a bird. Not like a slip of paper. He falls like a rock, like a cannonball. He falls so fast he's gone like a magic trick.

"Shit," Kate says, getting down on her knees to peer over the side. "Where is he?" When she turns back her eyes are huge. "He did it. Holy crap! Look," she says, pointing, "there he is." I kneel down beside her. Elgin is in the water, swimming away from the falls. "What an idiot," I say. I feel like shouting the words so they echo around the canyon.

"I'm gonna do it," Kate says, standing. She paces the cliff.

"What, now you're an idiot too?" I step away from the edge, shaking my head. "No, you're not jumping."

"He did it." Kate takes deep breaths, rotating her arms the way swimmers do before they launch from the block. She tightens her ponytail. "Look! He's fine." She points again like

I didn't believe her the first time. She's shaking out her hands. Far below, Elgin's sitting on a ledge swinging his feet. He sees us and waves. Kate waves back and grabs my hand. "We'll do it together. At the same time."

"Forget it." I shake her off and start walking away. "You want to go, go ahead. Go smash your brains on some rocks," I call over my shoulder, climbing up the large boulders leading up to the path. When I turn around I expect to see Kate following me, but she's still standing by the edge of the waterfall. "It's like our cliff game," Kate yells after me, "but there's something to catch you."

"We don't jump!" I shout down at her. "That's a pretty significant difference." I cross my arms and eyeball her while she looks up at me, chewing on her bottom lip. "Brad what's-his-name died here," I say.

"He didn't jump here." Kate keeps peering over the edge to check if Elgin is still there. She looks small and breakable from up here on the boulders.

"He did! He died right there." I'm practically shrieking now, pointing at the cliff. As I climb further up the embankment, Kate yells, "Hey!"

I turn back and we stare at each other. "He's just a guy," I shout down at her. "What do you need to prove?"

Kate puts her hands on her hips without saying anything, her mouth twisted in an amused smile. She thinks it's funny when I get angry.

"Do what you want," I say, sucking in my cheeks, and by the time I reach the path and look again, Kate is gone.

BAREFOOT, IT TAKES A while to get back to the suspension bridge—my flip-flops are still on the rocks by our towels. I push through the cluster of people in the middle of the bridge and scan the pool below for Kate. Just when I start to consider notifying the authorities, I spot her and Elgin swimming together around the waterfall. "Bitch," I mutter under my breath. People on the bridge are staring at me. My legs and arms start trembling from the cold, so I trudge to the other side to sit on a rock in the sun and scowl.

Almost an hour's gone before Kate comes running onto the bridge, yelling *chicken*. People grip the rails, giving her dirty looks as they're bounced left and right, but Kate's oblivious, glowing; Elgin trails behind her, grinning like a goon.

"You guys took forever," I yell over the glaring faces. The shivers start again. Kate strolls up to me and makes chicken noises in my ear. *"Bock, bock, bock."*

"I went down the waterslide," I say, jabbing her in the leg with my big toe.

"That was nothing, right?" Kate laughs, looking to Elgin.

"You missed out," Elgin says, throwing his arm around Kate's shoulder. "It was awesome." She hands me my flip-flops and my towel, which I wrap tightly around my shoulders, sulking into the terry cloth. There's a moment of silence as we all stare at each other. Kate gives Elgin a rough peck on the cheek. "See you tonight," she says, wrapping an arm around my waist and leading us with purpose out of the forest. When I turn to glare at Elgin, he's standing there with the stupidest smile I've ever seen frozen on his face.

When we're far enough away I ask, "What's tonight?"

"Party at the creek," Kate sings.

"Did you kiss him?"

"Of course!"

I MET KATE AT Outdoor School when we were ten years old. Outdoor School is a school where you learn about the outdoors. Once a year, they pile kids from elementary schools all over the North Shore into big yellow school buses and take them up past Squamish for a week to learn about animals and archery and canoeing and plants. It's all kind of confusing; one day you're sitting at your desk trying to figure out algebra and the next you're plopped in the middle of the forest, learning which berries you can eat if you're stranded in the wilderness. Max was my assigned learning partner. I was stuck beside him on the bus, a couple kids behind us made kissy noises on the backs of their hands, and he was never far from my side the rest of the week at camp. We had to share field notes, build a dam, and collect water skaters from a canoe. He called them Jesus bugs. He was strange and I was mortified, the way girls are most of the time when they're ten years old. Wherever I turned, he was there, lurking nearby. Kate was my salvation from that week forward. We were placed in the same cabin group, and I noticed her because she wore electric-blue nail polish, and also because on the first night, one of the girls in our cabin peed in the top bunk and Kate laughed at her behind her back. I thought it was cruel, but it also made everyone want to be close to her, including me.

Our second day there we learned about salmon. We learned how they reproduce, swim the stream, and die. Our wilderness instructor held up a flailing Coho, poking and pressing him to get the sperm out to fertilize the eggs. I sat beside Max on the cold hard benches outside, trying to concentrate on the wind turning up the bellies of the leaves, but I couldn't help watching the fish twisting above the bucket. He looked prehistoric, like he didn't belong in this world, like the bucket was a portal that would take him back to the right time and place. Kate was sitting in the front row. She kept groaning, pulling the sleeves of her sweater up over her balled hands and sinking her nose into the wool. When the instructor asked her if she wanted to hold the salmon, Kate pulled her hands away from her face and flat out said no, her voice as cold as the water in the bucket. At Outdoor School, we were expected to touch everything in nature that couldn't sting us or give us a rash. I'd already been forced to touch tree fungus and snake skin. As soon as Kate said no, Max started to laugh and couldn't stop. It was October, but all he was wearing was a white T-shirt and I could see the outline of his bony shoulder blades under the thin cotton. He put his head between his knees and howled while we all stared at him. For some reason the instructor thought I was the cause of all the hilarity, and he pulled me down to the front row, seating me right beside Kate. "Psycho," I whispered in Kate's ear, Max hiccupping behind us, and from that point on, Kate and I were friends.

With the salmon still twisting in the air, the instructor sent Max away on pig slop duty, which I think Max secretly enjoyed, because he had a smile on his face—and some people do like pigs. I felt bad for him—not Max but that salmon, all of us gawking at his thrashing and his sperm. There was nothing there to protect him; even the air was too much.

I just wanted the instructor to let him go, to hold him gently in the shallow river and feel the quiver of his body between his hands, a flicker of light through the water.

IN KATE'S CLOSET I sit on the floor, staring at her clothing piled in cubbies and falling off hangers. "I need something to wear," I say, digging through a heap of tops on the bottom shelf.

"Take whatever," Kate says into the mirror, naked from the waist up. She snaps on a pink bra with rhinestone-studded straps. Her breasts are perfect, round like halved peaches and bigger than those of most of the girls our age. Mine are practically inverted—I mean, like raisins poked into raw dough. Maybe not that bad, but nothing to prance around with top-less. "That bra's pretty," I say, turning my back to take off my shirt.

"Have it." Kate unhooks the bra and tosses it at me.

"It won't fit me."

"Stuff 'em." She walks to her dresser and pulls out some inserts, chucking them at me.

"Thanks," I say, my back still turned as I tuck the pieces of foam into pockets inside the bra and adjust the straps over my shoulders.

"No biggie." She puts on a lacy black one and a low-cut black tank top.

Earlier we napped in Kate's basement on the Hide-A-Bed, legs intertwined, everything cool and peaceful underground. The only noise was from the wheels of her sister's roller skates as she spun circles on the concrete floor. Her family is always in the basement. The TV's down there and the video game box and her dad's office too, which has been a shrine to their old family life ever since he moved out last winter. It actually isn't really an office at all, but just a space in the corner of the rec room with a desk, a swivel chair, and a maroon rug. There's a stash of porno mags on a top shelf above the desk, neatly arranged in grey file folders. Kate pulled them down once and showed me a page featuring buttholes. None of the girls had pubic hair and I realized I'd eventually have to get rid of mine. Since that day I've never liked Kate's dad.

"Put this on," Kate says, passing me a light pink tank top. "It matches."

We do our makeup in the bathroom, sitting up on the vanity. The canyon water washed my face bare: small eyes, pale lips, hair gone wild again. Nothing I can do will tame it.

"Be right back," Kate says, disappearing through the door.

I paw through the drawers and find some face powder, spreading a thin layer over my skin before snapping the compact shut and putting it back where I found it. The bathroom door swings open and Kate glides across the floor, pulling a half-full bottle of Grand Marnier from under her hoodie. "Drink up," she says, handing it to me. "It's all there was. That and whiskey." She unzips her hoodie and examines her face in the mirror.

"Your mom won't notice?" I ask, taking a gulp and passing the bottle back to her.

"She doesn't drink. It's my dad's old booze." She takes a sip, staring at me. "Your hair."

"I know." My hands involuntarily go up to my head.

"Overall it's better, though."

"I got this conditioner," I say, pulling the strands into a tight bun. "They use it on horse manes."

"At least you don't have that tumbleweed-on-fire look going anymore."

"Fuck you," I say, laughing. I put down the toilet lid, sipping at the Grand Marnier, getting used to the burn down my throat.

"Should I go on the pill?" Kate looks in the mirror like she's addressing herself.

"Why?" I ask before even hearing her question properly.

"You're so pure," Kate laughs. She hops off the counter and kisses me on the lips, soft and quick like a hummingbird. I blink, surprised, my cheeks flushing. She turns back to the mirror, sweeping her lids with shimmery pink shadow and flawlessly tracing them with black liner, smudging the lines so her eyes are shadowy and cat-like. "You need some of this," she says, handing it to me. Beside her I lean into my reflection, running the black tip of the pencil along each lid and rubbing the line with my pinky carefully, like Kate did. I sit back and look at myself: a pale feline, lonely dark eyes. It's better overall. "Meow," I whisper at the mirror.

"You're really weird sometimes," Kate says, digging into one of the drawers. She pulls out a pack of smokes, taking out a single cigarette and cranking open the bathroom window. "So?" she says, lighting it and resting her chin on the window ledge.

"What?" I brush thick coats of black mascara on my lashes. I can't stop staring at myself.

"What do you think of him?" Kate blows smoke out the

window.

"He's all right," I say, joining her. I take a drag from her cigarette. "You should wait."

"For what?" Kate says, smirking at me. "For you? That could take forever."

"Shut up!" I grab the bottle off the counter and take a longer sip, catching a dribble down my chin with the back of my hand. "Let's go."

"Show-off," Kate says, tucking the bottle under her hoodie. She kisses me again, a little harder. This time I'm ready, though. I smile and kiss her back.

WE ENTER MOSQUITO CREEK through Rana's backyard. She was my lab partner through most of grade eight, and she told me her mom is always complaining of either bears or teenagers in their backyard, shit or beer bottles. The beer bottles are better any day; there's nothing worse than bear shit. Rana likes to describe the scat in detail—berries, grass, fur, and bones.

Kate and I crouch low past the big picture window that looks out on their perfectly manicured lawn to the break in the hedges and the steep dirt path leading to the creek. On the trail, my eyes haven't adjusted to the dark yet and we forgot a flashlight, but Kate's an owl or a fox, dragging me by the arm as she skips ahead. Every few steps we stop to take swigs from the bottle, more for Kate than for me. It's her booze, I guess, and it doesn't matter because I'm already feeling a buzz. Kate trips over a stump, barely catching herself from falling, and I haul her back onto her feet. "What's the hurry?" I say, but she's already ahead of me.

We're past the neighbourhood and working our way up the mountain when I see the glow of a fire. We can hear music through the trees, but it's hard to judge how close things are in the dark and all of a sudden we're there. A group of grade elevens chat around a fire burning in a ketchup tin, and past them kids walk along the paths or sit on the rocks in groups of two or three. Deeper in the forest, at the source of the music, a larger crowd is gathered. We wander around the creek chatting with friends, trying to find a group we want to hang out with. Rana's sitting on a stump with a bunch of drama club kids and when she sees me she stands, waving me over. Kate and I join their circle and drink from the two-litre of shit-mix being passed around. When I spot Elgin coming toward us through the trees, I turn my back to him without saying anything to Kate, but she sees him anyway and squeezes my hand before disappearing with him into the forest. "Are they together?" Rana asks, passing me the two-litre, but I don't bother answering her.

A few minutes later, Kate comes back alone to lead me up one of the paths along the edge of the creek. At the base of a big evergreen a lighter flicks on and off and Elgin's voice calls out from the dark. I can see the outline of someone sitting beside him.

"Who's with you?" Kate says, still hanging onto my hand.

"Max," Max says. He lights a joint and the flame briefly illuminates his face.

"I can't see anything out here," Kate says, letting go of me and sitting down beside Elgin.

"Hi," I say to no one in particular—Max or Elgin—just

so everyone knows I'm here. I can barely see my own hand in front of my face.

"I know you," Max says, passing me the joint.

"Yeah?"

"We were in elementary together." He laughs like it's a joke.

"Yeah, I remember," I say, taking a puff. The smoke tickles my throat and my lungs tighten. I cough as I pass the joint to Kate.

"You liked My Little Ponies," Max says.

"No, I didn't."

"You did. At recess you'd be brushing their hair and shit."

Kate starts giggling and Elgin joins in. "Why do you remember that?" Kate says.

"I have a good memory," Max says, the joint back between his fingers, embers growing as he sucks in the smoke.

"Well, you don't," I say, "because that wasn't me."

"Whatever," Max shrugs.

"I think I'd remember that," I say. The glowing tip of the joint comes toward me and Max touches my hand as he passes it to me. I pull it back quickly and even in the dark I can tell he's smiling. The joint goes around the circle again before anyone says anything.

"This guy has the best weed in North Van," Elgin says, slapping Max on the back hard enough that he drops the roach. "Maybe the whole Lower Mainland."

"Fuck yeah," Max agrees, searching on the ground.

"We'll be right back," Kate says, grabbing my arm and pulling me over to the creek out of earshot. She's close enough I can feel her breath and the moonlight cuts down through the branches brightening her face. Her cheeks are slack and her eyes are wet like a sick dog. The pot's creeping into my face too. "I'm really stoned," I say, rubbing my wet eyes. We're both sick dogs.

"I'm gonna go with Elgin," Kate says.

"Okay."

"I'm not asking your permission."

"I know."

"Don't come find me if I don't come back," she says, heading back into the trees. "I'll find you later."

"What am I supposed to do?" I say, following her back toward the guys. Kate looks at me as if it's the stupidest question in the world and before she takes Elgin's hand she leans in close and whispers, "What about Max?" I'm still shaking my head *no* as they disappear into the dark. "Now what?" I say, sitting on a rock. I can hear the crack and snap of underbrush as Kate and Elgin make their way further into the bush. My eyes have adjusted to the dark and I can see Max's slouchy outline against the tree. He comes to sit beside me and I give him a weak smile he probably can't see. "Are they gonna fuck?" he says, relighting the joint and passing it to me.

"Why are you asking me that?" I take a toke and give it back to him. I can't decide how I feel about sitting with him, but I don't want to walk out of the trees with him either. It's easier to smoke weed until I figure it out.

"Curious, I guess," Max says.

"You're sick."

"I thought you guys talked about shit like that?"

"Not with you." When I look over at him, he's smiling his weird lopsided grin and I can't help laughing. "Should we go?"

"Let's finish this first," he says, blowing on the tip of the joint and we smoke in silence awhile, listening to the music down the creek. At one point I think I hear Kate laughing and my heart trips out of my chest, but the sounds are coming from a different direction. The weed is making me paranoid and I rest my head in my hands, taking some deep breaths. "Your stuff is strong."

"Yeah," Max says with pride in his voice. "Why do you tie your hair back like that?" All of a sudden, Max's fingers are squeezing the bun on top of my head. He's always been that way, inappropriate with physical contact. I remember him reaching into my pocket for an eraser when we were in elementary school.

"My hair?" I swat at his hand. "I don't know. It's easier."

"I like it out." He probes my bun.

"What are you doing?"

"Wait a sec." He has both hands on my head now, pulling my hair out of its knot. "There," he says, shooting the elastic into the brush.

"I need that."

"Who gives a fuck what people say? People suck." He massages my head until I start laughing.

"That feels pretty good."

He sits back, smoking quietly for a moment, and I can feel him staring at me in the dark. "It's cool," he says, before flicking the butt into the bushes. "I bet one day you'll really like your hair." We stand up and his lips brush against my cheek in the dark. "We don't have to go back yet," he says, turning in a circle as though there's a lot more to see in the forest.

"Okay, where should we go?"

We hike through the trees, higher up to a plateau where

there are large, flat rocks, and sit together, throwing stones. Far down the creek bed, shadows move around the fire. There's a waterfall nearby, the sound of frantic water pouring through my weed-wrecked brain. My head starts to spin and I lie back on the rocks. When Max lies beside me, I know I've given him a signal without meaning to, but I figure that's okay. For once I want to be like Kate freefalling in Lynn Canyon. "Are you cold?" Max says, leaning into me. I tilt my chin up and he kisses my neck, but then stops, waiting to see what I think. His saliva smells like beer. When I reach down to unbutton his jeans, he freezes for a second. He helps me slide them off, then he pulls off my jeans and I take off my bra under my tank top. His hands slide underneath my shirt to find my nipples. We kiss awhile, rolling on the cold rock, and when he reaches inside my underwear I don't stop him. He asks me if it's okay, if I want to do this, and I say sure. I keep my underwear on and he has to pull them to one side, his hipbones digging into my thighs as he pushes inside me. It hurts, but there's something wonderful about it, like I've finally accomplished something real. His face is pressed into my neck and I look up into the tree, branches criss-crossing the night. When he stops and asks me what's wrong, I realize I'm not making any sounds, I realize I'm barely breathing. For some reason, I need to concentrate really hard, and by doing that it's like I'm holding my body together, keeping everything in one piece. I tell him nothing's wrong, I tell him I'm really stoned. He starts laughing and I wish he'd stop.

Afterwards, we lie next to each other and Max talks about getting more weed, about maybe finding someone who has shrooms. The forest is black, trees stretching right into the night sky; they are the sky, but starless and tangled. I pull my jeans back on and look for Kate's bra, which has fallen somewhere between the boulders. Each time I stick my hand between the rocks there's a cold shock of water at my fingertips. "Do you need help?" Max says, standing over me.

"No." I plunge my hand into the creek. "I lost something. You can go back if you want."

"I'm not going to leave you here."

Eventually I give up and follow Max back through the forest to the party. In the morning a hiker will find Kate's bra downstream, glittering in the morning sunlight. When we reach the clearing where the dense trees open up onto the party, I veer off in the opposite direction from Max. He stops to look for me, stepping back into the forest to search for a moment, before disappearing into the crowd of kids.

I SPEND THE REST of the night trying to get Kate alone so I can tell her everything that happened. We're finally sitting together by the fire when I ask her how it was with Elgin. "Perfect," she says. At the exact same time, a spray of beer hits her cheek and soaks her top. Next to us a group of plastered grade eleven guys are shotgunning beers. Kate turns to them. "Quit it," she yells, wiping off her face. A guy wearing a yellow baseball cap punctures another can and points it right at Kate's head, hitting her in the ear with the spray. After that I'm not sure in what order things happen. Someone's swearing and someone's laughing. It all sounds normal at first, but then Elgin steps up and, with the back of his hand, knocks the grade eleven's yellow baseball cap off his head.

The guy picks up his hat and puts it back on, stepping up to Elgin. A crowd collects, the fight a magnet drawing everyone together. Another grade eleven in a black hoodie joins in, swings and smashes Elgin's nose. Blood gushes over Elgin's mouth and down his T-shirt. He wipes at his face and rubs his bloody hand on his cargo pants. Kate gets pushed to the other side of the crowd and Elgin staggers in the middle of the circle, blood still gushing from his nose onto his white sneakers. He stands there for a moment as it drips down his chin. He spits and smiles, his teeth red, and then the two grade elevens beat the crap out of him. Every time they beat him down, Elgin staggers back up like he wants more. The other guys in the front row are laughing at him. Kate tries to push herself to the front of the crowd, but she keeps getting forced back. Black Hoodie knees Elgin in the stomach and he falls to the ground, curled up with his bloodied fingers wrapped around his head to protect his face. This time he doesn't get up. One of the other guys gives him a couple kicks to his back and Yellow Baseball Cap pours the rest of his beer on him. On the outskirts of the crowd, Max watches, expressionless, and all of a sudden I feel ashamed.

WE DON'T TALK ON the way to Elgin's house. Kate and I each take one of his arms, but it's hard getting out of the dark crush of trees. We keep tripping, Kate keeps swearing, and Elgin asks over and over, "What the fuck happened?" We creep into Elgin's backyard and go in through the back door so no one will hear us. He leaves little drops of blood on the living room carpet. Above the TV there's a poster-size photo of a younger

Elgin playing hockey. He tells us to be quiet, not to tell his mom. We help him to the bathroom and he sits on the toilet seat, head in hands, his stringy hair falling all around his face. Kate pulls some toilet paper from the roll and hands it to him in a big crumple for the cut above his eye. She presses her lips to his forehead and then looks over at me. My hands suddenly feel empty. Elgin stands unsteadily and looks at his face in the mirror. He blinks a couple times like he can't believe his own reflection. "Fuck." He slams his fist against the wall. "Maybe you should go," Kate says to me.

"Are you sure?"

"Yeah. We're good." She turns back to Elgin, inspecting his cut.

"Okay, if you're sure." As I back out of the bathroom, I catch a glimpse of myself in the mirror. The black eyeliner has smeared, my eyes lost in dark raccoon circles. I'm a creature of the night. The loneliness is still there; it's worse now. "I'll call you later," I say from the hallway.

"Close the door," Kate says.

IT'S STARTING TO GET light out, a blue band growing behind the trees. I think about taking the shortcut through the forest, but I don't want to walk on the trail alone. I remember hearing something about bears feeding in the early morning. Or was it cougars? Maybe deer? It doesn't matter.

The houses are pushing up into the mountains. Or maybe it's the mountains pushing against the houses. I'm not sure which one it is, but their cold gigantic weight makes me anxious and I want to be somewhere else. An empty bus comes down the street and when I get on the driver doesn't look at me. I sit near the back. The bus is the only thing on the road and everything is quiet at this time of the morning—cars in their driveways, newspapers on front porches, heads on pillows full of rest. The bus driver and I are the only two dreamless, awake when we shouldn't be. I'm not sure where the feeling comes from, but all at once I need to talk to Kate so desperately I start to cry. I get off at Grand Boulevard and walk the rest of the way home. Across the inlet, in the distance, the city is a lit grid of neat cubes.

One of the cats has been left out overnight and he sits tall on the top step of the porch, watching me. As I climb the stairs, he paces and I bend down to kiss his soft, grey head. I slip my key into the lock and slowly and quietly open the door. The cat enters the house with intent, disappearing down the hallway as I creep up the stairs to my bedroom. My dirty clothes are everywhere. There are piles of dishes and a pool of hard candle wax across my desk. I close the door and go down the hall to my sister's room. Carlie's window is open and everything smells like a summer morning, clean and fresh with promises of lawnmowers and sprinklers. I slip under the covers beside her and in her sleep she makes a space for me. We used to do this if we got scared when we were little kids and shared a room. We have the same eyes and the same smell because I always borrow her perfume. If I wish hard enough, I can believe I was the one in here sleeping all night and Carlie was the one in the forest with Max.

Eventually I fall asleep, but at the same time I hear all the movements in the house. My father's alarm, the drum of the shower, the car backing out of the driveway. My mom's bare feet on the stairs, her hands through the dishwater, each piece of cutlery sinking, settling. It's the first day of summer vacation and there are two months ahead with nothing to do.

When I come downstairs later, Carlie doesn't ask me why I slept in her bed last night. We both pretend it never happened.

~

IT TAKES ME A WHILE to pick an outfit for the party—like over the summer I've forgotten how to dress myself—and in the end I go for something simple: jeans, a purple hoodie, sneakers. Mom's standing by the sink, hidden in a cloud of spaghetti steam as she dumps the noodles into the colander. "Take a jacket," she says. "Chilly tonight." There's a hint of blue left in the night sky and a purple stain where the sun has disappeared. As I round the corner of our block, I hear the bus pull away from the stop, so I decide to keep walking down to Lonsdale, where I can catch another one. Ambulance sirens whir out of the hospital on 13th Street and the sidewalks are empty, a cool wind—the first sign of fall—whistling down the street.

I flip up my hood and walk quickly, rubbing my arms for warmth. My slow-death summer is truly over. I spent it helping my dad with odd jobs around the house: painting the rec room, weeding the garden, clearing out the garage. I lost two months covered in cobwebs, hauling garbage bags of my parents' old hippie clothes for Goodwill. Mom made me drain the backyard pond because she didn't want to be held responsible for attracting West Nile virus mosquitos that could potentially wipe out the entire neighbourhood. God forbid my parents let me just lie on the couch, eating fruit cups topped with microwaved marshmallows.

So I wasn't dreading going back to school, but I wouldn't say I was cheery about it either. I wouldn't say I was skipping the whole way through the halls into grade nine homeroom. Over the summer there was some sort of tectonic shift beneath the school and I spent the first week wandering around like a new student, even though I spent a thousand hours in this purgatory last year. I was always on the wrong floor or walking into the wrong classroom, thirty pairs of eyes laser-zapping me in the chest. Things still aren't quite right, as though everyone is walking on a tilt — at least that's the way it looks through my eyes.

Kids are talking about what went on between me and Max, but it's hard to figure out exactly what they're saying because I get all my information from Kate and she was occupied with Elgin all summer. I thought things might be different now that we're back at school, but so far Kate's spent every lunch hour with Elgin in a little windowed alcove next to the library that no one knew even existed before Kate and Elgin started eating there. I walked by on the first day of school and Kate was curled in a ball on the floor, resting her head in his lap. It's probably the most romantic thing I've ever seen.

Today I found a note in my locker that said, *Quit spreading STDs* — anonymous, of course. I was scurrying by the alcove, ready to skip out and go home early, when Kate called out to me. "You coming tonight?" I had no idea what she was talking about, but I said, *Yeah, yeah, see you there*, and found out from Rana where the party was.

On the bus, I sit near the front, as far away as I can get from a group of kids from my grade. We all get off at the same stop, and I hold back, waiting for them to get far enough ahead so I can follow them to the party without them noticing me. The house is near the top of Montroyal, two blocks from my old elementary school, in one of those stuccoed Vancouver Specials kids always want to trash. As soon as I walk through the front door, I catch sight of Max's ratty old toque weaving through the crowded living room, so I head down a flight of stairs and end up in the laundry room, where it's so warm and cozy I think, *What's the harm in staying here awhile?* I turn the dryer on even though it's empty, the room filling with the smell of fabric softener and warm socks, and lie back, letting the vibrations jiggle my brain. It's a good solution because it's impossible to hear my heart thumping in my chest over the racket.

Max's name has become a joke—no one knows how it started. *MAX.* At the beginning of the school year, his name began appearing all over, scrawled on lockers with sharpie, dug into the wood tops of desks, scribbled on the doors of the bathroom stalls. It's nothing but his name, but it's become a swear word like *fuck* or *slut*. If his name ends up on your locker you scrub it off. Sometimes I hear it whispered at my back like a dirty secret. Lately I've been pretending to have headaches. It's good for getting out of things—gym class, school presentations, lunch in the cafeteria. My mother took me to the family doctor yesterday. "There's nothing wrong with you," he said. "You're in perfect health." It was almost an accusation.

Kate opens the laundry room door, music pouring in around her. "This is sad," she says.

"I was waiting for you." I sit up cross-legged to make room for her.

"You need to get a life," she says, hopping up beside me and resting her head on my shoulder.

"I have one," I say. "How was your summer?"

"Fantastic!" Kate doesn't mention anything about abandoning me. We pick up as though nothing has changed. She's in a great mood, better than I've ever seen, and it makes me realize how badly I miss her.

"Is he out there?" I ask.

"Yeah, he's out there," she says. Her cheeks are pink. Drama turns her on. "I'm not staying in here all night."

"I know," I say, bringing my legs to my chest and dropping my head on my knees.

"Fine, a few more minutes, but then we go out there."

Elgin opens the laundry room door. "What are you doing in here?"

"Now it really is a pity party," Kate says.

"I want him to disappear," I say, closing my eyes. I think they both assume I mean Max, but I actually mean Elgin.

"You guys are so bitchy," he says, sitting on a laundry hamper and pulling a baggie of mushrooms out of his coat pocket. "What's so bad about Max anyway?"

"There's nothing bad about him—" I say.

"He's strange," Kate says, holding out her hands.

"He dropped acid. He's so messed up right now he probably doesn't even know you're here." Elgin places a tangle of slug-like mushrooms into Kate's cupped palms. "I don't think *he* even knows he's here."

"You could've baked us some brownies or something," Kate says, grabbing the bottle of water Elgin hands to her and swallowing the mushrooms with one big gulp. "Didn't even taste them."

I do the same and taste the earth—dirt, dead leaves and the bottoms of everyone's shoes.

"I did mine already," Elgin says. "Let's go."

"You'll feel better around lots of people," Kate says.

"Right," I say, following them out the door. "Sure I will."

The living room is packed with kids, but Max is nowhere in sight. There's still a buzz in the house, though, like a mosquito in a dark bedroom. Rana sees me through all the people and waves me over to the couch where she's sitting. "I'm so glad you're here," she says, gazing up at me with this expectant look like she's waiting for me to do a cartwheel. Kate turns away to find someone else to talk to—she doesn't even pretend to like Rana. I shrug and squeeze onto the couch between her and two kids playing video games, my bum sinking into the crack between the cushions where there are crumbs and loose change.

Lately I've been doing more stuff with Rana and somehow she's come to the conclusion she's my new best friend, and maybe she is now. Maybe that's how friendships happen. The couple of times I did leave my parents' place over the summer, I hung out at Rana's house against my wishes—I was forced by total boredom. Her house is cold and smells like mildew and her mother always asks us to be quiet, but her Dad owns a sandwich shop, so at least there are always good cold cuts in the fridge. We sit at her kitchen table, whispering and eating deli slices rolled into tubes, and every half hour or so she asks me if I'm having fun and I tell her I'd have more fun if she stopped asking me that. We were eating mint chocolate chip ice cream one afternoon and when her father came home we had to hide our bowls on our knees under the table. The whole place makes me nervous. Rana acts like her house is the most normal home on earth and maybe to her it is. I sat with my bowl of ice cream melting on my knees while Rana's dad asked me questions about school—what subjects I liked, if I played a musical instrument, if I was interested in sports. When he left, Rana set her bowl on the table and went back to eating as if nothing was out of the ordinary.

"What are you guys doing?" Rana says, peering into my eyes and I wonder if I look high even though I'm not feeling anything yet.

"Shrooms." I look for Kate, but she's disappeared into the crowd. It's no fun being high with someone who's not—all you do is worry the whole time about being too high.

"Can I have some?" Rana asks.

The TV explodes in pulpy blood. "Dead!" one of the kids shouts, fist-pumping and punching his friend in the leg. "Next level!"

"Elgin gave them to me," I say.

"I'll find him." Rana gets up from the couch and weaves through a bunch of kids crammed around the stereo. I sink further between the cushions, watching the guys twist the video controls and grimace with concentration. Their faces are a weird combination of slack and serious, and I can't tell if they're stoned or just really into their game. I'm so caught up watching them, I barely notice Elgin slide in beside me on the couch. He has to tap me on the shoulder to ask me if I feel anything yet, and I say no. "Rana was looking for you," I say.

"Who?" Elgin lights a joint and passes it to me.

"No one," I say, taking a puff. "Forget it."

The voices in the room grow louder and I start going *sh, shh, shhh*, but no one seems to want to listen to me. Elgin looks over at me and starts laughing. "Now do you feel it?" he says, and I say, "Ah!" and let out a whole bunch of phony laughter even though I'm terrified.

"Cunt!" One of the kids has beaten the other and they wrestle on the couch. I move onto the armrest to get out of their way and Elgin disappears into the kitchen, coming back with a beer to finish watching the fight from a safe distance. One kid has the other in a headlock asking, *You had enough, pussy*, and the other one keeps saying *cunt, cunt*.

Last week in science class someone wrote *whore* on my desk in purple pen. There was a large, dripping penis under the word. I tried wiping it off with my hand, but it was permanent. When Max walked into class, he looked at me for the first time in a while. He looked really sad and it made me feel a whole hell of a lot worse. I poured Liquid Paper on the desk, and the teacher sent me to Paul, the school counsellor/drama teacher, who starts his classes with a circle massage. "Why vandalize?" He sat in a chair with his elbows on his desk, his hands cupping his chin, making an exaggerated sad face. It was ridiculous. He looked like a five-year-old. I didn't even answer him.

"I'm fucked." Elgin's in a ball on the couch, rubbing his knees. Someone grabs the joint out of my hand and goes running out onto the porch, saying, "Guys, you can't smoke in here."

"Why'd you give away my joint?" Elgin says. He's stopped giggling.

"Sorry." I scrunch my eyebrows together and concentrate

on him. "Why are you angry at me?"

"Cause you gave away my joint." He lies back on the couch. "Now there's nothing to do."

We sit together for a while without speaking, staring at the blue TV screen, and when I turn to ask Elgin how long mushrooms last, he's gone and in his place are two kids kissing. I walk around the house looking for Kate, catching glimpses of her, but by the time I get anywhere she's already gone. I start to worry she's doing it on purpose, and once I start worrying about Kate, I start worrying about a lot of other things. I think about the dripping penis and STDs. I wonder if Max was the one who told the entire school what we did at the bush party or if it was Kate because she likes to talk. The thought is on the verge of making me sick when I almost knock Kate over in the kitchen. She's leaning against the wall, shoulder to shoulder in deep conversation with Adrienne. My stomach flops and I catch her by the arm, Adrienne sneering at me as I pull Kate into the hallway. "Are you telling people things?" My body is so relaxed, I've lost control of my face. I feel like it's melting right down the front of my shirt, but then I realize I'm crying. My tear ducts become a problem when I'm messed up. They have a high probability of malfunctioning.

"Telling people what?" Kate's smile is twisting like a snake's tail.

"I think I'm having a bad trip."

"No you're not, you're definitely fine," she says, grabbing me by the shoulders. She shakes me. "You're fine."

"Yeah, keep shaking me. That feels good."

Kate walks me outside to the backyard where kids stand around in large groups or hang out in the tents, hot-boxing or making out. Max is walking around the yard making fireballs with hairspray and a lighter and pissing everyone off. Every time he gets close to us I grab Kate's arm. "Get lost," Kate says, shooing him as he passes us. He takes a step closer to me and without meaning to I scream. The noise frightens all of us. "I said fuck off," Kate says, stepping between us. "Can't you see how afraid she is of you?" He looks high out of his tree. "Let's go somewhere else," Kate whispers, wrapping her arm around me protectively and leading me along the side of the house. The front yard is empty, with only a few small groups of people chatting on the street. With the wide vacant yard and the stars flowing like streamers over my head, everything feels much better. Elgin's sitting on the porch alone, looking sad, so Kate hands him a joint and we all smoke a bit together and then everyone cheers up. "See, it all works out," I say, before spinning off across the lawn. Kate joins me, grabbing my hands so we can twirl together, but we fall so often that eventually we just lie in the grass.

"I can taste the moon," I say.

"What's it like?" Kate asks. She opens her mouth.

"Kind of acidic." I rub the back of my hand over my tongue. "It's horrible."

Max comes stumbling out the front door and trips down the porch steps, ignoring all of us. He wanders down the street away from the party and I feel happier than I ever thought possible. "I'm so much better now," I say to Kate.

We climb onto the stone planters beside the front steps and throw ourselves onto the grass, saying over and over, *It doesn't hurt, it doesn't hurt.* Elgin stretches out on the steps and closes his eyes. Without him watching us, things don't seem as much fun, so Kate and I sit in the grass side by side and stare at the house. It looks so boring from the outside, with the curtains drawn and the porch light flickering. A group of kids stream out the front door, down the steps, and into the street. A couple people say hi to Kate as they go by and Adrienne is with them, trailing at the back. She smiles at me and mouths the word *whore*. "You're the whore," I yell at her as she walks by, but she doesn't turn around. There's something about the way Kate sits in the grass—really still, focused on the tan stucco—that makes me feel so sad. "Why don't we hang out anymore?" I say, after all the kids have disappeared up the street.

"We can," Kate says. "It's not impossible."

"I wish things were different."

The porch light goes off and we're surrounded by the dark night. After a few seconds the stars get brighter.

"Different how?" Kate asks.

"Just easier," I say. "The way things were before."

Elgin sits up on the stairs and rubs his face. "Hello?" When he calls out, for some reason we don't move or say anything. He stands and goes back into the house, a sliver of light shooting across the lawn toward us before disappearing again.

"I'd never want things to be different." Kate lies back in the grass and stretches her arms overhead, smiling up at the sky. "I think the moon tastes nice. Like almonds."

I don't know how to explain to Kate how wrong she is about everything. This time I learn to control my tears and they only trickle out of my eyes silently. Kate leans over my face, her hair tickling my cheeks. She says, "Okay, let's be different then. We can just BE different." Right away the tears evaporate, and for most of the night I believe her, until I hear her later, when we're back inside the party, telling Rana she should BE different too.

I WAKE UP IN the morning on the grass in front of Kate's tent, shivering so hard my teeth clack together. The lawn is covered in dew and the sky's an uncertain silver, like the day hasn't yet decided what kind of day it wants to be. I unzip the tent to find Kate and Elgin buried under blankets. Inside the house, I step carefully around sleeping kids. I have to wake up some guy in the bathtub so I can pee, and then I dig through my pockets, lining up coins on the bathroom counter and praying for enough to get home on the bus.

I'm walking across the front yard when I find Max. He's in the bushes, halfway into the neighbour's property, like he's fallen asleep while trying to escape something. I shake his leg and then give it a tug. He sits up, staring at me like he doesn't recognize who I am. His arms are cut up, short, bloody slashes running diagonally from his wrists to his elbows. There's a piece of broken beer bottle in the grass. We both look at his arms like they aren't his own. I pull him up, taking him next door to find help, and it's like guiding a small child by the shoulders. I don't say anything. I don't say, *Max, what happened*, or *Max, are you okay*, or *Max, what the fuck, you can't do stuff like that*. There are so many things I could say, but I say nothing.

I guide him with the tips of my fingers, barely touching him, to a stranger's front yard. We stand on the porch together and Max stares out at the street while I ring the doorbell.

When an older woman in her housecoat answers the door, I realize I have no words to explain. I turn Max gently to face her so she can see what he has done.

ON OUR LAST DAY at Outdoor School they gathered everyone in the large field beside the parking lot for a game of Predator-Prey. They assigned all the kids an animal — bear, owl, skunk, coyote, squirrel. The point was to eat. The predators ate the prey by tapping them on the shoulder. The prey found cardboard food tickets in ice cream buckets scattered around the forest. The counselors were disease and they could eat anything. They set the boundaries for us: to the right, the river and mountains; to the left, the highway; straight ahead we could go as far as the power lines. Kate and I were deer. We stuck together from the start. I made sure to stand next to her before we were given the signal to hide — three long whistle blows. We had three minutes alone in the forest before the predators were let loose. You could hear them howling and barking. Max was a wolf. You could pick out his yowl, short and yippy like he really wanted to get out there, like he couldn't wait. While we ran, Kate laid out a plan. We'd find a spot to hide, and later, once the predators had tired themselves out, we would go find the food buckets. We ran past some kids hiding in a hollowed out tree, one of them laughing hysterically. "They'll find you there," Kate said, as we went by. "Idiots," she shouted back to me.

The whistle blew again: one long shriek, signalling the release of the predators. We found a path along the river that led deep into the forest and Kate pulled me down the side of a slope, both of us sliding through the mud, landing next to the river. The water was shallow and the riverbed bare in spots. We crept along the narrow bank until we found a small cave in the roots of a tree where water had eroded the dirt. Crouched in the tangle of roots, our shoes sunk in the mud, Kate pulled me close, hooking her arm around my waist. We plugged our noses against the stench of rotting salmon, the greasy humps of their decaying bodies all down the drained riverbed. Kate's eyes were sharp, her muscles tensed for a quick escape. I could feel my blood speeding through my veins. Above us we listened to the stamp of feet through the forest, the shouts as kids were caught. Counsellors yelled at the ones who were tackling. We shook with silent laughter and the exhilaration of hiding. Kate pressed a hand over my mouth. "Quiet," she whispered, but her eyes shone. We had found a good spot.

We huddled in our hole until the game was almost over, the forest gone quiet so all we could hear were the leaves turning and falling around us. Weaving through the trees, Kate spotted a food bucket behind a large pine, little tickets scattered across the ground in greedy hunger. Neither one of us heard Max coming up the path behind us as we stooped to grab as many tickets as we could, but Kate saw him first. She dashed off, crashing through a tight thicket of bushes, a trail of tickets fluttering behind her. I froze exactly like a deer would. I pressed my back to the tree as Max approached slowly, his breathing calm and shallow, his eyes over every inch of me as they looked for any twitch of an escape. He raised his two hands, palms cupped inches from each other as though I were a small bird he was trying to trap. As he got closer, I got smaller and smaller until his two hands came down, resting gently on top of my shoulders. "Got you," he said.

We all waited a long time for Kate to get caught. There must have been at least sixty kids sprawled out on the big field under the power lines, all of us waiting for her. Eventually, they had to send counsellors in to look for her. I never told anyone where Kate might be.

Max was the best predator, having caught the most prey. He paced the edge of the field, desperate to go out and find her, but the counsellors said no. They said the last thing they needed were two kids lost in the forest. One was bad enough.

~

KATE CALLS TO TELL me Max jumped off the Lions Gate Bridge. I'm sitting downstairs in the family room watching TV. Kate starts to cry on the phone. I haven't talked to her in months. She says, "I thought you'd want to know." She tells me they found Max floating in the water around Ambleside Beach and the memorial service is this weekend. I want to talk to her, but I just say thanks and hang up the phone.

On the TV, girls are pinching the skin on their thighs and stomachs. I go to the bathroom and try to throw up, but I can't. I look in the mirror and pull the skin under my eyes, but I don't cry. My hair is soft and wavy, the way it looks sometimes when I wake up. It looks good and I wish I had someplace to go, but lately on the weekends all I do is watch TV with my parents. Sometimes I go to Rana's to watch a movie or play Monopoly, but most of the time I'm too tired. Mom thinks I should go see the doctor again because I like to take long naps in the afternoon after I get home from school. She asks me why I sleep so much and I tell her it's schoolwork, but the real reason is because sleep is so easy.

I sit on the bathroom floor and stare at the quilted pattern on the toilet paper roll, trying to make myself feel guilty, but there's nothing inside of me. Even with all this emptiness there's no room for Max here. I pull one of the towels down from the rack and roll it into a pillow. I can sleep anywhere now.

AFTER THE MEMORIAL SERVICE, Kate stands smoking in the shade of the tall hedges beside the funeral home. I walk over to say hello and we stand together quietly for a minute looking past the cemetery and over the trees toward the highway. "I didn't sleep last night," Kate says finally. Her face is cool, almost cold. People gather and mill around the parking lot. Max's older brother is standing by the front doors talking with someone, absentmindedly plucking leaves from a bush.

"Can I bum a smoke?" I say. Kate hands me her pack. She tilts her head to examine me until I feel uncomfortable. I pause when I see there's only one cigarette left. "Smoke it. Enjoy," she says. She has a new expression, something she does with her lips, fattening them into a pout to punctuate her sentences.

When I introduced myself to Max's mother, I shook her hand and said, "Hi, you don't know me." She was walking down the long line of people waiting to get into the funeral home. I was staring at the poster board by the front door with Max's school picture from last year pinned to it, his hair

combed and neatly parted to the left in a way I've never seen
him do it before. Usually his hair hung down kind of scraggly
and the most he'd do was tuck it behind his ears. I was distracted thinking about how his hair was his best feature, when
his mother appeared in front of me with her hand extended. I
wasn't prepared for her dull, river-stone eyes, flat and lifeless.
I was grateful when Kate leaned past me and took her hand.

I smoke quickly. "Where's Elgin?"

"Elgin?" Kate seems confused by the question. "At home."

"Oh." I focus on the burning tip of the cigarette. "I thought
he'd be here."

"No." Kate shrugs, ashing in the hedge. "He hates funer-
als." She turns her gaze back to the distant highway noise. "I
felt this duty to come. We weren't close with him like you."

"I wasn't close with him," I say, maybe too quickly. I'm
glad I didn't cry during the service. I thought about whether I
should try to, but now I'm glad I didn't.

"Well, you guys did get together that one time," Kate says,
turning to look over the crowd, to look anywhere but at me.
"That must mean something."

"Yeah, but—" I look back at the funeral home. The doors
are closed and someone is locking them now. The cops said
Max wasn't high when he jumped from the bridge. I can't
decide if that's a good thing or a bad thing. I guess it doesn't
mean much of anything when the result is the same.

"I don't mean anything by it," Kate says. "I just mean it
must be harder for you."

"I know." My fingers fiddle with the hem of my shirt.

"And I didn't spread those rumours about you," she says
all of a sudden. She squints into the crowd as though she's

looking for the person who did. "I know you think it was me."

"What rumours?" I say, pretending to have no idea what she's talking about.

"You know, that you've slept with a bunch of people."

I nod; I've learned it's better to say almost nothing if you want to keep up a charade.

"I mean, I know you're not a slut or anything, obviously. I don't know why people are saying that," Kate says matter-of-factly.

"It's fine." I shrug my shoulders.

"I guess so," Kate says, "if you don't care."

Max's mother is standing at the edge of the cemetery, staring at a tree. She looks like she's being held up by a piece of thread. Someone should be standing beside her.

"So," Kate says, butting out her cigarette, "what are you doing tonight?"

"Nothing." I was planning to go to bed early, but I don't tell that to Kate.

"Want to go to the dam?" She's already heading for the bus stop, talking to me over her shoulder. "It would be good to hang out. We'll, like, remember Max and stuff."

"Okay." I have no idea if she hears me. I stand there waiting, smoking my cigarette down to the filter, until the bus comes and she gets on.

As I'm leaving, someone puts Max's mother into a car. They have to bend her knees and lift her legs inside.

THE BUS IS FULL of night skiers and boarders as it travels up Capilano Road. I get off near the base of Grouse. There's still snow on the mountain even though it's spring, and I stuff my hands in my pockets, making my way across the street. The mountains are so tall it's like they're folding over, the last colours of the day gone now, black inking itself out of the trees into the sky. At the base of Grouse, the reservoir is as still as a mirror, reflecting the icy caps of the mountains. It all feels like glass, as if any loud noise—even one from far away—could shatter everything to pieces.

When I get to the dam Kate's not there yet. I peer over the edge and watch the water pour down, a mist coating the bottom of the canyon and winding through the trees, making the rocks sparkle in the dark. I pull a stone from my pocket— I always bring stuff to throw into the dam—and toss it into the arc of water, losing sight of it almost as soon as it leaves my hand. The longer I stare at the spiralling water, the more I feel as though I'm falling, but I never find the rocks below, I just keep spinning out of control, unable to grasp anything or anyone around me. In a lot of ways I feel like Max dragged me down with him. If he knew he was going to end it all, why did he let me get close to him at Mosquito Creek? He could have said, *I'm fucked up. Stay away.*

I can hear Kate before I see her, her laugh ricocheting through the trees. I turn to face the dam to hide my disappointment when I see Elgin with her. "Sorry we're late," she calls as they walk toward me hand in hand. They're both drinking beer.

"I just got here," I say.

"Want one?" Elgin pulls a can from his knapsack and throws it at me without waiting for my answer.

"Thanks," I say, cracking it open and flicking the tab into the gully.

"We used to chuck things down there," Kate says, grinning as she peers over the edge. "Your math book and my crappy runners."

"I almost failed math," I say.

"Those runners were ugly. I had to quit track and field because my mom wouldn't buy me a new pair," Kate says, wrapping an arm around Elgin's waist. "We were so stupid."

Elgin leans over the edge and sticks out his tongue, trying to taste the mist. "This place makes me feel really insignificant."

"You're totally stoned," Kate laughs.

He grins, slamming back the rest of his beer and launching the can in a graceful arc over the falls. Kate climbs up onto the concrete wall and straddles it. "Remember when we used to play that game at the cliffs?"

"Kate," Elgin says, "get off there. You're high."

"Do you remember?" she says to me, ignoring him.

"It's gone now," I say. I didn't notice she was high at first, but now I can hear the effects of the weed in her voice, the heavy-tongued silliness.

"What do you mean gone?" Her voice echoes off the rocks below.

"Yeah. The cliff, it's like a condo development now," I say.

"What?" Kate pushes herself onto her knees, a cat on the fence. She looks sad, but I can't tell if it's genuine or an act or the weed making her phony. "But that was our place. We went there almost every day in grade seven."

"I'll give you a toke if you get down," Elgin says, lighting a joint and waving it in front of her face.

"I don't need your skunky pot." Kate slowly pushes herself

up to a standing position, holding her arms out for balance. "I was always better than you at that game," Kate laughs, loud and forced. "Braver."

"Get down," Elgin says, his voice sharp. Suddenly he looks sober. He grabs one of Kate's pant legs.

"Let go." She shakes him off and takes careful steps, placing one foot slowly in front of the other, pointing her toes like a ballerina. "You wouldn't do this, would you?" she says, smiling at me.

"Get down now. I'm serious." Elgin goes to grab her again and she takes a wide step back.

"Fuck off," she says, and I can see there are tears in her eyes. "Just look at me," she says, holding her arms above her head. "Do I look insignificant?"

"No," Elgin says. "You look really fucking special right now."

"Kate, you're going to fall," I say, holding out my hand to her. "Please."

"Fine." Kate does a pirouette then takes my hand and hops off the wall, casually wiping a tear off her cheek.

"Why do you do shit like that?" Elgin says. All the mellowness has left him and he's pacing now.

"For thrills." Kate plucks the joint from his fingers. "Don't you ever get bored of yourself?"

"I get bored of this shit." Elgin squints through a puff of her smoke. "You want to be fished out of that river and forgotten."

"What, like Max?" Kate says. She takes a long drag. "Max was messed in the head. He couldn't handle anything. He couldn't handle school and he couldn't handle his parents splitting and he couldn't handle girls. Right?" Kate says, look-ing at me for affirmation. "He couldn't even handle you."

"I don't know," I stammer, caught off guard by Kate's ques-tion. "I don't know why he did it."

"Leave her alone," Elgin says, turning back to the dam.

"What?" Kate looks at me, but I pretend not to notice. "I didn't mean anything by it."

"Just ease up, Kate," Elgin says over his shoulder. "You're the one who wanted to come here."

"Sorry," she says, stretching out the word and clasping her hands in a prayer. "I'm sorry for stating the shitty truth." She passes the joint back to Elgin.

"I don't want any more," he says.

"You know what the truth is?" I say, quietly. "The truth is, until the other day I hadn't thought about Max in months."

We all stand staring at the ground.

"I have to pee," Kate says, striding away into the forest.

"She's not dealing with this very well," Elgin says, without turning to me. He's still looking out over the reservoir. "She's been crying at night." I'm not sure if I believe him. There's silence underneath the roar of the water. After a while he turns to me and says, "Why'd you guys stop hanging out, anyway?"

I examine his profile, his thin lips and high cheekbones, his soft eyebrows and the curls of hair at the base of his neck. His eyes are always dark and intense, even when he's telling a joke. I think about saying because of you or making an excuse about being busy with school. I wait too long to speak, and then finally I say, "I don't know."

Elgin seems to accept the answer as the one he expected. I wonder if he's asked Kate the same question. "She's weird sometimes," he says, almost to himself. "She gets obsessed and then just sort of drops people."

"Yeah, I guess. It doesn't make her sad." I mean the last part as a question, but my voice comes out flat and dull. Elgin puts an arm around my shoulder. "I'm fine," I say, but he pulls me closer and wraps both arms around me. I nestle in closer to him, his breath in my ear. For a second it feels like he's going kiss me, but he doesn't. Kate's been gone awhile and I wonder if she's watching us from a distance—part of me hopes she is.

When she comes out of the trees Elgin doesn't move. I try to edge away, but he holds me tightly so I let myself sink back against him and try to look nonchalant. Kate stands in front of us with her hands on her hips. It's the first time I've seen her look awkward. She looks at Elgin then looks at me, propping herself up against the wall next to us. "You guys talking about me?"

"Yeah," Elgin says. I can tell by the way he says it he wants to mess with her.

"What'd you talk about?" she says.

"We talked about why you two aren't friends anymore." Elgin finally lets me go.

"What do you mean, not friends anymore?" Kate says.

"I never said that." I look at Elgin. "Tell her I didn't say that."

"I'll have another," Kate says. Elgin grabs two more beers from his backpack, handing one to Kate and cracking the other.

"So what, we're not friends anymore?" Kate says, looking at me.

"Elgin, why would you say that?"

He shrugs and laughs, suddenly indifferent to the whole situation. "I'm going back to the car. I'm gonna to put on some music and smoke some more weed. Come if you want." He walks off in the direction of the parking lot. "Come in peace," he yells over his shoulder.

Kate's watching the falls. She looks angry, the mist and the noise engulfing her. Her anger is mute, but I can feel it like a heat coming off her body. She chugs her beer. "Want to go to the car?" I ask. I say it so quietly I don't think she's heard me. When she turns, her eyes have gone cool again and she's smiling. "No, I don't want to go to the car," she says. I feel like I'm being lured into something and back away from her instinctively. "You know we came here for you," she says, her smile broadening. The words should sound kind, but they don't.

"What do you mean?"

In the parking lot Elgin has turned on the car, his high beams slicing through the forest.

"Elgin thinks you're lonely," she says, staring at me like she's looking for a reaction.

"I'm sad about Max." I can hear hip hop playing from the car and I take a step toward the music.

"I mean lonely all the time." Kate's smile is gone. "You should know, Elgin is being nice to you because he feels bad."

"That's not true," I say, looking Kate in the eye.

"He feels bad for you."

"We're friends."

"He's not your friend. He's nice to everyone. He's just that kind of guy," Kate says, and now she's smiling again, gently the way someone would if they were talking to a child. "I just don't want you to be confused. That's why I'm telling you this." She reaches out to rub my arm, but I pull away from her.

Elgin is making his way back from the parking lot, the headlights blacking him out. "Are you guys coming or what?"

$$\sim$$

ELGIN SAYS WE SHOULD go to Mosquito Creek to get out of the heat. It's too hot for late September—Indian summer. Everyone's prickly from it. We sleep late, skip classes. So far no one has missed us. We spend the morning in bed together eating dry cereal. The milk's gone bad. Elgin keeps the bedroom window shut against the highway noise and all I hear are our feet in the sheets and his deep breathing. We've had sex seventeen times. I keep track in my agenda book with a small x no one could decipher.

After his mom leaves for work—I wait for the shower, the teakettle, the mug in the sink, the car out of the driveway—I get up and Elgin stays in bed. He loves to sleep. The most he's ever slept is twenty-six hours straight, the night after his stepdad left. He told me he slept deeply, like someone had knocked him out. He says he never has dreams and I tell him that's impossible. Even dogs dream.

While he sleeps I look around the house. There's not much that's interesting, but it's not about finding something secret or dirty. I open the same boxes and drawers and find the same things. All their windowsills have my finger marks through the dust. The bedrooms are always messy. His mom's closet smells like body odour and something else—maybe the peppermint candies she's always sucking. They never have any fruit. I've only ever seen Elgin eat cereal and microwaved sausage rolls dipped in ketchup. The couch has deep sags, like there are invisible bodies watching TV. I don't know why it's exciting—maybe because it's not mine. Sometimes I feel like I'm not really here. It's like being a ghost or a tourist. Sometimes I think about Kate's bare feet in the exact same spots.

I crawl back into bed and run my finger along each of Elgin's eyebrows. "Wake up," I whisper. His mouth twitches and I run my finger along his lips. *Wake up, wake up, wake up, wake up.*

One year my parents took Carlie and me to Maui for Christmas. It was hot, but we strung Christmas lights on our balcony. I touched everything in the hotel room before we left—the TV, the lampshade, the towels, the hair dryer—like it was some sort of ritual. I wanted to because I loved it there. And maybe because I thought I'd never be back.

PAUL SHUTS THE DOOR and takes a seat behind his big, crappy desk. If it fell on you it would kill you instantly. I've thought about that a lot in this office. "How many classes have you missed since the beginning of the year?" He picks up a pen and taps it against his lip. I have to go see the school counsellor every time I'm late now. The secretary is so tired of giving me late slips she barely acknowledged my presence this morning. Usually she makes a big deal, staring me down, huffing at the other secretaries, her fluffy bangs fluttering around for what feels like forever before she'll fill out the slip. This morning she must have seen me coming; the late slip was sitting on the counter already filled out and she was back at her desk doing paperwork.

"I've missed a few classes," I say. "I've been sick."

"You look fine to me." When Paul smiles he shows a mouth full of abnormally long teeth. One of his incisors is dead, grey and creepy. "What made you late this morning?"

"I was sick to my stomach. Really sick. I was throwing up. Berries and seeds and something else, like animal fur or something."

"I don't think that's possible."

"No, probably not."

There's a photo sitting on the windowsill behind Paul's head. A woman sits at a table scattered with half-empty dishes. There are candles burning as though the dinner is a celebration, maybe a birthday. She's laughing and she looks young. Her hands are small like a girl's. "Is that your daughter?"

"That's my wife." Paul turns the frame away from me. "Do you have a doctor's note?"

"No. Do you think I should go to the doctor?" I look back quickly at the clock: ten to ten. Elgin's probably still sleeping. "Could I have leukemia? Kids my age get that all the time, don't they?"

"I don't think leukemia is common."

"I should get to class."

"Yes, you should, but you're here." He crosses his legs under his desk. Today he's wearing tan-coloured Birkenstocks. ˋ I find his toes offensive even from a distance. He wears sandals in the winter too, but with socks. It's hard to believe even when you're sitting right in front of him. Some girls think he's good-looking, but I don't see it. All I see is that dead tooth. "Why are you here?" Paul says. When I look up he's giving me the raised eyebrows and I wonder if he can tell I had sex this morning. He comes around and stands behind me where I can't see him and talks about my *opportunities,* my *potential,* my *budding possibilities.* He talks about flowers and loses me, then he asks me if I'm distracted by some of the guys at school.

"No," I say.

He asks me if I still think about Max, but when he says his name what I see is a puffy, bloated body busting up on the jagged rocks along Ambleside Beach, the same rocks Kate climbed down on her thirteenth birthday when we were drunk on a shared beer. Her party dress ballooned around her in the water.

"No," I say. "I don't think about Max."

Out the window Rana is smoking in the courtyard in plain view. Something has happened to her, like she decided to become a completely different person this year. She doesn't take any bullshit anymore and she gets away with everything. Somehow at school she always manages to stay below the radar. At home is a different story. She sees me sitting in the office and sticks her tongue into her cheek like she's giving a blow-job.

"You and Elgin Murphy are dating?"

I snap back to attention. "What?"

"How long have you been seeing each other?" He's sitting behind his desk once again, chin cupped in hand, leaning toward me like a girlfriend who wants all the gossip. His tactics are obvious to the point of being sad.

"We're friends." I examine Paul's face carefully and wonder

how he found out about us. When Kate and Elgin broke up the whole school was devastated, like the world stopped making sense and all hope was gone. It was a load of crap and I would have told that to anyone if anyone had bothered to ask me. Everyone wanted to know why, but there was no reason, things just died the way things do and Elgin and Kate went back to eating lunch in their regular spots, Kate in the drama room with friends, and well, no one ever really saw Elgin eat lunch before he was with Kate, so he just went back to wandering through the field and the smoke pit and now I guess he's with me. The alcove beside the library is still empty.

"We hang out sometimes."

Paul is smiling and nodding, wanting a little more. Could he actually be spying on me? Would Paul crouch in the pine tree outside my bedroom window? Can you climb a tree in Birkenstocks? I squint and he picks up his pen again and runs it along his bottom lip. "You're friends, though?" he says.

"Yeah, that's what I said."

"He's barely attended any classes this year," Paul says, flipping through attendance records. "Do you know what's going on with him?"

"Nope."

Paul looks out the window and catches Rana taking a long drag from her cigarette. She drops it quickly and heads for the cafeteria. "I worry about you guys," he says, shrugging his shoulders like it doesn't really matter whether he does or not. It's hard to tell who he's talking about specifically. "If you see Elgin, tell him I'd like to talk to him? Let's make grade ten a better year, okay?" He goes over to his bookcase and fidgets with the spines of the books, pulling one out and then pushing it back in. "I gave you my cell number if you ever need to talk."

"Sure." I pick up my books and make a phony attempt to look like an enthusiastic student.

"I'm here for you guys." He pats my shoulder and squeezes my arm. "Use me." The warning bell for second block rings. As I stride out of the room, I look at Paul over my shoulder and catch him staring right at my ass.

I MAKE IT INSIDE the portable before the second bell rings, but I can feel Mrs. Sasaki watching me the whole way to my desk. She makes some kind of joke about having to put an exponential number next to my absences. It's stupid and everyone laughs and then we learn how to graph the sine or the cosine or something like that. The portable is like a huge oven. I imagine the principal opening the door at the end of class and finding us all baked and crispy. Rana is sitting beside me gouging a big long mark down her desk with her compass. She turns to me and mouths *this sucks dick* and I wonder where she suddenly got such a foul mouth. She pulls her cigarettes out of her backpack, stuffing them into her pocket and raising her hand to go to the bathroom. I slump down in my chair and check my phone. Elgin's sent me two text messages already.

When the bell rings, I'm one of the first ones out of the class and I go stand in the thick weeds behind the portable to call Elgin. I twist a long piece of grass around my finger and after the first ring he picks up. "Let's go for a swim," he says. I can tell by his voice he's pacing. He hates being in the house by himself.

Mrs. Sasaki walks around the corner of the portable and I know she's trying to catch me smoking. I turn my back to her, but she walks around in front of me to tap her watch before heading back to the classroom. The bell sounds and I peek around the portable. The parking lot is quiet and everyone is in their classes. I can hear the sound of hundreds of pencils scratching.

CARS *WHOOSH* ABOVE ON the overpass as Elgin pedals hard up the steep part of the trail that leads to Mosquito Creek. I'm perched on the back of his bike, one hand on his shoulder for balance. The sweat collecting on his T-shirt forms a wet band down the curve of his back and two others under his arms. He stops by a natural pool deep enough to swim in and we strip down to our underwear. The leafy trees glow pale green in the heat and the evergreens look dry enough to ignite, like one misplaced cigarette butt could send the whole forest up in flames. In the distance I can still hear the cars speeding along the highway. My gaze floats up to the big pine trees and I think about how from far away the forest looks perfect, like every tree has been chosen for its spot on the mountain, but up close it's messier. There are rotten logs with hornets' nests and thick, sticky spiderwebs and dried pine needles stuck to everything. Kate and I used to come here when we were younger and I wonder if she's the one who first brought Elgin here. "I like this spot," I say, slipping into the pool, pretending I've never been here before.

"My mom and I used to pick blackberries under the highway," Elgin says, jumping into the water. "They always tasted like gasoline."

"That's disgusting." I float on my back, let Elgin slip his fingers through mine and pull me around the pool. "Why'd you eat them?"

"They were there," he says, releasing me and ducking underwater beneath my body, coming up the other side and spraying water droplets over me. "I kind of like the taste," he says. "I'll go pick you some."

"No, thanks." I close my eyes. He traces my body with his fingertips. The mushrooms we took at his house start to kick in, every sensation multiplying.

"You should stay over tonight," he says, his lips brushing my ear underwater, sending shivers over my scalp, down my spine to my fingertips.

"I don't think your Mom will like that."

"Who gives a shit?"

"She doesn't like me." For some reason this makes me laugh, maybe it's the mushrooms. The evergreens dip down and I stretch my arms up trying to touch them.

"What do you tell your parents?"

"That I'm at Kate's." The water feels like oil over my skin, colours itself pink and then back to green. "My shrooms are really working," I say, rubbing my hands over my face, staring wide-eyed at Elgin.

"Really? I don't feel anything. Maybe I need more." He wades over to his pile of clothes and pulls the baggie of mushrooms out of the pocket, eating another stem. "They still think you're friends?"

"With Kate?" I'm playing with my cheeks, hollowing them with my fingertips. "My parents don't know anything."

We climb out of the water and sit on a flat rock across

from each other, legs crossed, knees touching, transfixed, like it's hard to break eye contact. "If it's any consolation," Elgin says, "my mom hated Kate too."

"Sure, that makes me feel better."

"She called her a tramp." Elgin laughs at the word. "Who says that? She assumed we were sleeping together."

"You were." I reach out and touch Elgin's nose.

"Is that what Kate told you?" He kisses the tip of my finger.

"What do you mean?" I peer up into Elgin's face.

"Hey," he shrugs, "it's not like I didn't want it to happen."

"Why are you telling me this right now?" I hop off the rock back into the water and paddle a circle in the pool. "I'm so fucking high."

"You asked," Elgin says, kicking water at me. "Is it a big deal?"

"She lied." I swim up and pull Elgin back into the water, wrapping my legs around him.

"To who?" He pushes the wet hair out of my face.

"To everyone."

"Did she?"

"Jesus," I say. "I don't know."

A fat, angry horsefly circles the water, weaving between us. I swat at it, but it keeps coming back. It buzzes near my face and I throw myself under the water, my legs still wrapped around Elgin's waist. The iciness electrifies my skull, but I try and stay under as long as I possibly can, until the air presses against the walls of my chest and I start to get dizzy. The water is a shattered mirror and I can see Elgin, a million pieces of him, swatting and splashing at the bug. He stops and the mirror fuses. I glimpse something, more of a feeling than a sight, as he stares through the water at me. His hand reaches in and pulls me to the surface, the air burning my lungs. The horsefly dives at our faces as we climb up the rocks and grab our bundles of clothes. Elgin races down the trail like there's a cougar chasing us. I trip after him, twigs and rocks digging into the bottoms of my feet, the buzz filling my ears. We run down a hill and Elgin stops suddenly, wrestling me into his arms. He holds me close to him and covers my mouth. "What?" I say, muffled by his hand.

"Listen." The forest flutters around us in a gentle breeze, cool over my wet skin. There's nothing: no buzz, no horse-fly. Elgin takes his hand off of my mouth and kisses me, his tongue warm and heavy. When we pass back under the high-way, I pick a blackberry off the bush. Elgin was right—they taste like exhaust, but there's a sweetness in them too.

ELGIN BIKES ALONG THE highway on the way back to the house. Each car that passes brings a wave of hot air on my bare legs. He pulls over onto the grass shoulder, says, "I have to take a piss." I turn my back while he climbs into the brush along the side of the highway. A car honks as it drives by and my eyes follow unwillingly. Before I know what's happening, Elgin races out of the bushes and onto the highway. He jumps up on the meridian and pretends to surf, like the cars are ocean waves or sharks or something. "Are you stupid?" I yell, across the stream of traffic. "Come on," Elgin shouts back. He motions with his arms and almost loses balance. Something makes me think that if I am standing with him he won't fall. Cars blare their horns and people shout out their windows, *you idiot, get off the road, you're going to kill someone.* Their angry faces burst past in hot flashes. I wait for a break in the traffic and run across the highway. Elgin holds out his hands and helps me up onto the divider. "You're really stupid." I hold my arms out like a tightrope walker. Elgin takes my hands and we balance, grinning at each other.

"I love you," I say, letting the words lose themselves in the traffic. The cars whip past us, sending gusts of warm air through my wet hair. It's not how I imagined, not like flying at all.

~

PAUL'S TEACHING US SEX ED and whenever he says the word vagina I blush and hate myself. Most of our grade ten class is sitting on the gymnasium floor watching a slideshow with diagrams of deformed genitalia. Paul clicks through the pictures listing the STD that caused the damage — scabies, syphilis, gonorrhea. When a grotesquely swollen scrotum appears on the projection screen, some guy in the back row shouts *blue balls* and everyone starts laughing. Rana's sitting beside me scribbling notes on my arm. She doesn't seem to care that, from wrist to elbow, the only thing we've discussed is her hair, which now has pink streaks. Over the summer her parents separated and sold their house next to Mosquito Creek; her father moved back to Lebanon and Rana and her mother moved into a condo on the waterfront with a view of the city. The separation means Rana can get away with a lot more than usual right now (which is still hardly anything), but when she saw her mother crying at the kitchen sink this morning she decided she would wash the dye out tonight. I make tiny little braids with the streaks in the meantime. It keeps her from writing anything else on my arm.

Kate's sitting in the front row, her hair pulled back in her usual swishy ponytail, and when Paul hands out bananas and condoms she's one of the first to get one. The laugh that explodes from my mouth is a little louder than I intend. It makes Rana duck into her lap and Kate turn to scan the rows of heads accusingly. Paul gets fed up and says something like, "You guys better smarten up. This is part of your Career and Personal Planning mark."

Between bells Rana and I head to the washroom along the main hall. Usually I avoid that washroom because it's the largest one in the school and there are always long lines of girls waiting for stalls or standing at the row of mirrors. The place reminds me of a hive, but one littered with toilet paper and really bitchy honeybees and a constant buzz of gossip over the stalls. While Rana pees I stand at the mirrors fixing my hair and wait for the right moment. "Ran," I call in a clear voice over the top of the stall, "did you hear Kate lied about sleeping with Elgin? She's still a virgin." The bees pause for an infinitesimal second before resuming their activities. The stall door swings open and Rana comes stomping over to gape at me in the mirror. I use the word *pathetic* and Rana's laughing, hand over her mouth, going *holy shit, that's too good*.

As we walk down the hall we pass right by Kate's locker. She's pulling textbooks out and stuffing them in her backpack. Rana mutters the same word I used, *pathetic*, but it sounds harsher from her mouth. The strange thing is, Kate doesn't look at Rana—she looks right at me.

THE RAIN COMES DOWN hard so I stand under the awning, waiting for Carlie's blue Nova as the school empties around me.

"You look like shit," Carlie says, as soon as I buckle my seat belt. She's always pissed when she has to drive me to the mall. "When's the last time you brushed your hair?"

"I can't brush my hair."

"You can't brush your hair?" She taps her fingers on the steering wheel and throws herself back into the seat with a sigh whenever we hit a red light and I ignore her and watch the scenery: the condos, the gas stations, the antique stores. "How are you getting back?" she asks, putting on mascara while we wait at a light.

"I'll take the bus."

As the mall comes into view, Carlie accelerates, screeching around the corners in the parking lot like we're on a racetrack. She slams on her brakes for an old lady who is nowhere near the crosswalk, but almost hits two girls in tight white jeans trying to cross an intersection, honking at them as they run across the street. They give her the finger when they're safely on the other side. "You should buy yourself something," Carlie says as she pulls up to the curb. She motions to my head. "A hairband or a scrunchie."

"Shut up, Carlie." I get out of the car without saying goodbye and Carlie drives away before I've even closed the door.

The smell of sweet and sour pork, drugstore perfume, and new leather makes me dizzy as I walk through the revolving doors. The mall is dead, full of outdated stores selling greeting cards, sunglasses, and baby clothes. There are two stores selling vacuum cleaners, as if one isn't enough. Everything smells like greasy Chinese food or preteens or the elderly. Escalators lead nowhere and people either move way too fast or way too slow. At the lingerie store I dig through the sale bins and find three matching sets of bras and panties in my size. Through the window, I catch sight of Kate drifting by like a ghost, sucking on a giant Orange Julius. I duck behind one of the bins and the sales lady sneaks up behind me and asks me what I'm doing, as if I'm planning to stuff a bunch of thongs in my pockets.

I take the long way to the Bread Garden where Rana and I planned to meet up, strolling through some empty corridors and across the Bay so I'm sure not to run into Kate. The restaurant is nearly empty, rain streaking the windows, the sky fallen dark, and I pace at the glass display case while a pimply kid from my school waits unblinkingly for me to make a decision. I want to yell at him, *Blink, god dammit,* but I feel sorry for him too because his shift looks somewhat like eternal damnation. In the end I get nothing, deciding to wait for Rana to see if she'd rather split a cinnamon knot or a chocolate muffin. I take a seat next to the windows and while I'm dusting cookie crumbs off the table, Paul walks in. Something has happened to him; it's as though outside the school walls a metamorphosis has occurred that's broken him free from his cocoon of bad footwear and pitying gestures. As he stands at the counter with a newspaper tucked under his arm, ordering his coffee and picking out a danish, he seems like someone relaxed and cool and utterly unlike Paul. He's still wearing jeans, but he's also wearing a leather jacket and expensive-looking boots. It suddenly occurs to me that the Birkenstocks may be meant to connect with students, as though baring his gnarled toes shows some kind of vulnerability. When he turns to find a table, I'm staring right at him with a dopey grin on my face. "Paul!" I shout across the restaurant like it's been years since I've seen him instead of earlier this afternoon. Right away the image of a banana encased in latex flashes in my brain and I start to sweat.

"Studying hard, I see," he says, standing over my table, taking a sip of his coffee and balancing his danish on a plate in one hand.

"You can sit down," I say, pushing one of the chairs from the table with my foot.

Paul looks around the empty restaurant. "For a minute," he says, sitting down and folding his danish in half, taking a large bite. From across the table even his smell is different — pearly soap and forest sap. I watch him chew. He swallows and asks, "How are you doing? I assume better, since you haven't been to my office this week."

"Much better," I say, straightening my shoulders. "Really a lot better."

"You're attending all your classes?" Paul's chin dips to one side and he raises his eyebrows.

"Yep," I lie with a smile.

"Can't have a repeat of last year."

"Last year was really abnormal for me. It was an anomaly."

"Good word."

In the mall, outside the restaurant, I see Kate and Adrienne walk by together. Kate's oblivious, but Adrienne does a double take when she sees me and Paul. I watch them walk out the front doors, their coats pulled up over their heads against the rain. Something tingles inside of me as Paul stuffs the last bite of pastry in his mouth. "I should get going," he says, standing with his coffee. I walk out of Bread Garden with him and we stand under the awning, looking at the rain. I pull my jean jacket closed, trying to look especially cold and miserable, as I secretly scan the parking lot for Kate and Adrienne. "Do you have a ride?" Paul asks.

"Nah, I was going to take the bus," I say, looking over at the empty stop.

As I'm getting into Paul's car, Rana's coming up the street toward me, looking pissed and giving me a half-hearted wave. I pretend not to see her, bending down in the front seat to retie my shoes.

"I don't normally give my students rides," Paul says, shifting the car into reverse and pulling out of the parking spot. We drive slowly down Marine Drive, the rain enveloping everything and the wipers thwacking across the windshield. There's something about being in a car when it's pouring that makes conversation uncomplicated. Words are muffled, all the sharp edges softened and the empty spaces filled. We talk easily and for the first time about things other than school, about music and the best place for sushi on Lonsdale. I give Paul directions that take us out of the way, and when we finally reach my block I feel disappointed. I point out my house and Paul drives a little further, stopping behind a tall hedge. "Thanks," I say, as I get out of the car.

"Anytime," Paul says, smiling at me. The dead tooth could ruin everything, but for once it doesn't.

As soon as I get to my room, I call Rana to apologize. All she says is, *lucky slut.*

AFTER DINNER I GO to Elgin's to watch TV. We fall asleep on the couch, but when I wake up I'm alone in Elgin's bed and it's dark and I have no idea what time it is. I can hear his mother in the living room talking about me as I fumble for my clothes, quietly slipping them on under the sheets. She's talking about feeding me, asking why she has to work to put food in my mouth, and I can hear Elgin mumbling, but I can't make out the words. I try to find my socks, but give up and slip my bare feet into my sneaks. Their voices get louder, like they're right outside the bedroom door. "Why don't you sleep at her house?"

"Mom." Elgin's voice cracks. "Stop!"

"Let me in there. I'll tell her myself." I stand frozen at the edge of the bed, waiting for the door to swing open. There's a scuffle outside the door, then a slap, and Elgin shouts, almost growls, "Leave me alone." I've never heard Elgin like that before, like the angry words are being ripped from his guts. "I hate you. You fucking bitch." I hear spit flying and their bodies struggling against the door. His mother cries out and I open the window, highway noise flooding the room. As I hop out, and just before the bedroom door opens, I can hear Elgin sobbing, saying over and over, "I hate this house." I run across the backyard without looking back. Out the window his mother shouts, "Are you running, you little slut?" Next door a porch light flips on and I squeeze between the black-berry bushes, scratching up my arms.

At the edge of the highway, I tuck my hands in my T-shirt for warmth. I forgot my coat, but the rain has stopped, the night unexpectedly clear—moonless and cold. I wait for a break in traffic before running across the highway. Cars without drivers whip by on the dark road. I walk along the drainage ditch with my thumb out, hoping to God Carlie's blue Nova will magically appear. No one picks me up for a while, and by the time a red minivan stops on the side of the road, I'm shaking I'm so cold. A rosy-cheeked lady leans across the passenger seat, the door still locked, and sticks her head out the window. "You shouldn't be hitchhiking."

"I know," I say. "It's a bad idea." She sits in the car, exhaust spiralling up toward the stars. It doesn't look like she's going to let me in, so I start to walk down the highway to find another ride. The horn toots lightly and I walk back. "Get in," she says. "It's too cold to be standing out here with no coat." I open the door, letting the car swallow me into its warmth. There's classical music playing from the radio and a churchy feeling swells up inside me. "I'd like to take you right to your house," the lady says. "I don't mind if it's out of the way. Just make me a promise you won't hitchhike again. It's not safe for girls." I tell her the address and buckle my seat belt.

"That's not too far," she says cheerfully. She's either plump or bundled in too many layers of clothes. The buttons on her coat look like they're going to pop. "A long way if you're walking though." She looks like a mother. I know she's a mother.

"Thanks a lot," I say. She nods her head and puts on her turn signal, checking her blind spot twice before pulling out onto the empty highway.

I close my eyes and fall asleep.

THE WOMAN DROPS ME off at the entrance to the subdivision and I walk through the dead-quiet streets lined with identical homes. A mist comes up from the canyon and I get lost in all the cul-de-sacs before I find Kate's house. I walk around to the backyard and sit on the edge of the trampoline, trying to figure out how to get up to Kate's window. Someone passes back and forth behind the curtains like they're pacing or tidying up. The window casts a square of light on the grass and the air has that crackly electrical feeling like the static in my hair when I pull off my toque. A light is turned off in the room and replaced by a dimmer one, a bedroom lamp. Sitting in the middle of the trampoline with my knees pulled up to my chest for warmth, I cup my hands around my mouth and whisper, "Kate."

The room goes dark. It almost feels cold enough to snow.

THE WINTER I WAS in grade eight, it snowed for the first time in what felt like years. All night the fat flakes fell from the sky. Kate called my house all excited. She talked to my dad for a while about when the last time was it snowed like this—if ever—and my dad told stories about how they used to go skating on Lost Lagoon when he was a kid, how the water never got cold enough to freeze solid anymore. "Maybe we can go outdoor skating," Kate said breathlessly when I grabbed the phone.

The entire city shut down. I had to walk home from Lonsdale because the bus driver wouldn't venture off the main roads. Carlie and I stood in the garden grinning like dummies. In my head I kept hearing the words *winter wonderland, winter wonderland,* like I was high on drugs or something. We didn't want to move our feet the ground felt so precious. The cat came scooting by us headed straight for the door, his legs taking exaggerated leaps through the snow. I was so disappointed when Dad came barrelling through it all, dragging Carlie and me into the powder with him. The patches of grass showing through the white were so ugly. But I accepted it as something that happens—nothing could ever stay that perfect forever.

The next morning Kate called early and I was still in bed watching the snowflakes twirl madly down onto my skylight. I could hear my dad outside, the scrape of the shovel as he cleared the driveway. Kate came over and we put on winter clothes, even ski pants that we tucked into our boots. I loved the feeling of being untouchable, wrapped in wool and nylon; nothing could get to me, not the snow or the cold. I rolled around on the sidewalk, crawled through the street, lay on my back with my mouth wide open, eating the flakes like a two-year-old. "It's a perfect day," Kate said. She let herself fall in the snow, arms above her head, but for some reason she didn't look happy. The buses still weren't running and there were almost no cars on the road. Occasionally we heard an engine revving far off, but all the sounds were muffled, everything travelling long distances, as though sounds were coming right across Burrard Inlet.

We walked the whole way to Mosquito Creek. It took us almost an hour. Kate wanted to have a winter picnic. She had everything we needed in her backpack: a thermos of hot chocolate, ham sandwiches, and peanut butter cookies. The only people we saw on the way there were a group of kids near Grand Boulevard sliding down a hill on garbage bags, and an old person crossing 13th Street holding a broken umbrella with a perfect mound of snow collected on top. I kept suggesting other places we could stop for our picnic—we passed six or seven parks along the way—but Kate was determined. As we trudged up Lonsdale through the snow, she clenched her teeth, her jaw drawn in a tight line.

Once we got to Mosquito Creek, I took her mitted hand. The longer we walked, the more her enthusiasm for the day drained from her. By the time we reached the creek, she looked like she was ready to drop into a snow bank. She tried to pull her hand away a few times, but I hung on to her and we walked carefully over the boulders and rocks until we found a flat spot under the cover of some heavy evergreen branches. There was a fine dusting of snow on the ground under the tree, like someone had sprinkled icing sugar all over the pine needles. We spread out the blanket Kate had brought and unwrapped our sandwiches. The branches created a small cave of shelter and we chewed quietly, watching the snow pile up around us. "It's like a church," Kate said, pouring the hot chocolate. "I guess," I said, but I'd never been inside a church. When I looked at churches from the street, passing in a car or walking by, this was close to what I thought was inside—a quiet white perfection, something so simple and obvious. I imagined if we stayed there all day, the snow would seal up our cave and we would have our own confession booth. Kate smiled when I told her this, then she looked away, up into the tree. "My dad left this morning," she said.

For the past couple of nights, Kate told me, her mom had been sleeping in her bed. Every night, her dad came home after they'd fallen asleep, like he'd been waiting, watching from his car for the lights to go off. It didn't matter because Kate woke up every time the front door opened. Last night Kate's mom woke up too and she and Kate stared at each other for a second before her mother closed her eyes and Kate understood she should do the same. Kate pretended to sleep, but listened to her father open her bedroom door and stand there, staring at the two of them. She could hear his breathing and smell booze. Eventually he closed the door, so quietly and slowly Kate thought it might take him all night. Almost as soon as the door was closed, he opened it again and walked right into the room. Her father picked her up out of bed like she was a young child and shook her. He didn't say anything. He kept shaking her, Kate staring at him silently, and as he carried her out of the room, she saw her mother's eyelids flutter. In the living room her dad set her on a chair while he made up the couch for her to sleep on. "He was just drunk," Kate said. "But this morning he was gone and there was all this snow." It was the first time I realized Kate's life wasn't perfect.

～

"WHAT ARE YOU SUPPOSED to be?" Carlie's out the window smoking a cigarette. All I can see is her bum, but I can tell from her tone she thinks my costume is stupid.

"A corpse bride," I say, threading a needle to stitch feathers to the hem of one of Mom's white nightgowns.

"Aren't you a little old to dress up for Halloween?" Carlie says to the oak trees out the window.

"Aren't you a little old to still be living at home?"

"I'll pretend I didn't hear that." Carlie leans back into the room and gives me an uncertain once-over. "Hm."

"What?"

"You need a veil. I think I was ten the last time I wore a costume."

"Do I look like I care?" I say under my breath, concentrating on getting my stitches evenly spaced.

"Shit," Carlie says as Dad clomps up the stairs. She butts out her cigarette and grabs perfume, spritzing it around the room. I wave my arms in front of my face, saying, "Quit it." The door swings open.

"Dad," Carlie shouts. "Remember knocking?" He wrinkles his nose at the perfume, stepping back into the hallway and closing the door behind him before knocking. "Oh, for Christ's sake," Carlie says, zipping up her boots and grabbing her purse.

"Do you ghouls still need a ride?" Dad yells through the door.

"Let's go," Carlie says, flinging open the door and checking herself in the mirror one last time. She pops a piece of gum into her mouth and I hold open my hand for some, but she walks right by me. "What are you supposed to be?" Dad asks me, peering around the doorframe as Carlie stomps past him down the stairs.

"A corpse bride," I say, annoyed. I put the last feather on the slip and throw on my hoodie.

"Dad, let's go," Carlie shouts from downstairs.

The doorbell rings and I hear a bunch of little kids pushing each other around on the porch. "Trick or treat."

"Mom, where's the candy?" Carlie screams.

Dad asks me if I'm coming, but I tell him I'd rather walk and I follow him down the stairs as Carlie opens the door and

Mom brings a big bowl of treats from the kitchen. I squeeze past all the kids with their hands out. "You hoo, Frankenstein's Bride," Mom says, holding out a candy bar for me. I ignore her and make my way across the street. I can hear her behind me, saying, "Just one, now. Everyone gets one."

THE STREETS ARE SMOKY; bottle rocket squeals shriek across the night sky and the cul-de-sacs feel like war zones. I hurry along the sidewalks and cut through the park to stay off the roads, which burst with hot firecracker colours. Kids from another school are hanging out on the jungle gym. A girl with long blond hair smokes while she hangs upside down on the monkey bars, the tips of her hair brushing the dead leaves on the ground. There's a group sitting in a concrete tube in the middle of the sandbox, smoking weed. I can't see them, but I can smell the smoke and hear their voices echo out of the hollow cylinder and into the park. Someone's boots hang out one end and some guy's saying, "Can you see me? Can you see me?" Everyone's laughing like it's the funniest thing they've ever heard, but it doesn't sound like the guy is joking. Someone jumps out one end of the tube and stalks off through the park. "Fuck it. You guys are fucking fucks." From inside the tube a girl says, "Relax." The guy walks off to a car and sits in the front seat for a minute blaring metal and then comes back carrying something behind his back. A lighter flicks and he throws the thing gently into the tube. There's machinegun pandemonium as everyone shoots out the opposite end, whooping and screaming, *holy shit*. Loud pops and hot green light go firing through the tunnel and I leave the park and cross to the far side of the street. The guy who lit off the brick of firecrackers jumps onto the concrete tube and yells, "I'm the army, yeah! Fuck, yeah." One of the other guys pulls him down and they start fighting. Across from the park, little kids in fuzzy bear costumes and pirates dragging their swords knock on the neighbourhood doors, their voices sweeter than candy.

At the house party I don't recognize any of the kids sitting on the front stairs, so I duck through the hedges on the side of the house and go around the back. Kate and I were at a party here once. A bunch of guys built a bike jump in the backyard and they all smoked dope and fell off it all night. Kate got drunk on Slippery Nipples and puked in the bushes by my front porch. My mom thought it was the neighbour's golden retriever when she found the vomit the next morning.

Elgin's with friends in the kitchen, sitting on the counter beside a sink full of beer cans and a dinner plate overflowing with cigarette butts. He's dressed normally, but he has a cardboard sign around his neck that reads *serial killer.* "Good costume," I say, hopping up beside him. When I look around I realize most of the people at the party are out of high school and almost no one is wearing costumes. "What are you supposed to be?" Elgin says.

I take a sip of his beer, pretending not to hear him. "Where have you been? You haven't been at school all week."

"Thanks, Mom," Elgin smirks and his buddies laugh. While he talks with his friends about the new skate ramps they're planning to build, I pluck the feathers off my slip, letting them drift down to the kitchen floor. When I ask Elgin to follow me, he comes reluctantly, his fingers laced limply in mine while his friends make *blah blah* gestures at my back.

Outside, kids lie on their backs in a circle in the yard, their heads almost touching and their feet fanned out like the rays of a sun. Elgin leans against the side of the house lighting a cigarette and watches them. "By the way, I'm suspended," he says.

"What?" The kids are making weird movements with their hands in front of each other's faces — starbursts, elephants, waves. "For how long?"

"I don't know," Elgin shrugs. "It doesn't matter."

"What did your mom say?" I try to grab his hand, but he's stuffed it into his pocket.

"What do you think she said?" He slides down the side of the house and crouches on the walk.

"What happened?" I sit cross-legged on the cement in front of him so he has to look at me.

"What happened?" He raises his eyebrows and laughs. "Paul's what happened. You know anything about that?"

"Why would I know something?"

"Did you talk to him about me?"

"No," I say, unable to hide the hurt in my voice.

"You know people say you're sleeping with him, right?" He flicks his half-smoked cigarette into the bushes and watches my face closely, but before I can utter a word he laughs it off. "It's a joke," he says.

"What kind of joke is that?" I say, pushing myself up from the ground. I consider joining the circle of kids in the grass.

A door opens beside us and Rana stumbles out, bee-lining for me. "I've been waiting for you," she says, grabbing my arm. "You have to come with me."

"Not now," I say, trying to shake her from my elbow.

"Trust me," Rana says close to my ear. "You want to see this."

We all go back into the house through the basement, where kids are packed wall to wall, but when I turn to look behind me Elgin is gone. Rana leads me down a dark hallway, the noise from the party growing dimmer, and I can hear someone humming. At the end of the hallway, she shoves me gently toward a door that's partially ajar and I push it wide open. An older guy is sitting on the bathroom floor, his head against the wall and his eyes closed, tapping the beat he's humming on the tub. Kate's lying beside him on the lino-leum. She's passed out beside the toilet bowl, an arm wrapped around its base, her cheek pressed to the floor as the guy strokes her pale face absentmindedly. Her jeans are unbut-toned. The guy opens his eyes. "Do you know her?" he asks.

I shut the door and walk quickly down the hallway with Rana trailing behind me. I look in every room in the house, but Elgin is gone. Outside the kids are still lying in the grass. One of Elgin's friends pushes up the driveway on his skate-board. "Do you know where Elgin is?" I ask as he flips his board and goes back down the driveway. "Left," he says, glid-ing past me with a smile.

"Where'd he go?" I say. Rana grabs my hand and squeezes it.

"Didn't say?" He circles me on the board. "I've got weed. Wanna go somewhere?"

Before I can say anything, Rana's pushing me across the lawn, telling the skater to *get a life*. There's a bad feeling every-where, around the house, in the sky, climbing the walls of my stomach. The skater follows us on his board to the end of the road until Rana starts screaming bloody murder.

RANA IS STILL HOLDING my hand in the elevator on our way to her condo. She tells me she's too stoned and asks me if I will stay with her awhile. My heart is in my throat, but I say sure, why not. The weed was laced, she tells me, with something bad—crack, arsenic, Drano, rat poison. Before she opens the front door, she clutches my hoodie and tells me if I wake up her mother she'll kill me. I say sure, no problemo, I'll be a mute.

We take off our shoes in the hallway and slipper-foot over the condo's thick carpets into the dark living room with its view of the city stretching out on the other side of the inlet. "I'd rather be somewhere else," I say, pressing myself right up against the floor-to-ceiling windows, the way I always do when I visit Rana.

"Thanks, asshole," she says, rubbing my greasy nose marks off the glass with her shirt sleeve.

"You know what I mean," I say. "Do you have any food?"

We lie on the carpet because her mother's furniture is uncomfortable—all carved wood and expensive upholstery—and eat honeyed pastries, licking our fingers. Rana takes me out on the patio and we throw all of her carved pumpkins over the side of the building. We lean over the railing, laughing as they bust apart in the parking lot, fifteen floors below. "Imagine that was my head," Rana says. The cold night air creeps under my nightgown, making it billow around me, but we stay out there jumping up and down until we can't feel our fingers. Back inside we make up dance routines in front of the windows that look out at other darkened apartments. It's like everyone in the city is sleeping except for kids. It would be easier to synchronize our routines with music, but Rana always likes it this way, quiet so she can concentrate. She thrusts her hips from side to side and glides her hands over her body, over her breasts and her stomach and the insides of her thighs. My phone blinks on the couch and when I check it, it's a text from Elgin to meet him at Ambleside Beach. I tell Rana I have to go, but she barely looks at me. Her hands are in the air, and to her feet, and in the air again, and I leave her to dance alone.

WEST VANCOUVER IS DEAD at night. Even on Halloween the streets are empty, the windows of multi-million-dollar homes lit up with blue television glow. I zip up my hoodie and cross the train tracks, making my way down to the beach. Waves hit the shore hard and ahead of me Stanley Park looms, a darker shadow in the night, while the Lions Gate Bridge looks almost cheerful with its twinkling arcs of light. I walk down to the far end of the beach before finding Elgin sitting with his back up against a log. Instead of staring out at the ocean, he's looking at the bridge and smoking. I plop down beside him in the cold, damp sand and Elgin leans over, kissing me lightly on the lips. "I didn't want to be at that party anymore," he says.

"Me neither." I lean back on the log, looking up at the clear October sky. The waves roll in a few inches from our sneakers.

"It's not just a suspension," Elgin says, after awhile. "They want to put me in the work experience program."

"What's that?" I say, pulling my knees up to my chest for warmth.

"It's like decelerated learning," Elgin says, picking up a rock and hucking it at the ocean.

"Why do you need that?"

"Paul thinks I'm a moron," Elgin says, throwing another rock, harder this time.

"They won't keep you there." I stretch my arm around him and pull him toward me. He's cold, like he's been sitting here for hours. "They'll see right away you don't belong."

"No way in hell I'm going to that program. Not even for a day," he says, frowning at me then looking away down the beach. "My mom wants to send me to my dad's. That's what I was going to tell you." My heart stops quietly like a fist hitting a feather pillow. "I don't even know the asshole," Elgin says, butting his cigarette out in the sand, where a small collection is accumulating. When he turns back to me his eyes are wet. "He lives in Cranbrook."

"You're going to go to school there?" I push Elgin's butts further into the sand, burying them.

"I guess." He rubs his eyes hard with the back of his hand.

"Why?" The question catches and I clear my throat. "Because of us or because you got suspended?"

"It's a lot of things," Elgin says, standing up. "I think I'm going to take off for a while." He steps to the edge of the ocean, jumping back before a wave swamps his sneakers. "I wanted you to know. I didn't want you to think I was dead or something." He sits back down beside me and I try to catch each tear with the back of my hand before they get anywhere near my cheeks. "I'm fucked," he says. "I'm fucked, I'm fucked, I'm fucked. No matter what I do."

"Did you tell Kate?" I'm not sure why I ask the question, but for some reason I feel like she deserves to know as much as I do.

"She'll find out soon enough. Maybe you should tell her," he says, kissing me once more. Then he's up, hopping on the spot, and in a bogus cheerful voice he says, "You'll be happier when I'm gone." He jogs up the beach and when he turns back he has this look on his face—this shiny, phony hopefulness that makes me feel sick to my stomach. "You look happier already," he shouts, rubbing his hand under his nose. He's close enough to see I'm crying. "Look at you." He stands there for a second, the smile gone, his hands back in his pockets, and I know I'll probably never see him again. I watch him disappear into the darkness and then I turn to watch the waves roll onto the shore.

I CROSS THE TRAIN TRACKS and walk up 15th Street toward Marine Drive. A grease trap behind one of the restaurants is broken and a large, rank puddle has pooled in the middle of the parking lot. The smell is nauseating, like bile spilling into the air around me. I try not to breathe, walking a little faster, but I stop when I catch a glimpse of something moving. Next to a silver car a black dog bows, lapping at the reeking pool. The smell gets in my nose and I gag involuntarily. The dog looks up and freezes. I can see the white breath around his wet muzzle, and his dark eyes follow me as I back away slowly, breathing into my hands. When I'm nearly out of sight around the corner, the dog goes back to licking.

Down the street, the neon-lit steeple of the West Vancouver United Church glows and a message on the board in front says *GOD INSPIRES YOU*. I walk up the steps to see if the door is open and I'm surprised to find it is. As I walk down the middle aisle, I keep thinking I hear an organ—not really music, but one long note—and whenever I shake my head the sound disappears and fills with a silence so deep it's noisy. I walk around the large room, touching things. Nothing is old or creaky or white like I imagined. The floors are green carpet and the pews are caramel-coloured. The bibles look pretty new and I finger their crisp pages. There are no confession booths like I thought there would be. It's nothing like Kate's winter church, not even close. I hear a noise behind a curtain at the back of the room and walk quickly out the door. Out front I sit on the stairs and scroll through my cellphone. There's sand in my shoes from the beach and I tilt my feet, letting it collect near my heels. The screen glows softly in my hand and I wait only a moment before dialing.

PAUL'S CAR HUMS UP the winding roads of the West Vancouver hills, past homes hidden behind tall hedges and big iron gates, past the last few kids in costumes who should be too old for trick-or-treating. "It's a strange night," he says, driving by a zombie and a pink-wigged superhero. I rest my cheek against the warm leather seat and turn on the radio. I ask Paul if it's okay and he smiles at me. When I got into the car he asked me if I wanted him to take me home, but I told him I wasn't ready to go to my house yet. I made up some bullshit excuse about my parents fighting and my sister having a crazy boyfriend who made me afraid to sleep at night, and by the look on Paul's face I knew I'd gone too far, but I'm tired enough I don't care.

"Can I ask you something?" Paul says, looking over at me.

He drums his thumbs on the steering wheel. "Why did you call me?" He barely holds back a grin when he asks, like someone who is expecting a compliment.

"I don't know," I say. "You're the first person I thought of."

We pull into a short, circular driveway and Paul stops the car right in front of the door. The house is modest for West Vancouver, a rancher with big windows. Inside everything looks freshly varnished and I have the urge to go skating around in my socks, but I keep my shoes on and walk around the living room while Paul hangs his coat and moves around the house turning on lights. "Your place is nice," I say, smelling a vase of flowers and rubbing the petals between my fingers to check if they're real.

"Can I get you something to drink?" Paul's voice comes from somewhere I can't pinpoint.

"Sure. Do you have vodka?"

Paul pops his head around a corner close to where I'm standing. "Funny. Coke, Sprite, milk?"

"Coke's fine."

I run my hands over books, tables, chairs, before sitting down on the couch. Suddenly, being in my mother's nightgown feels ridiculous and I run my fingers through my hair trying to tame it. Paul comes into the room and sets a can of Coke on a coaster for me and sits at the other end of the couch. "Do you want to talk about your parents?" he asks. He has a drink in his hand and he sips it then rests the glass on his knee.

"No," I say, reaching for the can.

"Something else?"

"How can you afford this place?" I say, taking a drink, the carbonation bubbling in my nostrils.

Paul laughs and looks around the living room as though he's trying to remember how he got here. "My wife's family has money," he says finally.

"Where's your wife?"

"Edmonton," he says, resting his head on the couch and turning to look at me. "On a business trip." He stretches out his arm and turns his palm up as though he wants me to take his hand. "What are we going to do with you?"

"I don't know," I say. I reach out and grasp his hand. There's a glimmer in his eyes—something like alarm—before he smiles at me and squeezes my palm tightly. I close my eyes, because all of a sudden I feel embarrassed, but he hangs on to my hand and starts to tell me my parents did a good job of raising me, that I'm a beautiful girl, that I'm not indifferent or stuck up like other kids, that I need to surround myself with people who love and support me. Everything he's saying seems like a really nice antidote to sadness, and I can actually feel the words like they're a silky lotion he's massaging into my thumping heart. While he talks, he moves closer and I can smell booze on his breath. When I open my eyes, his face is right there with this need tightening the corners of his lips. It looks painful and I can see his dead tooth, and now I wonder why he's never bothered to fix it if his wife has all this money. I wonder if maybe he doesn't care about the right things and suddenly I'm not sure anymore how I got here, if it was my idea or Paul's. "Can I have some ice?" I say, pulling my hand away from him.

"Sure," Paul says, jumping up and heading out of the room. "I'll get you a glass."

I hear him opening cupboards in the kitchen. I hear the

hiss of the refrigerator and the crack of ice cubes tumbling into a glass. I hear him pour himself another drink and suddenly I don't want to be in his house anymore. My toes fiddle with the sand in my shoes. I pull my sneakers off, carefully spilling two piles of sand on the polished wood floor before putting them back on and walking over to the windows. They look out across the distant city lights, where streams of cars cross the bridge and neon signs flicker like stars in another galaxy. Everything is gentle and harmless from here. I place my hands flat on the glass and glide the sliding doors open, stepping out into the night, the perfect lines of the deck and the manicured lawn and clipped hedges. In the distance cars speed along the highway. I walk out onto the lawn and look back at Paul's house, a cold breeze moving across my face and under my clothes. He's still in the kitchen, but he'll be back soon. Most of the windows are lit, but I notice movement in one of the darkened rooms. It's hard to say, but there may be a child standing there, its small body pressed up against the window, the glass giving its skin an unnatural icy glow. The child stands there like a small statuette and for only a moment I'm frozen.

I WAIT AWHILE ON Marine Drive for the bus, but there are a couple of guys in a car across the street who keep staring at me. It looks like they're hot-boxing their car, so I start walking. I think about what could happen if I got in the car with them. We'd listen to music and I'd end up doing it with both of them. Or maybe one of them would leave and the other would fall in love with me. He would transfer to my school to be closer to me and we could eat lunch in the alcove every day. Or they'd rape me and leave me in the forest, where no one would ever find me. They'd have to have a funeral with an empty coffin or have the funeral in the forest. At the moment any one of those options would do me fine.

The walk along Marine Drive is long, but I can smell the ocean. I go into a gas station to buy smokes, but the clerk is already looking at me suspiciously so I spare myself the embarrassment of being refused. He keeps staring at my hands and my pockets, so I buy some gum to prove to him I have money. I stick three pieces in my mouth and chew furiously as I walk toward Taylor Way. After the intersection, I veer right, toward the Lions Gate Bridge instead of toward my house. The on-ramp to the bridge curves gently under a glow of orange street lamps. A car swoops past like a bat and speeds away, rap blaring from the speakers. I've been over this bridge in cars a thousand times before, but I've never walked across it. During the day it's beautiful, like an elegant, braceleted arm stretching over the inlet, but at night it's different. The bridge is empty, there's no steady stream of cars crossing, the birds are sleeping. Walking slowly, I let my hand slide over the cold metal railing. It's not what I expected, standing out here, no glass and metal to protect me. The wind pulls the air right out of my lungs, whips my hair into a thousand tiny knots that will never be able to be picked out. At the bridge's midpoint I lean out over the railing to try to see the ocean, but all I see is black. Max would've been diving blind. He would've never seen the water coming. There's nothing in my pockets to throw, so I step up on the bottom rail and hork my wad of gum over the side, leaning far over the edge to watch it disappear. I wonder how he fell; I imagine it grace-ful like the canyon jumpers, the sky brightening around his arrow-straight body, a milky white arc leaving a trail brighter than a jet tail.

"Don't move, honey." Behind me stands an older man, his greying hair floating around his head in wisps, the wind mak-ing him look like he's being electrocuted. He's wearing a con-struction worker's orange vest, the reflective lines glowing. "How 'bout if you step away from the side there."

I glance down at the ocean shifting dark and endless beneath the bridge and try to laugh, but the wind snatches the sound and it comes out like more of a gasp. "I wasn't going to jump."

The man inches toward me, smiling carefully like I'm a wild animal, like I may pounce or run scared. He nods as though he's waiting for me to show him something, but the joke is on him — there's nothing there. He keeps moving until he is almost right behind me and then he stops. "I'd feel a heck of a lot better if you moved away from the railing a bit." With one step back I'm pressed against him, his arms wrapped tightly around me.

I can see the red-blue of the police car coming over the crest of the bridge. Someone wraps me in a wool blanket and sets me in the back seat. We drive off the bridge, away from the wind and into the quiet suburbs of North Vancouver. All the homes cry perfect little songs into the night. The radio squawks with calls about kids causing mayhem. The officer is not friendly. He doesn't try to talk to me. I curl into the corner of the back seat and pull the blanket over my head like a hood.

"I miss my friend."

The police officer keeps his eyes on the road and I realize I wasn't speaking out loud.

What I miss is the feeling I had hiding with Kate by the river, our backs pressed into the muddy belly of the cave, curled like small animals, breathing hard, our brains sparking with instinct. I could smell the earth and the rotting fish and Kate's sweat. All the forest colours were vibrant. I could hear each leaf turn in the breeze and feel the blood pumping in my gums and taste the iron in my mouth. And with Kate holding onto me, neither one of us was afraid. Together we were simple and fearless and alive.

ACKNOWLEDGEMENTS

SOME OF THE STORIES in this book were first published as fol-lows: "Whale Stories" in *Event*, *The Journey Prize Stories 20*, and *Coming Attractions 10*; "Fishtail" in *The Fiddlehead* and *Coming Attractions 10*; "Thanks to Carin" in *Prairie Fire Magazine* and *Coming Attractions 10*; "Rabbit" in *Prairie Fire Magazine*. Special thanks to editors Rick Maddocks, Andris Taskans, and Mark Anthony Jarman for their care and attention. I'd also like to express appreciation to the Canada Council for the Arts for their financial assistance.

A hearty thank you to my publisher, Sarah MacLachlan, and the dedicated, energetic people at House of Anansi Press, particularly my gifted editor, Melanie Little, for her invalu-able insight, enthusiasm, and warm spirit. Thanks to Peter Norman for meticulous and thoughtful copyedits. Infinite praise to my agent, Marilyn Biderman, for her kindness and her lion heart.

A special recognition to the Department of Creative Writing at the University of British Columbia for their support and commitment, especially Rhea Tregebov, Steven Galloway, Andreas Schroeder, George McWhirter, and Lynne Bowen. I owe endless gratitude to Keith Maillard, who encouraged and inspired me from the beginning, and gave me the confidence, in those early years, to write stories.

Thank you to my parents, Robert Armstrong and Nicole Fraser Armstrong, for everything. Without their unwavering trust this book would not exist. To my sister, Aland, and my brother, Pierre, for their love and solidarity, and to so many others who have offered their support while I worked on this book: the Frasers; the Millikans; the Armstrongs, especially Jean Armstrong; Ria Voros; Anosh Irani; Mireille Lebel; Daniel Dubiecki; and Lara Alameddine. Merci, Mémère, pour toutes vos histoires d'autrefois.

"The Spider in the Jar" was inspired by a story recounted by my father and my uncle, Ed Armstrong. "Clear Skies, No Wind, 100% Visibility" could not have been written without the meaningful and extensive contributions of Andrew Graham. All the characters in this book are fictitious; any resemblance to real people is purely coincidental. Also, my deepest apologies to those I never asked for permission.

An endless gratitude to my husband, Jason O'Malley — my confidant, my abettor, my co-conspirator. Your love and faith are what keep me going. Since the beginning you have been my ally at the other end of the table. Thank you for tirelessly reading every version of these stories over the past several years, and offering discerning and perceptive observations. These stories are better because of you.

And finally, to Willa, for reminding me what's important. Thank you, my little love.

ABOUT THE AUTHOR

THÉODORA ARMSTRONG is a fiction writer, poet, and photographer. Her work has appeared in numerous literary magazines across the country such as *Event*, *Prairie Fire*, *The Fiddlehead*, *Descant*, *The New Quarterly*, and *Contemporary Verse 2*. In 2008, she won a Western Magazine Award for Fiction, and her stories have been included in both *The Journey Prize Anthology 20* and *Coming Attractions 10*. Théodora lives in Vancouver, British Columbia, with her husband and daughter. She is at work on her first novel.